The FAERIE QUEEN

KIKI HAMILTON

Book Four of
THE FAERIE RING Series

The FAERIE QUEEN
Copyright 2020 © Karen Hamilton
All Rights Reserved.

This book is a work of fiction. All of the characters, organizations, and events portrayed in this novel are either products of the author's imagination or are used fictitiously. No part of this publication can be reproduced or transmitted in any form or by any means, electronic or mechanical, without permission in writing from the author.

Gaslamp Books

New York   Seattle   London

Also by Kiki Hamilton:

The Faerie Ring Series:
The Faerie Ring
The Torn Wing
The Seven Year King
The Faerie Queen

The Midnight Spy

The Last Dance

Unwritten

The FAERIE QUEEN

Book Four of THE FAERIE RING series

Pronunciation & Meaning of Irish Words
(With thanks to irishgaelictranslator.com and Irish Language Forum)

An fáinne sí (un FAWN-yeh shee): the faerie ring

Grá do dhuine básmhar (graw duh GGWIN-yeh BAWSS-wur): love for a mortal person

Óinseach (OWN-shukh): fool/idiot (for a female)

Nimh Álainn (niv AW-lin): beautiful poison

Tánaiste (tawn-ISH-tah): second in command

Cloch na Teamhrach (klukh nuh TYARR-uh): Stone of Tara

Corn na bhFuíoll (KOR-un nuh WEE-ull): Cup of Plenty

Samhain (Sow WEEN): festival marking the beginning of winter, usually celebrated on October 31

Am Bratach Sith: the Faerie Flag

The FAERIE QUEEN

Dear Reader,

The story told within **THE FAERIE RING series** is a combination of fact and fiction. Known as "historical fantasy," I like to think of the books as a *"what if..."* kind of story.

Much of book one, *The Faerie Ring*, is grounded in reality: **Queen Victoria and Princes Leopold and Arthur** were real historical figures. In fact, the story was set in the year 1871 because that was the year Prince Leopold turned eighteen years old.

Many of the places referenced in the series: **Charing Cross Station, King's Cross Station, the World's End Pub, St. James's Park, the Birdkeeper's Cottage, Buckingham Palace, Hyde Park,** and **the Great Ormond Street Hospital**, are real and can be visited today—should you be lucky enough to find yourself in London.

Both book two, *The Torn Wing*, and book three, *The Seven-Year King*, take you to other parts of England, including **Glastonbury Tor** and the **Wychwood Forest**, which are both real and have legends that associate them with faeries, and in the case of the Wychwood, tales of hobgoblins, witches, and other creatures abound.

The British Isles are rich with faerie lore, and there are many artifacts that exist today said to be associated with the fey. Introduced in *The Torn Wing*, the **Hill of Tara** exists in Ireland, the **London Stone** is displayed on Cannon Street in London, and in *The Seven-Year*

King, you'll learn of the **Luck of Edenhall**, which is real and currently on display in the Victoria and Albert Museum in Kensington.

The Author's Note at the end of the book contains additional information you might find interesting regarding some of the people, places, and things mentioned in *The Faerie Queen*, though to avoid any spoilers, perhaps best read **after** you finish the book.

Now—on with the final chapters of Tiki's story ...

Chapter One

Palace of Mirrors, the Otherworld

"We found this in her rooms, Majesty." A humpbacked guard, his massive shoulders twisted to one side, stood before the UnSeelie king with a piece of fabric dangling from his claw-tipped fingers. "The Seelie queen left it behind when she departed for winter."

"Give me that." Donegal snatched the pale-yellow silk from the man and held it to his nose, inhaling deeply. His scarred face, one side melted like candle wax, twisted with distaste. "I can smell the stench of her—like summer flowers." He tossed the delicate chemise to the floor as if the fabric had burned him. "Bring me Bearach's hounds and do it *now*."

Barely ten minutes had passed before the guard returned leading two monstrous black hounds, held by thick chains tied to spiked collars. The animals slinked along beside the man in an effortless gait, their heads low. They glanced from side to side, red eyes measuring the occupants of the room, as if deciding who would be their next meal.

The guard yanked the hounds to a stop before Donegal, who sat on a golden throne in the shape of a dragon. A low growl issued from the throat of the first dog as the guard jerked her chain.

"Sit," he commanded.

After a long moment, the animal lowered her haunches but remained crouched and ready to spring.

"This is Cana and Bruk, Majesty, said to be the fiercest of Bearach's hellhounds."

Donegal pushed himself from the throne, his black garments shifting like ripples of dark water. "I recognize this one"—he pointed—"by the scar above her eye. Bearach often had the beast with him before he died." The Winter King snapped his fingers and pointed at the dress, still resting on the marble floor. A guard scrambled to pick up the silky material and handed it to the king, keeping a cautious distance from the fanged jaws of the dogs.

The UnSeelie king took the fabric and held it out. The female hound lifted her nose and sniffed the air, then was on her feet, curiously smelling the garment. The other dog followed, nudging his way closer to smell the fabric as well.

Donegal took a hurried step back, keeping his arm outstretched so the dogs could gather the scent. "On my signal," he said to the guard, "I want you to release them." He leaned forward and stared into the female hellhound's blood-red eyes. "Fetch," he said firmly before his voice turned venomous. "*Kill.*" He nodded to the guard, who unhooked the leashes and took several quick steps away from the giant dogs.

Cana's eyes regarded Donegal with a baleful, intelligent expression; then as one, both hounds turned and ran, silently slipping through the Great Hall like shadows blown across the face of the moon.

Chapter Two

No. 6, Grosvenor Square, London

November 4, 1872

"It appears you're leaving."

The voice woke Tiki. There were so many things on her mind, it had been difficult to sleep lately, and when she did drift off, even the most minute sounds woke her. At first, she thought Larkin was part of her dream, but then the faerie spoke again.

"Before you go, there are matters to be discussed."

Tiki jerked upright, suddenly wide awake. "Larkin, what are you doing here? It's the middle of the night."

"Exactly," the faerie said. "That's why I've come now. I knew we could be alone. It's time we talked about Clara."

Tiki's stomach clenched as she leaned over and lit a bedside candle. She squinted through the shadows at the nebulous form of the faerie sitting at the end of her bed. "What about Clara?"

"You need to know the truth." Larkin's eyes glittered in the half light of the wavering flame. "Clara is my daughter. Surely you've noticed the resemblance?"

It was as if Tiki's body had turned to ice. She couldn't have heard the faerie correctly.

Larkin laughed, the sound like wind chimes, and a slow smirk twisted her lips. "I thought you'd have figured it out by now. I'm quite sure William has known for the longest time." She was swathed in a black drape that hid her striking blond hair, making her indistinct, barely illuminated by the dim shaft of moonlight that cut a narrow path across Tiki's bedroom.

"I don't believe you," Tiki cried.

"Yes, you do," Larkin scoffed. "When have I ever lied to you? Do you think it was a coincidence that Clara was directly in your path on Craven Street that day? Have you never wondered why you were the one who found her among the masses who inhabit London?" She stabbed her thumb into her chest. "It's because I wanted you to find her. I, alone, knew who you were—what future awaited. I knew she would be safe with you, filthy little pickpocket that you were."

Though her hands were shaking, a surge of anger made Tiki strong. "I don't care if she's your daughter—you gave her up, and she belongs with me now."

Larkin gave a derisive laugh, as cold and deadly as a well-honed dagger. "I loaned her to you for a purpose, but that is beside the point. Should I choose to take the child, I dare you to try to stop me." The faerie's voice changed to a conversational tone. "However, as with most things in life, guttersnipe, you do have a choice. If you relinquish the Seelie throne to me, I promise I will never bother the two of you again. You can go off with your mortal family and never have another worry about those in the Seelie court." She gave a delicate shrug. "It's quite simple, really. But if you don't, then it's time for Clara to return to Faerie with me." Larkin lifted her palms. "It's up to you. Which do you choose: a child, or a kingdom?"

Tiki shoved the bedcovers aside and jumped to her feet, fingers clenched into fists. "Don't you *dare* give me an ultimatum," she snapped. "You abandoned Clara and I've cared for her—I saved her life when she would have died from your neglect. I love her!"

Larkin's eyes narrowed. "Love is for mortals and fools."

Tiki took a threatening step toward Larkin. "You can't take her just because you want to threaten me into doing your bidding. I won't allow you to use a child to manipulate me."

Larkin's mood shifted and she spoke through clenched teeth. "Someone has to take action against Donegal. The borders to the Plain of Sunlight are littered with dead Macanna, their bodies impaled on giant stakes for all to see. If you won't lead the Seelie court in this war, then I will—but what I won't do is stand by and watch my people slaughtered without a fight."

Tiki blinked, and the mercurial faerie was gone— replaced by a cool breeze that swirled around her bare feet, chilling her to the core. Had Larkin spoken the truth? Were the Macanna, those giant soldiers who'd followed her father Finn when he left the Seelie court, being murdered by the Winter King? Was Donegal that powerful now? And would Larkin take Clara as a bargaining chip to secure control of the Seelie throne from Tiki?

She raced for the door and yanked it open. Her bare feet echoed against the wooden floor as she sprinted down the hall and up the stairs. Larkin wouldn't dare take Clara to Faerie. *She wouldn't dare.* Yet, fear sank its claws into Tiki's heart as she ran, for if anyone would have the nerve to take the child from her, it would be Larkin.

Tiki's breath came in short gasps and her knees felt weak as she crested the stairs and plucked a small, gas-lit hurricane lamp from a nearby table. A phlegmy cough rumbled in her chest as she approached Clara and Fiona's bedroom, and she coughed into the crook of her elbow to quiet the noise. She'd been fighting this cold for weeks now, and each day she felt a bit weaker—at a time when she didn't dare be weak.

She gently pushed Clara's bedroom door open, her eyes riveted on the small bed where the five-year-old slept. Blond curls, lit by a shaft of moonlight that streamed through a gap in the drapes, fanned across the pillow. Tiki's shoulders sagged in relief. Clara was safe.

She tiptoed across the room and stared down at the precious face of the little girl she'd come to love so much. Dark lashes rested against cheeks the color of fresh cream. Her lips were parted as she breathed in the relaxed rhythm of deep sleep. A small, ragged pink dog was tucked under her chin and small fingers clutched the worn animal close.

Tiki's heart ached with a bittersweet longing as she reached out to smooth the child's curls. She'd found Clara buried in a pile of trash outside Charing Cross over a year ago and had nursed the child back from the brink of death more than once. In the process, she'd come to love the little girl like her own. Larkin's words echoed in her ears: *Clara is my daughter. Surely you've noticed the resemblance?*

Now that she was forced to face it, the resemblance between Larkin and Clara was apparent: the sun-kissed blond hair, the flawless skin, the enigmatic blue eyes—a combination that created a breathtaking, otherworldly beauty that was uncommon, even in a city as populated as London. Their laughs were similar—ringing out like the melodic sound of wind chimes—and probably most damning, Clara's inexplicable ability to see those not from this world. The combination was enough to make Larkin's revelation undeniable.

Tiki lifted one of Clara's curls from the pillow, the strands twisting against her fingers. "I will never allow her to take you from me," she whispered to the sleeping child, "*ever*." But like a match to kindling, a wisp of fear had begun to burn deep in her gut.

"Johnny's been ill all night," Fiona said the next morning, holding a steaming cup of tea as she slid into a chair across from where Tiki sat at the brown wooden kitchen table. Dawn was breaking across London, though the sunrise only brought the watery light of winter—barely strong enough to breach the hidden nooks and crannies of the townhome. "He's still very weak."

Tiki frowned as a sense of warning quickened her pulse. "Is it flu?" Johnny had just regained consciousness in the last few days after an extended illness brought on by the attack of the deadly *liche,* an Otherworldly creature who sustained itself by consuming the hearts of his victims. The *liche,* who had been able to move between the mortal world and that of Faerie, had taken an unnatural liking to Fiona. Johnny had thwarted his efforts to snatch the sixteen-year-old girl, but his bravery had nearly cost him his life.

Fiona shook her head, brushing a strand of wavy brown hair off her brow. "I don't know for sure. He said he started to feel sick last night after he ate. It's the first solid food he's had since his return from—" She hesitated and glanced over her shoulder to where Rieker's housemaid, Mrs. Bosworth, stood kneading bread at the counter. Fiona lowered her voice. "Well, you know. Maybe it has something to do with that."

Tiki unsuccessfully tried to fight back a cough, her slender shoulders shaking. She hadn't slept since Larkin's nighttime visit. As a result of their conversation, she'd spent the remainder of the night sitting in a chair at the foot of Clara's bed, keeping watch and worrying whether the faerie had told the truth about the deaths of the Seelie soldiers. Were Toran or any of the Macanna she knew among the dead? Had Donegal begun the final siege against the Seelie court?

At dawn's first light, Tiki had gone in search of Rieker. She needed to tell him there would be a change in their plans to depart later that day for an extended trip to Scotland. But Rieker wasn't at Grosvenor Square, and she'd been forced to wait.

"We're to leave mid-morning," Tiki said to Fiona. "Do you think Johnny will be able to travel?" She was anxious for the group to be underway. It was a well-known fact that Donegal, king of the UnSeelie court, wanted to claim the kingdom of Faerie for his own. To do that, he planned to eliminate the present queen of the Seelie court—who happened to be Tiki. As if that weren't enough, he personally blamed Tiki for the horrific scarring that marred half his face, a side effect of the *liche*'s death, to whom he had bound his own body to resurrect. Donegal would stop at nothing to make her pay.

As a result, they were leaving in the hope they could elude the Winter King before he took deadly action against Tiki or her family. What Tiki needed to tell Rieker, however, was that she had decided she would not be accompanying them to Scotland. She had a responsibility to the Macanna and the fey of the Seelie court that couldn't be left for someone else. She was the queen—she wouldn't be able to live with herself if she didn't help when they needed her most.

Tiki ran her finger around the rim of her cup, confident she'd made the right decision. Fiona blew on her tea, diverting the spiral of steam rising like a miniature storm in Tiki's direction. "I'll help him pack. He'll be ready to go."

Tiki nodded. She'd seen the rage and determination in Donegal's eyes. "I've got a bad feeling about what's coming, Fi. The sooner we can go, the better for all of us."

Chapter Three

It was only twenty minutes later that Tiki stood alone in Rieker's study. Fiona had gone upstairs to check on Johnny and to roust Clara and eleven-year-old Toots from their beds. At Tiki's urging, Shamus, Fiona's eighteen-year-old cousin, had elected to stay behind and move to Rieker's manor house outside of London with the rest of the staff while Rieker, Tiki, and the others were away. Of the group remaining behind, Shamus was the only one who knew where they were really going and why.

Tiki reached for a nondescript green-glass vase that rested on one of the bookshelves lining the walls of the study and lifted it down.

"What to do with you while we're gone," she said as she turned the ordinary vase in her hands.

"I'd be careful with that."

Tiki jerked around. A tall, handsome young man stood leaning against the door frame, his arms crossed over his broad chest, eyes bright with curiosity. He wore a brown jacket and black breeches with tall black riding boots. He looked the picture of a young English lord.

"Dain, you startled me. I didn't hear you come in."

A smile played around the corners of his lips as he shrugged off the wall and approached her. Blond hair swept across his forehead in a windblown fashion, as if he'd just returned from a ride. "You weren't supposed to hear me." There was a teasing note in his voice. "How can I spy on you if you know I'm there?"

Tiki gave him a direct look. "And why would you need to spy on me?"

Dain's lips twisted into a half grin and his eyes became hooded as he surveyed her, enjoying their game. "Because I believe you have secrets, my dear Tara"—he leaned close and whispered—"powerful, powerful secrets."

"Yes, well, if I do, they remain secret from me, as well."

"Give yourself time. You've only just learned of your heritage." His sky-blue eyes crinkled at the corners as he smiled down at her. "Perhaps understanding your destiny might take another week or two."

"My destiny," Tiki muttered. "Has it occurred to anyone that maybe I don't have a destiny? That maybe my life is meant to be as ordinary as the next?"

Dain tipped his head back and laughed. "Why would anyone suspect you might have a destiny worth noting?" He tapped a long finger against the side of his face. "Let's see—you've been confirmed as a true-born queen of the Seelie court by the legendary Stone of Tara. William confided to me that you *stole* the ring of *Ériu*"—his eyes twinkled with delight—"which means you've recovered two of the mythical Four Treasures."

He dropped his hand to run a fingertip gently down the side of the glass piece. "And rumor has it that you've recovered the missing third Treasure—*Corn na bhFuioll*—the Cup of Plenty. Is it possible you might have glamoured the cup to look like this ordinary green vase?" He checked her reaction.

Tiki tightened her grip on the glass piece. "How did you know?" She hadn't yet told Rieker where she'd hidden the Cup of Plenty.

Dain straightened. "Actually, if you remember, you told me that you'd recovered the cup, and if there's one thing I know about you, my queen, is that you protect what is yours." His smile softened. "I think it's what I respect most about you."

Tiki forced a smile. Rieker's fraternal twin brother was the same height as the young lord—both taller than most, with similarly broad shoulders. They moved with the same effortless grace and could be charming and witty, but rather than identical, their faces were more of a mirror image of each other: similar, yet subtly different. Where Rieker had dark hair, Dain was blond; where Rieker's nose was straight, Dain's bore an almost imperceptible hook to the bridge. Rieker's gray eyes were often shadowed with secrets, while Dain's eyes were strikingly blue and seemingly guileless.

"May I see it?" he asked.

Tiki only hesitated for a second before she whispered the words that would remove the glamour disguising the cup. The green faded away to be replaced with clear glass covered in sparkling swirls of blue, yellows, and browns.

Dain sucked in his breath as he reached for the vase. "It's breathtaking." The colors and gold gilding on the rim glittered as he carefully turned the glass piece in his hands, examining every inch of its surface.

"*Corn na bhFuioll*—the Cup of Plenty. Said to hold the four essences of life: healing, inspiration, wisdom, and sustenance." He tilted his head at Tiki, his blond locks shifting to one side. "By my estimation, Girl Without a Destiny, you've gained possession of the first three treasures just as Donegal is set to drag the courts into the bloodiest war we've seen in centuries. Legend says the Four Treasures will be found when Faerie is in greatest need, and our fate has never been at greater risk than it is now."

Dain's expression, for once, was serious. "Tara, it is your destiny to solve the paradox of the treasures. It is you who is meant to find the Fourth Treasure and reunite Faerie."

Tiki's cheeks warmed. She had reached the same conclusion—but how could she admit that she had no idea how to go about using the first three treasures of a mythical legend to find a fourth that could be anything, hidden anywhere? What if she failed?

Sensing her discomfort, Dain reached into the interior of the vase. "What is this?" He lifted out a card between two fingers.

"Oh, that." Tiki took the vase from him and whispered the words to change its appearance back to an ordinary green shape before pushing the container back onto the shelf. "I have no idea what it is. The Court Jester gave it to me when we parted for the season." She shrugged. "It's probably nothing."

Dain tilted his head. "The jester gave it to you?"

"Yes. Why do you sound so surprised? It seems the man's purpose is to be an enigma. He takes special pleasure in speaking rhyme with no reason." She paused, imagining the gaudy, colorful clothing of the Court Jester who resides throughout all the seasons in the Palace of Mirrors. "Though I must admit, he did give us a clue about the Stone of Tara when we were searching. Some muddled conundrum about fate and truth." She shook her head. "I swear he acts the fool just to hide his brilliance."

"No doubt his wit keeps him alive, though he also has extraordinary talent with magic. I've seen him create birds from fire. Dangerous birds at that." Dain turned the card over in his hand, revealing several intricately drawn designs that resembled stained glass windows. He frowned as he ran a fingertip over the images. "Tara"—his tone changed—"do you recognize these images?"

Tiki leaned close to stare at the card. "That looks like a queen in the middle, and I know this"—she pointed to a drawing of a single upright stone positioned between the spokes of a Celtic cross—"is the *Lia Fail*, the stone from which the *Cloch na Teamhrach*, the Stone of Tara, was said to have originated." She moved her finger to the next spoke in the wheel containing a picture. "This is the *Corn na bhFuíoll***,** the Cup of Plenty, and this"—her finger tapped the image of a ring capped by a glowing red stone—"is the Ring of *Ériu*. But I have no idea what the meaning of the fourth image is. Do you?"

Dain rotated the card to better see the fourth drawing, a castle of golden bricks with a tower on one end. "Why would the Court Jester give you a card with drawings of the Four Treasures?"

Tiki laughed. "That is exactly my point—those *aren't* the Four Treasures. It's a picture of three of the Treasures and a castle. How could a castle be one of the treasures? It makes no sense. His wit is shrouded in puns with hidden meaning and murky innuendo. I think he amuses himself by confounding those he is meant to entertain."

Dain stared at the card, continuing to turn it in a circle to view each of the images. "What did he say when he gave it to you?"

Tiki raised her palms. "I don't remember."

Dain was oddly persistent. "Try."

She let out a low groan. "Let me see—it was on Samhain, when control of the court was to return to the UnSeelies. Something about the winds of change." She stared blindly at the floor as she searched her memory. After a moment, she snapped her fingers. "I've got it. *When the clock strikes twelve, may the winds of change blow you in your true direction.*" She gazed at Dain's face. "Does that make any sense to you?"

Dain tapped the card against his thumb. "Not exactly, but—"

"There you are." William Richmond entered the room, his wavy hair blown back from his face, cheeks rosy from the bite of the winter air. His broad shoulders were clad in a brown tweed jacket and he wore tall riding boots with dark pants that revealed his long, muscular legs. "Are you ready to go? Have you packed?"

Tiki plucked the card out of Dain's hand and slid it into her pocket as she stepped away from the bookcase. Her heart beat erratically at the idea of telling Rieker she wasn't going with them. It would not be a pleasant conversation. "We're almost ready. Fiona went up to wake the children."

Rieker threw an arm out as she walked past and caught her around the waist. He lowered his head, his eyes searching. "Good morning, my queen," he whispered, before he pressed his lips against hers.

Tiki returned his kiss, marveling at Rieker's willingness to show feelings he had kept hidden for the longest time. She pulled back, her lips curving in a soft smile, and ran a hand along the stubble on his cheek. "Good morning, my lord."

"Are you still committed to our grand adventure?" His smoky eyes were deep with an emotion he had only recently begun to let Tiki see.

"Where's my good-morning kiss?" Dain's question dispelled the intimate moment. They turned to find him with his arms crossed over his chest, chin tilted in a petulant angle.

Rieker released Tiki to take a step toward his brother, a wicked grin on his face. "So, it's a little snogging you want this morning, eh?"

Dain laughed and threw his hands up to protect himself. "Not from you, you nutter, I was talking to Tara …" The boys began a mock battle with Rieker trying to catch Dain to kiss him.

"William—"

Rieker stopped his horseplay and swiveled to look at Tiki, a questioning expression on his face.

Her words came out in a burst. "I'vegivenitalotofthought—" She took a deep breath, trying to calm her nerves. "And I'm not coming with you to Scotland."

Chapter Four

Situated at the far end of St. James's Park, the Birdkeeper's Cottage sat near the edge of the lake, nestled among the reeds and flowers that flourished there. Prince Leopold stood inside the cottage, hands clasped behind his back, contemplating the view that stretched across the water to Buckingham Palace, the building shimmering through the trees like a faerie-tale mirage.

"Mamie, did you have a chance to meet William's friend, Dain?" Leo glanced over his shoulder at the elderly woman who sat in a nearby rocker, a marmalade-colored cat curled in a ball on her lap. "He introduced him as his cousin, though I'd never heard of him speak of a cousin the same age before."

Mamie's voice was quiet, with a singsong quality that reminded Leo of bells. "No, dear, I didn't meet him."

Leo turned back to contemplate the view. "I'd never heard William speak of any family other than Thomas and James before," he mused. "And after their deaths, I never heard him speak their names again. Too painful, I suppose." Leo rocked back on his heels, a faraway look in his eyes. "There was a striking similarity between William and Dain. If I didn't know better, I'd say they could almost be brothers."

"What did you think of this young man?"

"He seemed a right enough fellow, though I'm concerned they're involved in something quite serious."

"These are serious times," Mamie replied, reaching for a teacup that sat on a nearby table. "I worry about William too—and his pretty friend, Tara."

"Yes." Leo nodded and let out a long sigh. "And then there is Tara." He turned to face Mamie, his arms crossed over his chest. The brown jacket he wore hung on his thin frame, a result of his recent battle to regain his health after the attack by a *liche*, sent by Donegal to London with the intent of killing Queen Victoria. "Dain said something I found quite curious."

"And what was that, dear?"

"He referred to Tara as a *queen*." Leo was silent for a long moment. Images of Tara as the scroungy young boy he'd first met in St. James's Park, and then as the breathtaking Elizabeth—a beautiful young woman who had appeared at a masked ball in Buckingham as if by magic, only to disappear as mysteriously as she had arrived—merged into the enchanting young woman he had come to know, the one with whom his dear friend, William Richmond, was obviously in love.

If he didn't know better, he suspected William's "cousin" might be in love with Tara, as well. "Tell me the truth, Mamie. I've known and trusted your wisdom all my life. You've advised my mother since she took the throne. I know you have knowledge of otherworldly things—is Tara a queen in that other realm?" A thread of disbelief echoed in his words.

The wooden glides of Mamie's rocker created a mesmerizing *hush-shush* as she rocked back and forth, the sound accompanied by the purring cat. Together, they created an odd melody, giving Leo the disconcerting sense that he had somehow left London far behind and now existed in an unfamiliar world where time stood still.

Mamie slowed her movement and patted a chair next to the rocker.

"Come sit, dear boy, and listen carefully to what I have to say, for I dare not say it more than once."

Leo hurriedly slipped into the chair. The elderly woman's white hair was a halo around skin gone soft with wrinkles, but her brilliant blue eyes snapped with intelligence and an unusual wisdom.

"What I'm about to tell you cannot leave these four walls, do you understand? There are far too many lives at stake."

Leo's pulse jumped, and he jerked his head up and down in assent. "You have my word."

"Your friend, Tara, is not only a queen but a true-born queen, acknowledged by *Cloch na Teamhrach,* the Stone of Tara. She is more powerful than even she can imagine."

Leo's teeth tugged at his bottom lip. "That mark around her wrist?"

Mamie nodded. "Yes, *an fáinne sí.* A rare mark that follows the lineage of the true high kings of Tara, the Irish royalty of the Otherworld. Her existence was only a rumor for many years."

"But where has she been?"

"Hidden, here in London, by parents who were doomed—who understood the destiny that waited for her." Mamie let out a long sigh. "The only one who knew where she was, and *who* she was, watched from a distance, waiting for the time when Tara's return would be most beneficial."

"And who might that be?"

"She goes by the name of Larkin now. A more cunning faerie has never existed. Her sister, Adasara, was Tara's mother." Mamie began rocking again, the wooden frame creaking with the movement. "Larkin was always terribly jealous of Adasara."

"Was Adasara a queen?"

"No. Tara's father, Finn, carried the royal blood." Her crooked fingers smoothed the cat's orange fur as she rocked, her voice softening with memories. "It was a tangled web that existed among the three of them. I'm not sure anyone but Larkin knows the truth anymore."

Her eyes narrowed. "In the end, though, Finn and Adasara both died, and Larkin disappeared. I'd never heard what became of her until last spring when you and Tara told me she'd become a spy in the UnSeelie court. Now she has returned to the Seelies and is leading them in a battle against the Winter King—the same king who wants to murder your mother." Mamie leaned her head against the back of the rocker and stared into the distance, seeing things not in the room. "But powerful though she may be, Larkin can only win this war with Tara's help."

Leo rubbed his sweating palms along his thighs. "Does Tara know she's part of this battle?"

"She's being forced to learn." Mamie slowed to a stop before Leo. "It is a deadly and dangerous war that is being waged in the Otherworld, and I fear for Tara. She may be a true-born queen, but she has not lived in that world, she's not been raised to think—or manipulate—like they do. I warn you, Leo—Donegal, the king of the UnSeelie court, will stop at nothing to claim all of Faerie, and England along with it, if he can."

Leo thumped back into his seat. This war Mamie spoke of had existed on the edges of their reality for as long as he could remember. It was a secret only spoken of in hushed tones and among a select few of the inner family. When his mother's precious Ring of *Ériu* had been stolen last December—by none other than Tara herself, he suspected—the balance had shifted and the Otherworldly war had spilled over into London, affecting all their lives, forcing them to acknowledge its existence in a way they hadn't before.

Leo sat upright in his chair. The idea of beautiful, charming Tara facing this battle alone and unprepared made his stomach roil. "We can't just sit by and helplessly watch them attack. What can I do?"

Mamie rested her fingers against the bare skin of his arm, her grip surprisingly strong. "You must speak to your mother, and *only* your mother, about this matter. You can't be sure who can be trusted. Ask her about the other secrets held within the ring of the truce that William guards. *That* is the information Tara will need to win this war." Mamie's eyes were shadowed with worry. "Those secrets might be the only hope Tara has."

Chapter Five

"Sullivan, have Bearach's hounds returned?" Donegal stood on the steps leading to the entrance of the Palace of Mirrors, his hands clasped behind his back, looking out over the shadow-shrouded Night Garden. Gnarled branches cast stark silhouettes against the watery moonlight that lit the landscape. Between the thorned bushes and razor-edged leaves, magnificent flowers bloomed with an alluring glow. It was only upon closer inspection that one could see the blood stains on their jagged petals—an ominous reminder of their lethal intent.

"No, Majesty. They've not been seen since they were released to hunt the Seelie queen yesterday." Sullivan stood next to the Winter King, mimicking his posture. He was taller than Donegal, but much thinner of limb, with silver hair that brushed his shoulders. "They must still be hunting her if they haven't returned." He cast a sideways glance at Donegal. "Have you considered they may not be able to find her? On Samhain, the queen took the body of the Seven-Year King and left. There's no way to know if she went to the Plain of Sunlight with the rest of the Seelie court or elsewhere. Given her history, she could have returned to the mortal world."

"I've thought of that." Donegal shifted his position to face his new *tánaiste*. Sullivan was one of his inner circle—one of the three men whom he trusted with his life. The fourth, Bearach, had been murdered while transporting a Seelie prisoner. A cold rage burned in the pit of Donegal's stomach as he planned his vengeance. "That's why I want you to take the hounds to London. In the past, she's lived in a place called Grosvenor Square. Check there first."

Chapter Six

"You are *not* going back to the Otherworld without me." Rieker was furious, his eyes blazing with anger as he stood with hands on hips, glowering at Tiki. Dain stood nearby, for once silent.

"William—" Tiki tried to clear her throat, but her words came out sounding raspy and raw—"I can't just walk away from my responsibilities there. I can't leave fey who are starving." She didn't want to mention the dead soldiers. That information might make a difficult conversation impossible to win. "The members of the Seelie court are counting on me, even the Macanna—they've been waiting and hoping for someone to lead them against Donegal. I thought I could leave them all behind—I *wanted* to leave them all behind—but I can't. They need me. And I need to do what my parents would have expected of me."

"Why can't we stay together? We've done fine so far," Rieker spat out.

"You know I can't take Clara and Toots to Faerie. That means they need to be with someone who will protect them with their life. Someone who understands the evil we're up against." She begged him with her eyes. "There is only you."

Rieker turned away with a growl. "I don't like it. I don't like any part of it."

Tiki moved to stand with her back to the fire, rubbing her arms to gather warmth. "Dain has lived in the Otherworld his entire life. He's been a spy in the UnSeelie court. He can give me the best advice on how to accomplish what needs to be done."

Rieker whipped back around. "Wait a minute. You're not saying Dain is going with you?"

Tiki nodded, bracing herself. "There is no other way."

Rieker clenched his long fingers into fists, the muscles in his jaw flexing as he ground his teeth together. "There is *always* another way. I can't stand the thought of you being there without me—unprotected."

"I'll protect her." Dain's voice was low but sure. "With my life."

In less than an hour, Shamus, Juliette, and the Bosworths had loaded up one carriage along with Geoffrey, their driver, and departed for Richmond where Rieker had an estate. Clara, Toots, Fiona, and Johnny were settled in the second carriage rigged with a team of four, prepared for their journey to Scotland. Only Rieker had yet to board. He stood before Tiki, his black hair hanging low on his forehead and shadowing his eyes. The day was overcast and gray, black storm clouds threatening on the horizon as if in reflection of his mood.

"I'm going to get them settled and come find you," Rieker said, his own larger hands engulfing Tiki's and holding them close to his chest.

"You can't leave them with strangers," Tiki said gently. "You know that. What would help me most is to know that you are all safe, so I can concentrate on what I must do." She pulled her fingers free and cupped one side of his face with her pale hand. "I'm stronger than I look. I'll be fine." Tiki's heart lurched at the heartache she saw in Rieker's eyes. "I love you so very much, William Becker Richmond—I'll always find a way to return to your side. Believe in me."

"Time to go." Dain interrupted them. "The longer we're out here, the longer Donegal has to find us. Best to keep moving."

Tiki stepped back, but Rieker shifted his stance to stop her from moving away. He settled his arms around her shoulders to pull her close. He kissed her with an urgency that spoke of his torment until Tiki was sure her lips would be bruised.

When he lifted his head, his warm breath grazed her ear as he whispered, "The Ring of *Ériu* is around your neck now. Use the inspiration from the cup to draw the secret of the Fourth Treasure from the ring, as only you are meant to do."

Tiki's knees felt weak. Even when he hated her decision, he understood it and supported her.

He rested his hands on her shoulders. "If you need help, call for me. Somehow I will hear and find you." Then he pushed away from her. He reached for Dain's hand and clasped it tightly. "With your life," he said tersely. Then, in a blur of motion, he vaulted up onto the driver's seat and urged the horses underway.

Tiki bit hard on her bottom lip to stop her tears as the carriage drove away. Clara, Toots, and Fiona peered through the small back window, and it felt as if part of Tiki's heart was leaving with them. Against her chest, the Ring of *Ériu* dangled from its thin gold chain to hang between her breasts, the metal still warmed from Rieker's skin.

"It was the right decision."

Dain stood next to her, his brow pulled down in a frown as he watched the carriage disappear around a corner. Once again, he reminded Tiki of a blurry image of Rieker, and his presence reassured her. She straightened, feeling stronger.

"Yes, it is. Now, we should prepare to depart. We have work to do."

A low growl sounded.

Tiki and Dain turned at the same time.

Behind them stood two monstrous black dogs. One had its head lowered with lips curled back in a feral snarl. The other had its snout raised, nostrils flared, sniffing the air. The rumbling that emitted from their chests was so fierce, it seemed the ground shook beneath Tiki's feet.

Bearach's hellhounds.

Before she could react, they charged.

Chapter Seven

A scream ripped from Tiki's lips as a viselike grip clamped around her upper arm and yanked her off her feet. Growls filled the air along with the sound of fabric tearing as the fangs of one of the giant dogs pierced her skirt. A burning sensation streaked down her leg as she catapulted through the air.

In a blink, Dain was between her and the beasts, his arms wrapped around her body as he dove sideways with her in his arms. Her breath exploded from her lungs in a painful gasp as she and Dain landed on the ground with a jarring thud.

Though Dain landed on top of her, he was on his feet in a blink, a whip now clutched in his hand as he turned a quick circle. Tiki scrambled to stand next to him, expecting to be attacked, but the hounds were gone, as was Rieker's townhome and the storm clouds that had blackened the sky above Grosvenor Square. Instead, they stood among the deepest shadows of a forest, the deafening growls of the hellhounds replaced with the babble of a nearby brook as it tumbled over its stony bed.

"Where are we?"

"The Wychwood." Dain's back was to her as he surveyed the surrounding forest.

"But how did we get here? I thought you had to go through the gates …"

Dain glanced over his shoulder. "When Larkin transported William and I from the Wychwood the night of the sacrifice of the Seven-Year King, she taught us how to transport between certain spots at will. Said our lives were going to depend on the ability to escape quickly. It seems she was right—again." He held out his hand to her. "Come along. We can't be seen here. We've got to keep moving—those beasts won't stop, though it will take them a while to trace you back here."

Tiki shivered. The air was much cooler and the nearby trees were bare, their branches stripped of leaves and coated in white frost. Heavy shadows lingered beneath their canopy, and the forest was much darker than the last time she'd visited.

"Those hounds—were they—" A gust of wind struck her in the face, making her turn away from the icy air.

Dain didn't seem to notice as he led her down a faint trail, his head swiveling, watching for any movement. "Yes. Bearach's hellhounds. They've tracked us before but this time, they were a bit too close for comfort. We were lucky to get away. If Donegal sent Bearach's hounds to Grosvenor Square, then he knows far too much about you."

He turned and contemplated Tiki. "I think we better give them something to ponder." He bent to one knee and tore a section from the front of Tiki's blue dress. With deft movements, he tied the piece of fabric in the center of a thick bush. "All right. That's a start. Let's go."

As they hurried down the path, Tiki became aware of the acrid scent of burning. "What is that smell?"

Dain's answer was terse. "Donegal must still have a fire burning in the Wychwood. Part of his plan to force the outliers into the UnSeelie court in this battle with the Seelies." He stopped and held out his hand. "Another piece, please." Tiki hurriedly tore another strip of blue fabric from her dress and handed it to Dain who climbed a tree, shoving the material into the crotch between two limbs and leaving a section dangling. "Hopefully, those beasts will smell your scent, but won't be able to reach it." He pressed his lips together. "That might delay them, but not for long."

They proceeded for another mile through the forest, leaving bits of Tiki's clothing as a trail for the hellhounds to follow. As they hurried along, Tiki searched the forest, certain the creatures of the Wychwood watched their passage, yet if they did, they remained unseen.

Dain stopped in the middle of the trail. "We need to place the final decoy and then leave this place."

Tiki glanced down at what remained of her shredded dress. Much of the fabric below her knees in the front had been torn away, making the back of her dress appear to be a long train. The cool air swept around her ankles, chilling her.

"Do you want me to tear another section?" she asked.

"No. I want the whole dress."

Tiki jerked her head up in surprise. Though Dain's expression was serious, his eyes danced with mischief.

"Fine. Turn around."

Dain raised one eyebrow. "Must you take all the fun out of it?"

Tiki grabbed his shoulders and forced him around. "And stay there until I tell you to move."

"Yes, Majesty." Dain chuckled as Tiki yanked the ties at the back of her neck to loosen the dress enough so what was left of it could fall to the ground around her ankles. She stepped free of the garment and whispered the words to make her sheath and undergarments melt into clothing woven from the fabric of the forest. Bark-colored trousers clung tightly to the contours of her legs. A dark green jacket with a mottled weave made her blend with the surrounding trees. Her long, black hair, which before had hung around her shoulders like a cloud, was now braided neatly down her back. On her feet were boots of the softest leather, with soles that would make no sound nor leave a trace. The slender hilt of a dagger protruded from the ankle of each boot, within easy grasp should she need to defend herself. In a matter of seconds, she had become all but invisible within the forest.

"All right, you may turn around," she said as she scooped up the dress.

"Nicely done." Dain nodded in admiration as he took in Tiki's curves. "Inspiring, really." With a flick of his wrist, Dain's clothing, which had been appropriate for London, dissolved into an outfit almost identical to Tiki's, except he now carried a quiver on his back with a bow slung over one shoulder and a knife in his hand. The whip he had carried was hooked to his belt, along with another wicked-looking knife with a long, curved blade.

In a few graceful swings, he sliced several long lengths of vine that hung from one of the trees that towered above their heads and wound them into a neat circle before shoving them inside his jacket.

"What's that for?" Tiki asked.

"You'll see." He motioned at the faint trail that wound through the trees. "Let's keep moving—it's not far from here."

"Where are we going?"

"A spot on the far side of the Tor called Dry Falls. Centuries ago, before the Palace of Mirrors existed, a waterfall used to plummet from the top of the Tor and over time cut deep valleys into the rocks, forming odd cliffs and caves." As he spoke, he veered onto a small trail that wound up the side of the mountain.

"This isn't the trail we took when we escaped from the Palace of Mirrors, is it?"

"No, that's on the other side of the Tor. We're below the encampment."

Tiki concentrated on her footing as she followed Dain up the boulder-strewn path and tried not to think of the encampment of homeless faeries that congregated on a rocky outcropping of the Tor. Most were so thin, they wouldn't survive another winter without food.

Many of the rocks were jagged and sharp, making it impossible to move quickly, though Dain seemed to know where he was going and walked the narrow footpath with confidence. As they climbed higher, the ground dropped away in a dizzying plunge that made Tiki's heart race and her breath come in short gasps. They were almost a third of the way up the rocky cliff when he finally stopped.

"Here's where we're going to leave your dress." He pulled the vines from the depths of his jacket and carefully plucked the leaves before tying one end to the shaft of an arrow. Threading the arrow into his bow, his raised his arms and fired across the rocky precipice. The point of the arrow quivered upon impact with the stone wall as the tip embedded itself in a crevice on the other side.

"Now, we'll slide your dress onto this ..." Dain threaded the vine through the neck and arm holes of the dress. Clutching the end of the tether, he climbed up the rocky slope and shook the makeshift line so gravity made the dress slide down toward the middle until the garment hung above the open canyon.

He hurried back to where Tiki waited and secured the vine to the trunk of a gnarled tree that grew from between the rocks. The gown, suspended on the line, billowed and moved as though dancing with the wind. It was easy to imagine someone wore the dress and floated above the rocky ravine.

"There," he said with satisfaction, hands propped on his hips as he surveyed his handiwork. "Perhaps those dogs will be stupid enough to think they can get to you and instead will jump to their deaths. If nothing else, it's enough to make them believe they've cornered their prey and they'll stay here to guard you."

"Dain O'Brien, you are brilliant." Tiki smiled at the young man. "Well done."

Dain turned to her, a puzzled frown on his forehead. "O'Brien?"

Tiki hesitated. "It's the name Larkin called you in the High Chamber. When she said you and William were the sons of the late Lady Breanna of Connacht."

"She said my last name was O'Brien?"

Tiki clearly remembered the conversation because it had been a new clue in Rieker's mysterious heritage. "Isn't that your name?"

"O'Brien is my middle name."

Tiki's brows pulled down. "She said you and William were the twin sons of Lady Breanna and a mortal lover. I assumed she meant William's father. Does that mean your last name is Richmond?"

Dain shrugged. "I'm not sure. Just before he disappeared, Kieran told me I was a Winterbourne. I didn't know what he meant—I'd never heard the name before. I rather got the feeling he regretted telling me, so I never mentioned it to anyone. Then he disappeared before telling me anything more." Dain stared out over the forest below, a faraway look in his eyes. "I've been meaning to ask William about it."

He shook his head, as if to shake the memories away. "But that's not what's important right now. We need to get to the Plain of Sunlight and find out what's happening with this war."

"Yes. I want to talk to Larkin and make sure the fey are being fed, especially now that winter has arrived."

Dain slid his warm hands around her cold fingers. The humor that often lurked in his eyes was absent, and Tiki was struck by the sheer beauty of his aristocratic features. The bruises had faded from the beatings Donegal had inflicted, no longer distracting from his high forehead, vivid blue eyes, and sculpted cheekbones that were like a work of art—one she didn't often notice because he was either mocking her or making a joke. When he was serious like this, he looked like someone she barely knew—the handsome enigma she'd first met as Sean and come to know as Dain. A person she would admire, respect, and if he weren't Rieker's brother, potentially fear, for she sensed he had the potential for great power.

"Tara, before we return to the Plain of Sunlight, I need to tell you something."

Tiki stiffened. "What's that?"

"Larkin will most likely be there, and I think it's important for you to realize that Larkin will make sure she gets what she wants before you get what you want."

Tiki's shoulders relaxed. Dain wasn't revealing anything she didn't already know. But her tone was cool when she responded. "I thank you for your warning, but you must realize that Larkin is not queen here—I am." Tiki raised her chin. "*I* will make the decisions on who gets what they want."

Chapter Eight

They arrived in a sunlit meadow, the air pierced by the sharp trills of a meadowlark. A familiar grass-covered mound stood before them with an arched stone entry. Tiki took a deep breath of the warm, succulent air, rich with the fragrance of honeysuckle, and for the first time in a long time, she didn't feel the urge to cough. It was as if they had stepped through time into summer.

"Welcome to the Plain of Sunlight, Majesty." Dain swept his arm out as he bent in a stiff bow. "The Seelie court's home away from the Palace of Mirrors."

Tiki inclined her head in a mock bow, matching his formality. "Thank you, kind sir." She looked at the horizon where the impressive hulk of Wydryn Tor rose against the sky. The top of the Tor was concealed by dark clouds that spilled down into the Wychwood Forest below, as though a storm overflowed the top of a teacup. Tiki was glad to be far away from the troubles that simmered there.

She pointed to several oddly shaped silhouettes in the distance. "What are those?"

Dain squinted in the direction she pointed. Without responding, he whirled around and took her arm, motioning to the entry to the Seelie court's underground lair. "Never mind. Let's find Larkin."

"What do you mean, *never mind*?" Tiki glanced over her shoulder at the odd shadows again. "What are they?" Dain trudged along in silence until Tiki pulled her arm free. "Tell me now."

An unfamiliar look crossed Dain's features, and Tiki's stomach clenched, not sure what to make of his strange reaction.

The muscles in his jaw flexed before he spoke, as if he struggled to keep the answer captive. "They are what remain of the border guards. Donegal continues to attack, and when he captures one of our soldiers, he impales their bodies on large stakes. They line the perimeter of the Plain of Sunlight as a grisly warning of his intent."

Tiki spoke in a horrified whisper. "Why haven't they been taken down?"

"The UnSeelies lie in wait for those who might rescue the fallen. It's suicide to try to take the bodies down right now."

A terrible thrumming rumbled in Tiki's head. Dead bodies left to rot where they'd been impaled as a threat. She could think of nothing more barbaric. With each bit of knowledge she gained about the Winter King, the outcome of this war became clearer and clearer: Donegal had to be stopped—at whatever cost.

Dain led Tiki through the arched stone entry into the underground chamber of the Seelies. The passageway was lit by wall-mounted torches, their flames flickering and wavering as they passed. The hallway smelled of fresh dirt, but the walls were hard-packed and almost stone-like, as if they had existed for too many years to count. The path led steeply downhill to a plank door. The guard who stood there recognized Tiki immediately.

"Welcome home, Majesty," he said, bowing as she passed.

"Thank you." Tiki nodded, surprised by his reaction.

They moved farther along the corridor and the hallway widened, changing from dirt to stone with columns lining each side. The next guard stamped his staff on the floor and bowed. "We've been awaiting your return, Your Grace."

A buzz built as she and Dain continued down the winding hallway, the news of her arrival somehow spreading through the Seelie court as if by magic. Each of the red-coated guards they passed on their way to the great underground hall where the Macanna gathered bowed and stamped their staffs as she passed.

"We are yours to command, Majesty."

"Feel safer knowing you're here, Queen Tara."

Tiki nodded and smiled, surprise warring with gratitude in her chest.

Dain looked over at her. "Do you want to go directly to the hall, Majesty, or to your rooms first?"

Tiki noticed how formal his tone and manner had become, now that they were around others from the Seelie court. The teasing spark that usually lit his eyes was gone.

"Let's find Larkin first."

"How nice of you to join us." The mercurial faerie's voice was unmistakable.

Tiki whirled. Nothing about Larkin should surprise her, yet somehow, the faerie always managed to remain unpredictable. The other girl was dressed in the same dark drape she'd worn when she'd paid Tiki her recent nighttime visit. Even dressed in black, Larkin's exquisite face was as breathtaking as ever, her porcelain skin and enigmatic eyes emphasized by the contrast with her clothing.

"Yes, well, I was strongly encouraged to visit," she replied. It was hard to draw her eyes away from the faerie's ethereal beauty, and Tiki straightened her spine, as if preparing for battle. "There are matters on which I'd like an update. Is there someplace where we can have privacy?"

"Follow me. Dain," she said over her shoulder, "I'd like you to join us as well." She didn't wait to see if they would follow. Instead, she swept down one of the seven corridors that stretched away from the circular main hall like spokes in a wheel. Her footsteps were silent, and there were moments when she became as indistinct as the shadows that clung to the huge columns lining the hallway.

Larkin swung around a corner and stopped. "For my own protection, I conceal my chambers. Do not reveal this location to anyone"—her eyes narrowed—"you may need to hide here yourself one day."

She disappeared behind a wall of greenery. Dain raised his eyebrows at Tiki and made a face as he took her hand and pulled her into a shadowed space behind the plants not visible from the hallway. Before them, a moss-covered door stood ajar, a sliver of light escaping from the room.

Dain motioned for Tiki to enter. "After you, Majesty."

Tiki walked past the faerie, unsure of what to expect. The only other time she'd visited the Plain of Sunlight, she'd seen little more than the main underground hall. She looked curiously into the room, then stopped and stared, her heart fluttering with surprise. To her amazement, the room was furnished almost identically to the drawing room in Grosvenor Square. A cheery fire burned in the grate, with an identical rug on the floor before the hearth. A similar couch and chairs were grouped in a comfortable half circle with pastoral paintings on the walls that matched those in Rieker's townhome. Resting atop familiar cabinets, several candles were lit within hurricane lanterns, throwing a yellow circle of light that was both inviting and reassuring. Whatever Tiki had expected— this wasn't it.

Larkin marched into the room and sat in one of the chairs, snapping her fingers at Tiki to sit on the nearby couch. "Fifteen more dead. Staked on the border to taunt us. While Donegal's army grows, ours is being decimated."

The hair on Tiki's arms rose as chill bumps covered her skin. "I saw them when we came in. What do you want me to do?"

"I want you to be the queen you were born to be," Larkin snapped. Her words seemed to echo off the walls of the small room.

"Larkin," Dain said, his tone a warning. "Tiki has come back to help. You need to help her understand how to do that."

Larkin took a deep breath and looked at Tiki expectantly. "We need to plan an attack. We can't continue to let Donegal grow his army, or the Seelie court won't stand a chance. Did you bring the cup?"

"I—" Tiki hesitated, feeling foolish, especially after Larkin's insinuation that she'd not been living up to her responsibilities. "No, I—"

"We were forced to leave London unexpectedly." Dain's hands rested along the back of the couch and his long fingers brushed Tiki's shoulder in a reassuring way. "Donegal set Bearach's hounds after Tara, and they found us in Grosvenor Square." He spoke as if unaware of the tension that choked the air around them. "I'm sure I could easily retrieve the cup from wherever Tara has stored it."

"Go now," Larkin commanded. "Donegal has taken all the homeless faeries captive. Those who are able to walk are now UnSeelie soldiers. He's forced any hobgoblins he can find into service—the rest are hiding for their lives in the Wychwood. The redcaps, spriggans, Jack-in-Irons—the whole lot are combing the forest looking for Tara and either impressing any Seelies they find into their ranks or killing them. While we need to go on the offensive, we don't have the manpower to compete with the UnSeelies. I fear our only hope to win this war is to find the Fourth Treasure—and to do that, we need the Cup of Plenty."

Tiki turned to Dain and put her hand on his arm. "You know where it is. Go now and bring it back. It doesn't seem we have time to lose. Be careful."

"As you wish, Majesty." He bent his head and exited the room.

Larkin's eyes were hooded as she contemplated Tiki. "You trust him with such precious secrets now?"

"He has earned my trust," she answered.

Larkin's beautiful lips twisted in a smirk. "Do you think William trusts him as completely as you?"

"Of course, he does," Tiki replied indignantly. "They're brothers."

"Let me assure you, my naive little queen"—the bitterness in Larkin's voice was unmistakable—"blood does not buy loyalty."

Chapter Nine

"I'm going to Windsor." Leo stood in the open doorway to the drawing room and waited for his brother's reaction.

Prince Arthur looked up from where he sat polishing a rifle, pausing mid-stroke. At his feet, a small black-and-white cocker spaniel lay sleeping. "Why? I thought you still weren't feeling well."

Leo had just returned from visiting Mamie. He debated whether to tell Arthur the truth, but Mamie's warning was still fresh in his ears, and he decided that nothing would be gained in telling his brother the real purpose of his trip.

"Actually, I thought the clean air might help my recovery. I swear, these low-lying clouds have trapped the soot and debris right on top of the palace. I can barely draw a breath when I go outside." Leo coughed to emphasize his point. "I'm going this afternoon."

"That's fine. Why don't you stay for a few days? I'm sure Mother and Baby will be pleased to see you." Arthur grinned as he resumed his work. "And I'm sure our little sister would be quite happy to take more of your money in cards."

"Don't be a prat, Arthur," Leo said. "I'll be back for the poker game on Friday night, and I plan to make you eat your words."

"That's right, cards this week. Is Wills joining us?"

"I don't know. I'll go round Grosvenor Square and invite him when I'm back from Windsor. I'm curious how he and his cousin are faring."

"And I'm sure the thought of visiting the beautiful Tara has never crossed your mind."

Leo chose to ignore his brother as Arthur snorted with laughter. "I'm going to ask Wills if he wants to bring Dain. He's a bit of a mysterious chap. I'd like the chance to ask him a few more questions."

"I'm glad I caught you alone, Mother," Leo said the next day as he closed the door to the small library in Windsor Castle. The weather outside was wet and dreary, making the wood-paneled room and warmth of the fire that much more inviting. "I'd like to talk to you."

Queen Victoria looked up from her book, a guarded expression in her eyes. Like usual, she wore a high-necked black gown and had her hair pulled back from her round face, knotted tightly at the nape of her neck. "On what subject, Leopold?"

"On the matter of your ring that went missing—the ring of the truce that William Richmond now guards."

Victoria's eyes narrowed. "Is there a problem?"

"Not directly, but at Mamie's suggestion, I've come to ask you about the other secrets in the ring." Leo perched on the edge of a chair, too excited to pretend nonchalance. He sensed that his mother held information that no other mortal knew. Would she share her knowledge with him?

His mother marked the page she was reading and closed her book, her motions slow and deliberate. "So, Mamie told you there were other secrets in the ring?"

"Yes."

"Was that all she said?"

"She said Wills' friend, Tara, needed to know those secrets. It sounded like it was a matter of life or death."

"Tara? What role does she play?"

Leo took a deep breath. "Mamie said she was a true-born queen."

Victoria raised her eyebrows. "I suppose it's possible. She's about the same age I was when I ascended the throne. Does William still guard the ring?"

Leo nodded. "I'm sure of it."

The queen crossed her hands over the book that now rested on her lap and stared into the distance. When she finally spoke, her words were hushed. "Mamie is the only other person who knows there is more than the truce in that ring. We vowed never to speak of the other secrets unless we felt imminent danger to the British throne existed."

Leo exhaled slowly. So, there was something more in the ring. He leaned closer. "What are the secrets?"

His mother shook her head, her expression serious. "I don't know all that is held within the ring—they were never our secrets to keep. Part of our alliance with the fey allowed them to safeguard information in our world. In exchange, they protected us from those who would do us harm. Until recently, that is." Her gaze shifted to his face. "But I believe, as Mamie has indicated, whatever those secrets are—they are very powerful."

Leo pushed himself out of the chair. "Thank you, Mother. I'll let William and Tara know straightaway." He hurried to the door.

"Leopold."

Leo stopped and glanced over his shoulder. "Yes?"

"There is one secret I do know."

His breath caught in anticipation. "What's that?"

"One must use a mirror."

His brows pulled down in a frown. "Come again?"

"There is a particular mirror that hangs in the private passageway to the White Drawing Room in Buckingham. It is round with an unusually carved frame—one of a kind. Our family has had it since long before I was born or my mother or my mother's mother. It came into our protection at the same time as the ring. I've always thought of it as the Faerie Queen's Mirror, because it has what looks like the head of a faerie queen carved into the top. That mirror is tied to the purpose of the ring."

Leo slowly shifted around to face his mother. "How so?"

"As the ring is a secret-keeper for the faerie world's kings and queens, the mirror is their fail-safe should the ring ever be stolen. We were told that one cannot decipher the secrets held in the ring without the mirror." Victoria opened her book, signaling their conversation had reached its end. "I suggest you go immediately and find William Richmond and his friend, Tara, and tell them what you know. Perhaps it is time for the mirror to be put to use."

Chapter Ten

It was still light in London when Dain shimmered into the foyer of Grosvenor Square. Storm clouds gathered overhead, however, and long shadows stretched through the empty rooms, giving the townhome an unnaturally vacant feeling. Dain hurried to William's study where Tiki had stored the Cup of Plenty when they'd left the previous day. Perched on a bookshelf and glamoured as plain green glass, Dain marveled at how something so powerful could appear so insignificant.

"A lesson, I suppose," he muttered to himself as he reached for the cup. "Much like Tara. The world is not always what it seems." He carefully cradled the vase in his hands as he twisted the cup to examine the piece, but the glamour hid the iridescent swirls of colored glass that normally adorned its sides. "Healing, sustenance, inspiration, and wisdom," he whispered. "You are a powerful little piece of glass. How do we get what we need from you?"

A pounding sounded from outside the room, and Dain jerked around in surprise. He placed the goblet back on the shelf and hurried to the door and peered down the hallway. Shamus and the others had left for William's estate in Richmond yesterday. Had someone remained behind? The pounding sounded again, and this time it was obvious that the noise came from the front door.

Curiosity got the better of him, and he slipped down the hallway and into the foyer. Standing to the side so he wouldn't be seen, he moved the curtain shielding the sidelight window ever so slightly to view the street. An ornate carriage stood before No. 6. There was no mistaking the gold and red, nor the liveried footman who stood at all four corners of the coach. Someone from the palace was calling on William.

Dain stepped back and stared at the door as if he might be able to see through the wood to determine who stood on the other side.

The pounding was replaced with the sharp rap of the brass door knocker.

"Wills!" a familiar voice called in a muffled tone. "Are you home?"

Pure instinct fueled Dain's reaction and he yanked open the door.

Leo stood frozen with his fist in the air, poised to pound on the door one more time. "Oh. You startled me. I thought everyone must have gone." He dropped his hand and tugged on the bottom of his jacket.

"Prince Leopold." Dain gave a sharp bow. "How nice to see you again. I'm William's cousin, Dain. We met on a very wet and stormy night not long ago."

"Yes, hello, Dain. I remember—nice to see you again. Is Wills about?" Leo tilted his head to look around Dain's broad shoulders.

Dain stepped back and swept his arm out with a flourish. "Would you like to come in, Majesty?"

"My mother is the Majesty—not me. Friends call me Leo. It would please me if you would do the same." The young prince stepped over the threshold and looked up and down the hallway with obvious familiarity. "Where's Wills? I need to speak to him immediately."

"I'm afraid William isn't here at the moment." Dain edged around the thin prince to shut the door, the skin on his arms prickling. "Has something happened?"

"No. Yes." Leo shook his head. "I must speak to Wills. I have information he needs." The prince focused on Dain. "Where is he?"

Dain hesitated. How much of the truth should he reveal? William had turned to Leo when they needed to hide from Donegal in those last hours of Samhain, so clearly his brother trusted the young royal, but to what degree? How much did Leo really know about the Otherworld? About the threat Donegal posed?

Dain drew a deep breath. If William trusted Leo, so would he. "I'm afraid he's on his way to Scotland," he said quietly.

Leo looked stricken. "Scotland?" he said in a horrified whisper. "Why would he go *there*? Is Tara with him?"

There was something about the prince's manner that struck a warning note with Dain. "I can take a message to him, if you'd like. I'll be joining him soon." It wasn't the absolute truth, but the statement held a sliver of fact. Eventually, he would see William again—he just wasn't certain if it would be this month or next. Assuming he survived Donegal's attack.

Leo went silent, indecision evident in his frown. Dain took a chance.

"Does this matter have something to do with—the *Otherworld*?"

Leo's eyes shot to Dain's face. "You know of that?"

Dain nodded. "William has confided in me. What have you learned?"

Leo hesitated.

Dain leaned closer. "It's a very dangerous time between the worlds right now, Prince Leo. If you've learned something you think might help William, best to share it with him straightaway."

"How long will he be gone?" Leo asked.

"It could be months." Dain motioned to the empty townhome. "The entire staff has departed—for their own safety. I've just stopped by long enough to gather something William needed and then I'll be joining him." He stared hard at the prince, willing him to do his bidding. "What information can I pass on to him?"

Leo took a quick glance around the dim foyer. "You swear on your mother's head you will tell no one but William or Tara?"

"I do."

The prince took a deep breath. "There is a very special ring—it holds a truce between our world and—*that* world." Leo's expression grew intent. "William guards this ring with his very life."

"The Ring of *Ériu*." Dain nodded. "I've heard of it."

A look of relief shot across Leo's face. "You have? Excellent. I've learned there is other"—he hesitated—"*information* ... in the ring. Important secrets that William and Tara need to know."

A vague sense of disappointment washed over Dain. The prince didn't have any knowledge of value after all. "Is that the message you'd like me to relay? There are other secrets in the ring?"

"No. I suspect Wills and Tara already know that much. What they don't know"—he glanced up and down the hallway before he whispered—"is they need a mirror to decipher the secrets. *That's* what I need to tell Wills."

Dain's brows pulled down in a frown. "A *mirror,* you say? Are you quite sure?"

Leo nodded. "But not just any mirror—a special mirror—one that hangs in Buckingham Palace. My mother refers to it as the Faerie Queen's Mirror."

Less than twenty minutes later, Dain and Leo arrived at Buckingham Palace. The carriage driver stopped in the inner Quadrangle and the two young men rushed from the vehicle into the palace.

"Mother said it hangs in the White Drawing Room," Leo said over his shoulder as they hurried along the corridor. Elaborate gilded designs covered the soaring walls, interspersed by oversized pictures of royal ancestors. Their footsteps echoed on the stone floors as Dain followed the prince, scarcely able to believe the turn the evening had taken. A mirror needed to decipher the secrets in the Ring of *Ériu*? If what Leo said was true, that in itself was a well-kept secret—no doubt another layer of protection by Eridanus and Finn to guard the ancient power of the Seelie court.

"The mirror is very distinctive."

"How's that?" Dain looked over at Leo.

"She said the top of the frame bears the carved head of a faerie queen."

"Really? I'm looking forward to seeing this."

Leo stopped before a pair of immense maroon-and-gold carved doors inlaid with huge rectangular mirrors. With a tug, he pulled one open, revealing a room that seemed to have been spun from gold sugar. The White Drawing Room was one of the most opulent spaces Dain had ever stepped inside. Lavish gilding dripped from square columns and carved ribbons of gold stretched around the room. Light from floor-to-ceiling windows, as well as from the glittering, cut-crystal chandeliers, reflected in the elaborate gold-framed mirrors that lined the walls, making the room appear to be drenched in sunlight.

Dain tipped his head back to stare in awe at the intricate design of the breathtaking domed ceiling. Gilded circles with triangles embedded in their centers supported a shelf where rows of winged cherubs had been carved. Faeries, perhaps? His lips twitched in amusement. Diamond-shaped embellishments decorated the arches leading to the center square of the ceiling far above their heads. Not an inch of the immense space was left unadorned. In a way, the room reminded him of the Palace of Mirrors when the Seelies were in control.

Dain looked about the room in amazement. "There are mirrors everywhere—do you know which one we're looking for?" He pointed at a grand mirror that sat atop a fireplace, its frame decorated with lavish scrolled gold carvings. "Could it be that mirror?"

"No. That one is much too big," Leo said. "And do you see a faerie queen on that frame? The mirror we're looking for is hidden."

Dain shifted to the prince. "Do you know where?"

In response, Leo hurried to the end of the spacious room and stopped before an ebony-veneered cabinet with a tall mirror stretching high above it. He reached behind the gilded edge and to Dain's amazement, the entire cabinet and mirror swung away from the wall as one.

Leo glanced over his shoulder with a wicked grin. "In our secret passageway."

Dain's jaw dropped in surprise. "Where does that lead?"

"To our private rooms. We use this drawing room for state receptions and the like. This hidden corridor is a way to come and go discreetly." Leo's voice became muffled as he disappeared into the passageway behind the cabinet.

Dain followed the young prince through the opening into a small hallway. At a curve in the passageway, Leo stood before a small, round mirror that hung upon the wall. Dain hurried to his side.

The mirror wasn't large. At its widest point, it couldn't have been more than twelve inches. What had once been a gold frame was now aged to a mottled, green-blue patina. But most interesting—at the top of the intricately carved frame was a woman's face, with wings on each side.

Leo motioned at the carved figure. "Now this is a faerie queen."

"Indeed," Dain said in a low hush. His eyes caressed the mirror, for he knew innately that this mirror was connected to his world. The design, the detailing, the age—this was another piece to an ancient puzzle. He focused on the figure located at the bottom of the mirror. The image was that of a man with ram's horns protruding from each side of his head. An arrogant expression twisted his features, and he wore a headdress with a golden jester's mask at its crown.

At the same moment, Leo pointed to the figure at the bottom. "Who do you suppose that is?"

Dain answered with uneasy confidence. "The UnSeelie king. The dark to her light." He motioned to the mirror. "May I?"

Leo moved aside and Dain shifted so he stood directly in front of the frame, but instead of reflecting his image, the surface of the mirror shifted and undulated until it looked like a fire burned within the glass.

"What could be the purpose of a mirror like this?" Dain mused as he examined the piece. "One that does not provide reflection, but instead shows us something not in this room."

"I don't know." Leo reached for the frame and lifted it from its hook. "But there's only one way to find out." He proffered the mirror to Dain. "You must take this to William and Tara—they'll know what to do."

Chapter Eleven

Dain rode alone in the back of the carriage as Leo's driver returned him to Grosvenor Square. The mirror rested on his knees, carefully wrapped in a blanket and hidden inside a fabric bag. The Faerie Queen's Mirror. What luck that he'd been at William's townhome when Leo had come calling.

He ran his long fingers over the fabric that protected the mirror, marveling at the secret he guarded. All his senses told him that this was important—a critical link to understanding the powerful clues that Finn and Eridanus had left to the future ruler of the Seelie court—to Tara. Could this little mirror mean the difference between glorious victory or soul-crushing defeat for the Seelie court? But only if they could decipher how to use it.

"I will take you to my beautiful faerie queen," he said to the bundle on his lap, "and she will make sense of your true purpose." He imagined the intricate design of the frame, with faces carved into the mirror's border. The Summer Queen and the Winter King. Should he include Larkin when he shared what he'd discovered? Though he'd trusted the faerie with his life more than once, he was well aware of Tara's distrust and even dislike of Larkin. Perhaps he should leave it to Tara to decide who would know of the mirror.

He lifted his head to look out the window as the *clip-clop* of the horses' hooves echoed against the cobblestones. The streets of London were always thick with a diverse crowd: from gowned women in their elegant attire to streetwalkers, one side of their skirts hitched in their belts, plying their trade; from coal-dusters and black-faced chimney sweeps to the finest top-hatted men; and always the street children, so dirty, it was all but impossible to tell boy from girl, scrabbling among the mix, trying to survive. London was home to all.

But here, in the quiet, tree-lined streets between Buckingham Palace and Mayfair, a bubble of gentility existed as though insulated from the darkness of the world. As if air was more plentiful here and one could draw a deeper breath—but Dain knew it was an illusion. There was no safe place in London or the Otherworld while Donegal lived.

An hour later, Dain had returned to the Otherworld and stood in Larkin's drawing room that was so similar to Grosvenor Square. He had hidden the Faerie Queen's Mirror in his own rooms upon his return to the Plain of Sunlight, waiting for the time when he could give it to Tara alone. On the other side of the drawing room, Larkin held the Cup of Plenty. The glamour had been removed, and brilliant colors swirled on the outside of the glass, glowing in the firelight.

"How does it go again?" Tiki looked over at Dain. "The paradox of the Four Treasures?"

Before he could speak, Larkin answered as if reciting a poem, never lifting her eyes from the sparkling glass she held. "One must possess the first three to find the fourth. The secret of the Fourth Treasure is held within the third: the Ring of *Ériu*. One must use inspiration from the second, the Cup of Plenty, to procure the secrets from the ring. But one must be a queen named by the first, the Stone of Tara, to retrieve the information." She lifted her head. "So, it's up to you, Tara. Use the inspiration of the cup to draw the secrets from the ring so we may find the Fourth Treasure and defeat Donegal."

Tiki sank onto the couch and closed her eyes. "I just need to … think for a moment."

Dain looked over at Larkin. "Have you got a blanket? And perhaps something for Tara to eat before I leave? It's been a difficult time lately."

Tiki's eyes flew open and she clutched at his hand. "Leave?"

"Yes. I need to—"

A knock sounded against the wood.

"Come," Larkin called as she set the cup on a small coffee table in front of where Tiki sat. The door silently swung open and a small figure came in, hidden behind the voluminous crimson-colored dress bunched in its arms.

"Your dress, Lady Larkin," a scratchy voice said.

Tiki turned with a jerk. "Ailléna?"

"I'll take that before you wrinkle it any further." Larkin plucked the dress from the diminutive figure's arms revealing the face that had been hidden by the material. A long beak nose stretched from a wizened face with fang-like teeth jutting up from the little goblin's lower jaw. An uglier creature probably didn't exist.

"Majesty?" Ailléna dropped into such a low curtsy, her forehead thumped the floor. "I didnae know you were back." She raised her head and clapped gnarled fingers together, jumping up, her stubby legs pushing her a few inches off the ground. "We're saved!"

Tiki held out her hands and wrapped her long fingers around the little goblin's. "Perhaps not saved yet, but we're working on it. I'm so glad you were able to come to the Plain of Sunlight. I thought you said you weren't allowed …"

"That is enough," Larkin snapped at Tiki. "Release that dirty redcap before she bites you."

Ailléna yanked her hands free and took several hurried steps back from Tiki. "Yes'm." She pointed a clawed finger at the Cup of Plenty sitting on the coffee table. "I see you brought the cup with you." She drew in a long breath, the oversized nostrils on her beaked nose flaring. "Still smells as delicious as ever."

A tantalizing scent wafted through the air as if a hearty soup cooked nearby.

Tiki frowned and inhaled. "You're right." She looked from Larkin to Dain. "What is that smell?"

"I don't know, but it's making my mouth water." Dain nodded at the little goblin. "Have you brought food with you?"

"No, sir," Ailléna said, her frightened eyes shifting to Larkin. "I'm not allowed to eat the food in the big house—just the scraps they throw in the fields."

Tiki pushed herself off the couch. "What? They don't feed you here?"

"Of course, we feed her." Larkin pointed at the door. "Be off with you. You've done your job. Now scat."

Ailléna smiled at Tiki, which looked more look a horrible grimace with her jutting underjaw and huge fangs reaching over her upper lip. "Pleasure to see you, Majesty." Then she scampered out the door and disappeared.

Tiki turned to Larkin. "Tell me you're feeding her."

"Obviously, since she's alive, isn't she? Now let's get back—"

But Tiki persisted. "How is it that Ailléna has come to be at the Plain of Sunlight?"

Larkin lifted her slim shoulders in an elegant shrug. "I guess we needed some help around the place. Labor has been in short supply since Donegal converted the beggars to UnSeelie soldiers." She let out a derisive snort. "Though we could probably buy off the lot of them with a loaf of bread."

"That smell is gone now, have you noticed?" Dain raised his nose and sniffed. "How strange. Maybe the goblin had been in the kitchens and the smell clung to her clothes."

"This isn't the first time that has happened. When we were in the Palace of Mirrors, the same thing occurred—Ailléna was with us and the room smelled like fresh soup." Tiki stared at the cup with a perplexed frown. "The cup is said to provide sustenance—" She reached for the little glass goblet and peered into its depths but the vessel was empty. She tipped the cup as if to pour liquid, but nothing emerged.

"Maybe it only provides sustenance when there is someone in need nearby," Dain offered.

Tiki lifted her head. "That's brilliant, Dain. We'll have—"

"Let's focus on the main purpose of the treasures," Larkin interrupted.

Dain pulled a blanket from the back of a nearby chair and handed it to Tiki. "Wrap up in this. Larkin will order food and you can rest until I return."

"Where are you going?" Tiki asked with concern.

Dain pushed his blond hair from his forehead. "I've got to find William so he can bring the Ring of *Ériu* back here. It won't do us any good to figure out the inspiration of the cup if we don't have the ring to pry the secrets from—wouldn't you agree?" He slid his hands into the pockets of his trousers and looked from Tiki to Larkin, waiting for a response.

"That's exactly right, Dain," Larkin replied. "Do you know where to look for him?"

"He was headed to Edinburgh, I believe. I could …"

Tiki interrupted. "We don't need William."

Dain's nodded. "You're right, we don't need William," he said, grinning, "but we do need the ring he guards."

"No," Tiki said. "Leave William alone and let him remain safe." She tugged on the thin braid of gold that hung around her neck and pulled the ring from beneath her clothes. "I guard the Ring of *Ériu* now."

Larkin moved so quickly, Tiki barely discerned her movement. One minute the faerie was across the room, the next she was standing too close, mesmerized by the bloodred stone that hung from Tiki's neck. She reached out a hand. "May I?"

Tiki lifted the ring and looked at the flickering flame that burned in its depths. She didn't remove the chain from around her neck, but instead, held the ring out for Larkin to see.

Dain let out a low whistle, his expression filled with awe.

"A true-born Seelie queen named by the *Cloch na Teamhrach,* the Cup of Plenty, and now the Ring of *Ériu*, all together in the same room. Three of the Four Treasures are within my sight at this moment." He grinned like a little boy on Saphrenmas morning. "Larkin, did you ever dream you'd see this day?"

Larkin's eyes narrowed. "I have been planning this day for half my life." She contemplated Tiki. "You held the cup while wearing the ring—did you *feel* anything? Sense anything? Gain wisdom you didn't have before?"

Tiki heaved a dejected sigh. "If there are secrets within this stone, they are hidden from me—and I have no idea how to retrieve them."

Chapter Twelve

"We've found a blue gown, hung from the rock cliffs on the far side of the Tor." Sullivan's hair shimmered like liquid silver, brushing his bony shoulders as he approached the Winter King.

Donegal turned from the window where he had been staring at the band of light on the horizon. "Was it hers?"

"It had her scent"—Sullivan scowled—"but the hounds lost her trail among the rocks."

Donegal smiled, the scarred side of his face pulling down in a grimace. "She knows she's being hunted and has sent someone to lay a false trail as a diversion."

"I think you're right. We had spies in London who saw several of the mortals who live with her in Grosvenor Square leave by carriage just before the hounds arrived. She didn't go with them."

"How fascinating. Who were they and where did they go?"

Sullivan shrugged. "It was the male who is often seen with the queen as well as three children."

Donegal's black eyes flared with interest. "Children?"

"I believe they live with the queen in the mortal world."

"Did someone follow them?"

"Yes—MacDonald and Brady."

"Where did they go?" he asked with a sudden urgency.

"I haven't heard back yet."

"I want to know the second you have word. This is our opportunity. The queen has sent off those she loves thinking she's protecting them." A guttural laugh escaped his lips. "She will soon learn there is no protection from my vengeance."

The Winter King turned back to the window and nodded toward the Plain of Sunlight where a golden glow reflected in a thin band across the horizon. "Tara MacLochlan will be back in the Otherworld soon, if she hasn't already returned." His words were as raw as a blade drawn against a stone. "This time I won't leave it to someone else to kill her. I will do it myself."

Chapter Thirteen

"Finn would not have made this an impossible task." Larkin dropped the ring against Tiki's chest and began to pace. "The cup offers inspiration, healing, sustenance ... how can a piece of glass inspire us?" she muttered as went from one side of the room to the other.

Tiki sank back and closed her eyes, willing herself to concentrate. The ring held the secret to finding the Fourth Treasure. The cup would provide the inspiration to release the secrets from the ring. They had used the cup to help Johnny before ... Tiki's eyes snapped open. Could it be that simple? Did she just need to drink from the cup to gain the needed inspiration?

She sat up and reached for the glass goblet.

Dain watched her from where he stood near the end of the couch. "Tara, what are you doing?"

Larkin paused in her pacing.

Tiki didn't answer as she lifted the glittering goblet to her lips and opened her mouth. The cup had appeared empty when they'd held it to Johnny's lips, but within seconds, fluid had poured from the goblet into his mouth, providing healing when he was in need. It had saved his life. Would the cup answer her need for knowledge in the same way?

She waited. Ten seconds. Fifteen. Twenty.

There was nothing.

A full minute went by before Tiki lowered the glass from her lips. "I thought …" The words died in her throat.

Dain strode over and sat on the couch next to her. "Well done, Tiki. You've answered an important question. Now we know one doesn't gain inspiration by drinking from the cup. There must be another way to gain the necessary knowledge."

"But what?" Tiki stared at the swirling colors that lined the exterior of the vase. "What do I need to do? Where do I need to look to know how to find the Fourth Treasure?"

The words had barely left her lips when a thin strand of smoke rose from the center of the goblet.

"What's that?" Dain pointed.

"There's something burning inside the cup," Larkin said, stepping closer.

Tiki tipped the goblet and stared into the center. In the depths of the glass an image floated, as if on water, even though a few moments ago the vessel had been empty. She peered closer.

"I see something … I think it's the ring of the truce—" The familiar shape undulated above a flickering flame and from the heart of the bloodred stone, a thin wisp of smoke curled into a mysterious shape as it rose above the rim of the glass and dissipated. "There's a fire below it."

"A fire *below* the ring? Are you sure?" Dain asked.

"Yes," Tiki said, "there's a flame beneath the ring. Smoke is rising from the stone and it looks like"—she squinted—"*something*, but I can't quite make it out."

She lifted her head. "What do you think this means? Do we need to light a fire beneath the ring?"

"Let me see." Larkin pressed her blond head close to Tiki's dark one to peer into the goblet.

Dain's brows pulled down in a quizzical frown. "Are you sure you're not seeing the fire that exists *within* the ring?"

"Of course." Larkin straightened with a jerk and stepped back, making way for Dain to peer into the cup. "Fire is one of the four great elements. As some fey have a natural affinity for earth or wind or water, Finn was always drawn to fire. It's why he hid the truce within a flame. What provided him with strength was also a natural defense against his enemies." She shook her head. "Brilliant. I should have thought of this long ago. To have a flame release a secret as smoke makes perfect sense."

"Try this." Dain plucked a candle from a nearby table and blew on the wick. A small orange flame sprang to life. "Why don't you take the ring from around your neck and hold it over this—see what happens."

Tiki pulled the delicate chain from around her neck and gazed at the fire that flickered in the stone's depths.

"Time to reveal your secrets," she said. "Where do we find the Fourth Treasure?" She held the ring out so it dangled an inch above the small tongue of fire. After a few long moments, the ring began to move. Slowly, at first, then more steadily, until the gold-encased stone swung in a small arc above the candle flame.

"Are you doing that?" Dain whispered.

"No." Tiki shook her head. "My hand has remained still."

The ring spun faster and faster, the arc widening as it gained speed. Ever so slowly, a wisp of smoke rose from the stone.

"I don't believe it," Tiki whispered. The smoke wreathed and curled, gathering as though to form a picture, yet remained indistinguishable. "Does that mean anything to anyone?"

"Not me," Dain muttered.

"No," Larkin said. "We must be missing something. I'm sure the cup gave us the correct inspiration." She waved her long fingers in the small space between the whirling stone and the flame, then through the smoke that had gathered above the spinning ring. "We must need to do something else—but what?" She gritted her teeth in frustration.

"Wait a minute—I know." Dain jumped up and darted from the room.

"Where's he going?" Tiki asked with a frown.

"I have no idea," Larkin muttered, clearly annoyed. "Always had a bit of mischief in him."

Tiki turned back to the small arc of smoke rising from the ring. "There's something there ... don't you agree?"

"Yes—but it's just out of reach. Just a bit too blurry to see what it is ..."

Dain sprinted back into the room.

"We need to use this," he cried, holding up the Faerie Queen's Mirror. Bits of gold glimmered through the heavy patina that covered the mirror's frame.

"What's that?" Tiki said, standing up to see what Dain held. As she moved away from the flame, the movement of the ring stilled.

"This is the Faerie Queen's Mirror." Dain quickly related the story that Prince Leo had shared.

"How curious." Larkin took the mirror from him and held it with both hands. "I've never heard of this artifact before. Do you suppose Victoria has remembered the history correctly?"

"Leo seemed most definite about what his mother had told him," Dain said. "Apparently, Queen Victoria said the mirror was a fail-safe should the ring ever be stolen. The thief would need both ring and mirror—and know how to use both—to glean the secrets from the ring. Leo was most insistent that I deliver it to Tara and William."

Dain moved to stand behind Larkin and looked over her shoulder. Rather than the faerie's reflection, the center of the glass churned with storm-tossed waves crashing to a rocky shore.

"Strange how it doesn't show a reflection, isn't it?" he said.

Tiki held out her hands for the mirror. "May I?"

"It shows a reflection," Larkin said cryptically, "just not always of a person's face."

Dain glanced at her curiously. "How's that?"

"So like Finn," Larkin mused, dropping the mirror to her lap, "unable to trust, even in death. He confided in only a handful of people in his lifetime: his best friend, Fraoch, Eridanus, Adasara. Perhaps some Macanna. It's hard to know anymore." She shrugged.

"He was a complicated man and we live in a complicated world. There were many who wanted him dead."

"What about you?" Dain asked, his expression unexpectedly somber. "Did Finn trust you?"

Larkin turned away, and Tiki eyed the faerie's back curiously.

From over her shoulder, Larkin spoke. "Let's just say Finn entrusted me with the important things."

Dain raised his eyebrows. "Such as?"

"It hardly matters now. What we need to focus on is deciphering the message within the ring and hope this mirror holds the answers." She motioned at Tiki. "Put the ring above the flame again and let's see what happens."

Dain moved to stand behind her as Tiki dangled the ring above the candle flame.

"Where do we find the Fourth Treasure?" she murmured. As before, the movement of the ring began with a gentle swaying that soon evolved into a spinning arc above the flame. It didn't take long before the ethereal strands of smoke had gathered in a tangled mass above the ring.

Larkin held the mirror at an angle so the smoke was reflected. "Can you see anything?"

To Tiki's surprise, the twists and turns of smoke formed a word that was legible in the mirror's reflection. She and Dain spoke at the same time:

"Dunvegan."

"*What?*" Larkin sounded stunned. "Hold this"—she thrust the mirror toward Dain—"I want to see."

They quickly changed places. For once, Larkin had a truly surprised look on her face. "I don't believe it."

"What does Dunvegan mean?" Tiki asked.

"I've heard that word before," Dain said. "It's a place, isn't it?"

"Yes." Larkin nodded. "Dunvegan is on the Isle of Skye in Scotland. An ancient castle built on a rock near the sea. I should have thought of it before." She paced again, her gown swishing behind her as the skirt swept the floor. "Of course—it makes perfect sense."

Tiki caught the ring in her hand as the smoke dissolved and pulled the chain back over her head. She tucked the stone inside her blouse, where it lay warm against her skin. "Who lives there? What does it have to do with the Fourth Treasure?"

"Clan MacLeod has occupied the castle for centuries."

"You know them?" Dain asked.

"Know *of* them. They are part of a story—a mortal tale that most fey grow up hearing. A mirror of the faerie tales mortal children grow up learning, I suppose."

A thrill of excitement shot through Tiki. "Are the MacLeod clan mortal, then?"

"Yes." Larkin shook her head. "So, like Finn—he so desperately wanted to blend the worlds that he and Eridanus hid the greatest treasures of Faerie with mortal keepers. Even in death, he has pulled the two worlds together." Larkin tapped a long finger against her chin, lost in thought. "No one would ever dream a clan of farmers could hold something of such great value."

Dain moved closer to Larkin, his blue eyes bright with excitement. "You know what the Fourth Treasure is, don't you?"

Larkin's lips twitched as if she was trying to hold back her smile, but the corners of her mouth curved up and she sounded breathless when she answered. "I do, though it never occurred to me that it might have such significance—that it could be one of the most legendary treasures of our world."

"What is it?" Tiki asked, her heart skipping in anticipation.

Larkin inhaled. "It's a flag. The Fourth Treasure of Faerie is a flag."

Tiki slumped in disappointment. A flag didn't sound very powerful. She looked at Dain to see if this news held any significance for him, but his face was blank.

"Go on," Dain urged.

"The Faerie Flag of Dunvegan Castle is ancient—and one of the MacLeod's most prized possessions. We will have to be extremely clever to get them to allow us to take it."

"*Faerie* Flag?"

"Yes. The flag was a gift, given by a faerie who had fallen in love with one of the MacLeod ancestors. She promised him that on three separate occasions, he could unfurl the flag and many armed men would come to the flag-bearer's aid. So far, the flag has only been unfurled twice."

Dain let out a low whistle.

Tiki sucked in her breath. "An army."

"An army to defeat Donegal," Dain echoed.

Larkin's blue-green eyes glowed as she jerked her head in sharp assent. "Precisely. The Four Treasures of Faerie will appear or be found when Faerie is in greatest need."

Chapter Fourteen

It was agreed they would leave for Scotland immediately.

"Best to stay together at this point," Larkin said in an imperious tone. "It will be up to us to stop Donegal. We're going to need each other. I can transport us as far as the Faerie Bridge on the Isle of Skye—we'll have to walk or garner a ride to Dunvegan from there."

"What should we do with these?" Dain pointed at the glamoured Cup of Plenty and the Faerie Queen's Mirror.

"We have to hide them somewhere," Tiki said. "Should I take them back to Grosvenor Square?"

"No. It's not safe there anymore." Larkin searched the room. "We need to hide them in plain sight. Glamour the mirror to match that one." She pointed to a plain round mirror that hung on the wall. "And"—she swept the cup up in her grasp—"we'll leave the cup as a green vase on this shelf right here." She deposited the cup on a nearby bookshelf as if it were no more than a decorative goblet.

Tiki did as she asked and hung the glamoured mirror on a wall adjacent to the other mirror. At a glance, it was impossible to tell the difference. No one would ever suspect one was an ancient treasure.

"There," Larkin said with satisfaction. "Safe for now."

As they were leaving the underground compound, a red-coated soldier approached. He was armed with a curved backsword and a razor-thin rapier.

"Majesty." He bent to one knee in front of Tiki. "Blessings on your health."

"Toran, how nice to see you," Tiki said. The tall guard had been assigned as one of her bodyguards when she'd first been named Seelie queen. He had been a second to Callan, an earnest guard who had made every attempt to stay constantly with Tiki to protect her. When Callan had been murdered by Donegal, Toran had taken his place as her primary bodyguard. It was only because Tiki had tricked him when she returned to London that he had been forced to stay in the Otherworld. She motioned at him. "Please rise."

The guard stood, his expression grim. He was younger than many of the guards and took his job very seriously. "I am here to protect you, Majesty. We've just received word that the hobgoblins have been routed from the northern part of the Wychwood. At Donegal's request, the redcaps set fire to their fields and homes. Those who survived are said to be headed this way."

"I hope Gestle and his men are all right," Tiki said. The hobgoblin leader had helped her and Rieker locate Dain when he'd been held prisoner in the White Tower.

"There's a storm over Wydryn Tor that extends down into the southern part of the forest. It's so black, you can no longer see the top of the Tor."

Larkin brushed passed Toran and continued down the hall. "It's Donegal, and he won't rest. It will be up to us to stop him."

"Toran," Tiki said kindly. "I'm going to need Aeveen. Could you gather her for me, please?" She felt bad about tricking the faerie again by asking him to get Dain's horse, but he couldn't possibly come with them to Scotland, and she didn't want to be delayed trying to convince him.

"Majesty—" Toran's expression was fraught with worry. "It's very dangerous right now. You shouldn't leave our stronghold here. Donegal has gone mad. They say he will kill anyone and everyone to get what he wants. I've heard he has even imprisoned the Court Jester and plans to feed him to Bearach's hounds. You should stay here where it's safe and we can protect—"

"*What*?!" In the space of a heartbeat, Larkin was next to the man, gripping his elbow. "What did you say?"

Toran's eyes widened in panic. "That the queen is safer—"

"No. About the jester."

The guard shot a quick glance at Tiki before returning to Larkin. "We have word that the Winter King has imprisoned the jester and plans to feed him to the hounds at the full moon."

Tiki let out a cry of dismay and covered her mouth with her hands. The jester was a fixture at court in the Palace of Mirrors—a colorful character who entertained whichever sovereign held the throne. Though an enigma who spoke in riddles and puns, he had been instrumental in helping Tiki and Rieker in the past, and she'd grown quite fond of his humor and idiosyncrasies. He was one of the few in Faerie who seemed to hold no malice toward Rieker and their relationship.

Larkin swore under her breath. "I will kill Donegal with my bare hands if that's what it takes," she growled. It was rare for her to show any emotion other than disdain, yet it was obvious she found this news about a man she referred to as "the Fool" terribly distressing. "Where are they holding him?"

"That I don't know," Toran replied. "Olcán is undercover in the palace. Perhaps he knows."

"Find out," Larkin snapped. "I want to know by sunset tomorrow. We've only seven days to the full moon." She jerked around. "Everyone but Toran come with me."

Tiki nodded at the young soldier. "Do as she asks. We need to know. I'll be fine." She followed Larkin down the hall, filled with a sudden uneasiness. Dain fell into step next to her. As they walked, Tiki silently mused why the jester, of all people, would elicit such a reaction from Larkin.

The transport to Scotland was effortless. Larkin had them link arms and then the world dissolved into gray, swirling clouds. To Tiki it seemed a stiff wind rushed against her body and turned her in a slow arc. The clouds cleared, and she was there.

They stood on a small stone bridge that arched over a river amid gently rolling hills of sparse fields. It was much cooler than the Plain of Sunlight, and Tiki shivered against the chill.

"It's winter in the mortal world," Larkin commented, "and especially cool up north here in Scotland. Best to glamour some layers while no one is about."

Tiki added a sweater and a long cloak, pulling the hood up around her head. She scanned the horizon. "Which way is Dunvegan?"

Larkin pointed. "North."

"Can't you transport us there?" Dain asked.

"I can't transport to where I haven't been," Larkin said. "For now, we walk."

An hour into their trek, a wagon came by, pulled by two small, shaggy plow horses.

"Where ye goin', lads and lassies, in all yer finery?" the driver called out.

"To Dunvegan," Larkin replied. "Have you room?"

The old man threw a thumb over his shoulder. "The whole wagon is open fer the takin'."

It was from the back of the wagon that Tiki first laid eyes on Dunvegan Castle. They came over a small rise and there in the distance, the castle stood on a cliff of rock above a reflective loch, the golden bricks of the fortress glowing in the watery afternoon sun.

Tiki let out a sharp gasp and covered her mouth with her hand.

Larkin and Dain both turned to look at her. "What is it?"

"I've seen that castle before."

Larkin frowned. "Where?"

Tiki stared at the imposing structure, searching her memory. She'd never been to Scotland, but the sight before her was familiar—she knew she'd seen Dunvegan Castle before. Suddenly, it came to her.

"The card."

"What?" Larkin asked.

"The card the jester gave me." Tiki looked over at Dain. "Remember? I showed it to you just the other day. In the section of the Celtic cross that should have had the Fourth Treasure, it was a picture of a castle—*this* castle."

Dain twisted to look at the castle again. "By God, I think you're right, Tiki."

Larkin moved closer, intent upon Tiki. "When did the Fool give you this card?"

"It was the night of Samhain—when we sacrificed the Seven-Year King and turned the court back over to the UnSeelies." Tiki looked at Larkin. "You were there. He gave me the card and said, 'When the clock strikes twelve, may the winds of change blow you in your true direction.'"

Larkin stared at the castle, her brow knitted in thought, long, golden strands of hair teased by the wind. "He knew, then."

"Knew what?" Dain asked. "Surely, you're not saying the Court Jester, the *Fool*, knew where to find the Fourth Treasure?"

Larkin's fingers were clenched on the short wooden walls of the wagon so tightly, her knuckles were white. The muscles in her jaw flexed as though she fought to keep the words from spilling out.

"What is it?" Tiki asked. "What do you know, Larkin? Speak the truth, because none of us are guaranteed to see tomorrow. If we aren't honest now—when we've only got each other to survive this war—then we will never be honest with each other."

The tense moment stretched between them, filled by the creak of the wagon wheels and the steady clomp of the horses' hooves on the dirt road.

"Why yer a'travelin' to Dunvegan?" the driver called over his shoulder.

As quickly as her face had revealed her emotions, Larkin's features shifted into a mask that hid her thoughts.

"We need to see the MacLeods about a personal matter," she replied in an imperious tone.

"The MacLeods, you say?"

"Yes. The lords of Dunvegan."

The driver let out a low chuckle. "They'd be happy to have you call them lords, miss, that's fer sure, but you ain't gonna do it at Dunvegan."

"And why is that?"

"Because the Potato Famine took everything the 'lords' of Dunvegan had. Old Man MacLeod moved his family to London back in '51. No MacLeod's been livin' at Dunvegan for over twenty years."

The driver stopped at a fork in the road and swiveled around to look at them, his brown felt hat shading his wrinkled face.

"This is the turn to the castle."

"Thank you for your kindness," Larkin said, as they scrambled from the back of the wagon.

"Much obliged," Dain said, reaching up to shake the old man's hand.

Their driver gave a slow nod. "Heard tell a few years back that Old Man MacLeod was a bank clerk in a place called Lombard Street, though, no tellin' if he's still there or not." He lifted his shoulders in a shrug, then readjusted his hat. "Good day to you folks." The reins snapped against the rumps of his two shaggy ponies. "Hi'yup."

"Now what?" Dain asked as the wagon trundled off in the distance and the three of them stood at the fork in the road. "If no one's been living at Dunvegan for twenty years, it's unlikely they would have left their most prized possession there unguarded."

Tiki remained silent. It seemed odd that the ring had released the word *Dunvegan* if no one lived there anymore, but their driver had seemed quite sure the MacLeods had left long ago.

Larkin studied the wooded trail that led to the castle, her face etched with indecision. "London does seem the better choice, given the circumstances."

"What are the chances we'll find them?" Tiki asked.

"We know one of the MacLeod men work on Lombard Street as a bank teller. We'll start there," Dain said.

"There are a lot of banks in London," Tiki said doubtfully.

"It's all we can do." Larkin held her arms out. "Gather round. We'll go together. We can't waste any more time here."

"No."

Dain and Larkin looked at Tiki in surprise.

"We're here—we need to at least go to the castle and see what we can learn. The cup gave us the clue. It must mean something."

Dain spoke first. "You're right. It would be foolish to leave without investigating."

Tiki expected an argument from Larkin, but the faerie surprised her. She swept her arm out in the direction of the castle. "To Dunvegan."

Chapter Fifteen

The trek to the castle took longer than Tiki expected—the trail wound up and down the swales of barren land in an undulating path, much longer than it appeared from a distance. As they neared the castle, the landscape became wooded, obscuring the panoramic view until they reached the entrance and from their perch atop a ridge of rock could see far into the distance. The castle was balanced on the edge of a great loch like a sentinel, the silence only broken by the cries of the seabirds. Before them the hills stretched as far as one could see.

They walked through an arched entry into a main courtyard with a parapet on one side that looked out over the vista.

"It's like we've arrived in another world, isn't it?" Tiki murmured. "After the hustle and bustle of London, it's hard to imagine that life exists like this."

Dain stood close by her side, his hands resting on top of the stone barricade. "I feel like we've gone back in time—to a place perhaps Eridanus and Finn knew."

"I agree. It's like we've reached an intersection of old and new, ancient and present—a crossroads of time and space." Tiki placed her hands next to where Dain's rested. His fingers were long and tan—a stark contrast to the petite size and pale color of Tiki's. She glanced up at the side of his handsome face. "Do you suppose it's destiny that has brought us here? Are we meant to find what has been hidden for so long?"

"Don't deceive yourself." Larkin's words broke the spell as she came to stand on the far side of Dain. "Destiny is simply the intersection of hard work and opportunity—nothing more, nothing less. If you put your mind to something with the intent of pursuing the goal at all costs, you create your own destiny."

"Can I help ye?"

Tiki whirled to find a wizened old gentleman dressed in a kilt standing ten feet away.

"The castle's not open to visitors at this time," he said, "though it's been years since we've had any." He tilted his head. "Have ye lost yer way?"

"Mr. MacLeod sent us," Dain answered, stepping forward with his hand out. "I'm Brendain Winterbourne and this"—he motioned to Tiki—"is Tara Dunbar MacLochlan, and Larkin." Tiki nodded and gave a short curtsy. "Mr. MacLeod said we could visit the castle. Are you the caretaker?"

"Rory Campbell, I be. Caretaker, groundskeeper, head inn master, and other assorted titles." He gave a gap-toothed grin as he gripped Dain's hand, then tipped his mac at Tiki, then Larkin. "Glad to make your acquaintance. You've come to learn about the castle, then?"

"Yes, we'd love to hear what you know about Dunvegan," Tiki said. "We've been told there are even some stories about faeries."

The old man let out a gleeful chuckle and jerked his thumb over his shoulder. "Why else would we have a faerie tower?" He cocked a shaggy eyebrow at them. "There are many treasures here at Dunvegan, but the Faerie Flag is our most prized possession."

Tiki clapped her hands together. "Would you tell us how the MacLeod's came to have a flag from a faerie?"

"Certainly, little miss. Would the three of ye like to join me for tea?"

Tiki and Dain grinned at the old man. "We'd love to," they chimed together.

Rory Campbell led them into the castle into a small room that doubled as a makeshift kitchen. "Pardon the mess." He swept a few periodicals off the table and dusted the wooden seats. "It's not often I have guests."

The three of them sat down on the chairs, as the caretaker moved about the kitchen and Tiki let out a grateful sigh. "Thank you," she said. "It was a longer walk than we thought. It feels good to sit."

"Where ye from?" he asked over his shoulder as he put a kettle on to boil and pulled four mismatched teacups from a small cupboard. "I can tell by your accents you don't live on the Isle."

"London," Dain said. "We're just in Scotland for a short visit. How long have you been caretaker here at Dunvegan?"

"Since the chief had to pack 'er up and go to London." He shook his head, an expression of great sorrow on his face. "I'm the only one who stayed." He looked around the small room. "Somebody has to keep the place alive."

"Can you tell us about the Faerie Flag?" Tiki asked. "I've never heard the true story of how it came to be in the possession of mortals."

"Yes, please do," Larkin added. "It sounds fascinating."

"'Twas a gift, ye see." Rory threaded his gnarled hands together and rested them on the small wooden table. "A very precious gift, indeed." He stared at the table, as if gathering the threads of the story he was about to tell. When he was ready, he lifted his head and began.

"It was long ago, hundreds of years before now, when one of the chiefs of Clan MacLeod fell in love with a young woman. What the chief didn't know at the time was that the woman was a *bean sidhe*—a faerie—but I doubt that would've stopped 'im. They was in love, ye see, and there's little that can stop true love. They married an' lived happily for several years. Had a baby boy what was their greatest joy. But the chief didn't know his wife had made an agreement with her father—she could only stay for a certain length of time. At the end of that time, she had to return to the Otherworld and bring nothing from the mortal world with her."

His voice was low and melodic, and Tiki sat mesmerized by the tale he told, his words creating images of people she'd never met.

"Well, the time up and came where the faerie had to depart. She and her husband bade a tearful farewell at the Faerie Bridge"—he pointed out a little window—"right down yonder, not far from the castle. Before she left, she bade her husband promise that the baby would never be allowed to cry, for she would be able to hear his cries in the faerie realm and it would break her heart. Her despairing husband agreed, and they parted ways.

"One day passed into another, and the chief remained distraught at the loss of his love. His clan was so concerned, they organized a party for him. A young nursemaid was assigned to take care of his son, but the party went on well into the night, and the young maid had never seen such a revelry. There was music and dancing under the stars and she crept from the baby's room to watch the goings-on. It was then that the baby woke and began to cry."

He stopped and lifted his cup to his lips.

"And what happened?" Tiki asked.

"O' course, the mother heard the wee babe from far away in that Otherworld and she appeared at his cradle. She wrapped her baby in a piece of fabric—some say it was her shawl, others say it was a flag—but she sang a sweet lullaby to her son until he slept again. When the chief came to the baby's room to check on his son, he found him wrapped in a golden silk sewn with what looked like red elf berries."

"She didn't take him back to Faerie?" Tiki asked.

Rory shook his head. "When the child grew to be a young man, he told his father that the flag was *Am Bratach Sith*—a gift from his mother. Should they ever find themselves in danger, they should wave the flag and armies from the faerie realm would come to their aid." He held up a crooked finger. "However, there was a condition—the Faerie Flag could only be used three times, and then it would disappear and return to Faerie."

"Oh my," Tiki said. "That is quite a story."

"Has the flag ever been waved?" Dain asked.

"It's been used twice: once when the clan was in battle against the MacDonalds and once when the MacLeod cattle herds were stricken with plague and the clan members were dying of starvation. Both times, the chief waved the flag and the faeries saved them."

Larkin smiled at the old man. "Sounds like the flag has one last go in it."

"Yes, indeed. It's there for when we need it most."

"Where do you possibly keep such a valuable treasure?" Tiki asked innocently, lifting her cup to sip her tea.

The caretaker didn't blink. "You'd have to ask Chief MacLeod. That secret is not mine to keep."

Chapter Sixteen

"Wills!" Leo's jaw sagged. "What a surprise! Your cousin told me you'd left for Scotland."

"You saw Dain?" Rieker's expression mirrored the surprise on the young prince's face.

"Just yesterday." Leo grabbed Rieker's arm and pulled him into the small sitting room. "Come in here so we can talk in private."

"Uh—Leo—" Rieker resisted the tug on his arm.

"What is it?"

"I'm not alone."

Leo frowned. "What? Who's with you?" He leaned out the door to peer down the hallway.

"They're not out there. The guards thought it best if I came up by myself."

"And who have you brought to visit?"

Rieker glanced over one shoulder and then the other. "The children. We were headed for Scotland for their safety—but I wasn't far outside of London when I realized we were being followed."

"Followed! By whom?"

Rieker pressed his lips in a thin line. "I don't think you want to know."

Leo's eyes widened. "You're serious?"

"This was the only place I could bring them where I knew they'd be safe. Do you think the children could stay with you for a bit?"

Leo's mouth opened and closed and opened again before any words came out. "Of course. We've plenty of room—"

"I know it's a lot to ask, but there's no one else I trust."

"Say no more." Leo held up his hand. "It's past the supper hour. Have any of you eaten?" He pushed past Rieker and marched down the hallway before Rieker could answer. "Bring the children to the lower drawing room and we'll feed them before we send them to bed. Then you and I must talk."

It was several hours later when they reconvened in a small sitting room on the second floor near Leo's private chambers. They sank into a pair of leather chairs, and Rieker leaned his head back against the cushion with a sigh of relief.

"Thank you for taking us in, Leo. I wasn't quite sure what I was going to do. Having to care for the children changed everything."

"Yes, I can imagine. Probably better to have staff for that sort of thing."

Rieker gave a short laugh. "I can see where it would come in handy at times."

"What is your plan now?"

Rieker ran a hand through this hair. "I need to find Tiki, except I don't know exactly where she is." He looked at his friend. "It could take me a while."

Leo waved a hand through the air. "The children can stay. No worries. You do what must be done. It seems that the, uh ... *situation,* has taken a turn for the worse."

"Yes. You said you'd seen Dain? Where was this?"

"It was yesterday, late afternoon. I called on your townhome and he answered the door. I'd just had an enlightening conversation with Mamie and my mother and had stopped by to share what I'd learned."

"And Dain answered the door at Grosvenor Square?" Rieker asked in astonishment.

"Yes. In the morning, you should travel directly there and find him. I gave him something very valuable intended for you."

"And what was that?"

"The Faerie Queen's Mirror."

Rieker's eyebrows shot up. "Leo, I think you'd better explain."

"Mother told me about it ..."

The next morning, Leo shared the table with Fiona and the children over a breakfast of poached eggs balanced in delicate china egg cups and a plate of buttered toast. They ate in an elegant parlor decorated in bright yellow and white that made the room light and sunny, a sharp contrast to the stormy weather outside. Waitstaff in black tails stood at the ready.

"Is your friend Johnny feeling better? He's hardly eaten a thing since you arrived."

"I know he would have been at breakfast if he could, Prince Leo," Fiona replied, staring down at her plate.

"Should we call for the physician?"

"Do you think it would help, sir?" Fiona and Toots looked at him hopefully.

"Well, he's certainly having a devil of a time. I feel for the poor chap—throwing up everything he tries to get down." Leo used the edge of his spoon to crack the top of the egg and pulled the little dome away. "He'll blow away in a stiff breeze at the rate he's going."

"We don't need a physician," Clara piped up in a matter-of-fact tone. "We need to call Larkin."

"Who's that you say, child?" Leo turned to Clara with an indulging smile. The five-year-old's wavy hair was like a golden halo around her head, and she looked as pure and delicate as a little angel. A grubby pink stuffed dog sat in the empty chair next to hers.

"Clara," Fiona warned as Toots choked on his bite of toast.

"Larkin is a friend of ours," Clara said, ignoring Fiona. "She's very clever. She'd know right what to do to fix Johnny up."

"Fi—" Toots choked out, his green eyes as wide as two lily pads floating in his freckled face. "Clara's right. That's exactly what Johnny needs—he needs Larkin."

They were still at the table when Rieker entered the room. Snow coated the shoulders of his dark coat, and a gust of cool air swirled into the room with his arrival.

"Any success?" Leo asked.

Rieker shook his head. "If Dain was at Grosvenor Square, he's gone now. And to make matters worse, there's a bloody hell of a storm on. The winds are howling, there's a sea surge that could flood the coastal areas, and it's starting to snow."

"It's probably worse up in Scotland," Leo said philosophically. "Why didn't Tara plan to accompany you there?"

Rieker sighed. "It's long and complicated. She felt I was the only one she could trust to look after the children while she took care of some problems that others felt only she could solve. But I'll tell you, Leo—I can't shake the feeling I shouldn't have let her go without me." He slapped his leather gloves onto the table. "I knew better than to let her go. Now I don't know where to even look for her."

"I'm going to call Larkin," Clara said brightly, gripping a glass of milk in her small hands. A white mustache covered her upper lip. "On account of Johnny, o' course. When she comes, you could ask her how to find Teek."

Rieker sat up abruptly. "Clara—you are brilliant! That is exactly what we need to do."

Chapter Seventeen

"There's nothing for it but to go," Larkin said after they left Rory Campbell's small apartment. "It's obvious he knows nothing, and even if he did, he'd never tell us."

"I have to agree," Dain said. "We'll never find it here on our own. Besides, it's possible the MacLeod's took the Faerie Flag with them to London."

Tiki looked out over the loch. She felt sure they needed to stay. Why else would the cup have released the word *Dunvegan*?

"Tiki?" Dain touched her elbow. "What do you think?"

"Yes, I suppose you're right. It's just that—"

"We need to find MacLeod and get some answers," Larkin snapped. "We are running out of time! Hold on to me and we'll go now."

They arrived in London within the small, abandoned clockmaker's shop that Tiki had called home just a year prior.

"We're in Charing Cross," Tiki cried in surprise.

"There are too many people in the City for all of us to arrive together," Larkin explained. "We can leave here one by one and not draw any unwanted attention."

Tiki looked through the shadows at the familiar space, a strange mix of emotions tugging at her. When she looked around the room, she could imagine Shamus, Fiona, Toots, and Clara here with her. Memories of the many nights they'd snuggled amongst the rags they'd called blankets, reading stories by candlelight, flitted through her mind. How many of those nights had they gone to bed hungry? More than she could count. A pang of longing twanged in her chest as she thought of Rieker. He was as much a part of her memories of this place as the rest of her family.

The overturned wooden apple crate with a plank of wood that had served as their table still stood next to the rickety chairs they'd taken from a burnt-out flat in Drury Lane. The small box stove at the back that had cast out enough warmth so they didn't freeze in the winters was now cold and dark.

This place had been a haven when she and the others had lived here, yet now it was so barren and desolate—barely more than four walls, a floor, and ceiling. She imagined the elegant beauty of Grosvenor Square as well as the opulence of the Palace of Mirrors, and a surge of gratitude welled in her throat. Thanks to Rieker, she had a very different life now.

Dain reached for Tiki's hand and squeezed her fingers. "Loads of memories here, I'll bet."

Tiki nodded. "It seems like last week we were plotting how to get the ring into Buckingham and then back out again. I guess we figured out those answers."

"Yes—" Dain's brow flickered, and it was as if a shadow had crossed his face. "But there are still some answers I wished I had—like, what happened to Kieran and who was Breanna?" He ran his hand through his hair in a move so reminiscent of Rieker, Tiki's heart jumped. "But I guess I'll be thankful for having a family again."

"Rieker mentioned he has questions too. Maybe when the two of you have a chance to talk, you'll both learn something."

Larkin interrupted, her words clipped. "I can't go into London with you. You'll need to go on without me."

"Why?" Dain tilted his head to gauge her strange comment. "I thought finding the Faerie Flag was the most important task we had."

"It's too complicated to go into now, but I must find the jester first."

Tiki's mouth dropped open. "The *jester*? But Toran said Donegal had captured him. You don't even know where to look. Where would you start?"

"There are only so many places Donegal keeps his prisoners," Larkin said tightly. "The White Tower, the Plain of Starlight, or the Palace of Mirrors. Trust me—the jester is being tortured in one of those places."

"But that's a death sentence to try to enter any of those locations right now," Tiki said. "Donegal is trying to kill us all. You'd walk right into his arms and offer yourself up?"

"Don't be foolish," Larkin snapped. Her eyes narrowed and her fingers clenched in tight fists. "You think I've survived this long without knowing who and what I'm dealing with?"

"A'ine Fiachna Erinn Lasair, come to me." The words were faint, as if spoken from a great distance.

Tiki looked around, her eyes wide with panic. "Who said that?"

Larkin looked as startled as Tiki. "I need to go."

"No. Wait." Tiki blinked but the space where the faerie had stood a second ago was empty. Larkin was gone.

"Where'd she go?" Dain looked around in surprise. "I still have so many questions—"

Tiki gripped Dain's arm. "Did you hear that voice?"

He nodded, glancing around the room one more time. "Yes. It was very odd—"

"It was *Clara*. She knows Larkin's true name. She can call her—"

"But how is it we could hear her? Isn't she in Scotland?"

"She's supposed to be," Tiki said. "Something must be wrong. We need to go check on her."

"How? We don't know where she is."

Less than fifteen minutes had passed when Larkin returned, and she wasn't alone.

"William!" Tiki cried. "Is it really you?"

"He had Clara call me," Larkin said, her face twisted with displeasure. "The child was out waiting in the snow."

"She enjoyed it." Rieker's hair was windblown, his cheeks ruddy with cold. He was dressed as if for London's winter weather in a black coat, with a gray-

and-black-checked scarf loose around his neck. "She was trying to build a snowman before you insisted she go inside."

"Are you all right?" Tiki cried as she hurried to him. "What's happened?"

Instead of taking her hand as she expected, Rieker wrapped his arms around her and pulled her close, pressing her tight against his chest. Cold radiated off him, causing Tiki to shiver. "Thank God you're safe, Teek."

"You're freezing," Tiki said as she slipped her arms inside his coat and pressed against his lean body to share her warmth. "Where are the children?"

"They're fine. They're safe." He rested his hands on her shoulders and looked into her face, his eyes dark with worry. "I couldn't leave you to do this alone. I just couldn't do it."

Conflicting emotions warred in Tiki's chest. She was relieved to see him, yet, there was nowhere she considered safe—where could he have possibly left Johnny, Fi, Toots, and Clara?

"I'm glad you're here too," Tiki said gently, "but the children—"

"They're with Leo. Playing pony, no doubt. Safe in Buckingham Palace and having the time of their lives." Rieker gripped Tiki's hands. "It was the only spot where I was sure I could leave them without worry."

"Brilliant," Dain said, striding forward to clap Rieker on the back. "Glad to have you back. We're going to need you."

"It's disturbing that you don't trust me inside Buckingham Palace, William, but better that you're here," Larkin said. "We've got much to do."

"And Leo didn't mind?" Tiki searched his face.

"No. He said they could stay as long as we need." Rieker ran the backs of his fingers along her cheek. "And what of you? Have you learned anything?"

"I have learned something," Larkin said. "The boy you took in—the pickpocket—is dying."

Tiki sucked in her breath. "Johnny?"

Larkin shrugged. "I suppose that's his name. The one the *liche* brought to the Otherworld. I tried to warn you when you fed him faerie drink from the Cup of Plenty—"

"I was trying to save his life," Tiki sputtered.

"But it also doomed him to life in Faerie. You should know by now that magic has consequences for a mortal. The boy can't live in this world any longer—the food and drink are killing him. If you truly want to save him, he'll have to live in Faerie the rest of his days."

"No," Tiki whispered as unwanted images danced before her eyes. "What about Fiona?"

Larkin's lip curled. "Wasn't it you who said, 'Better alive in Faerie than dead forever'? The boy won't last much longer. He needs to be returned to the Otherworld and cared for there. I'll take him with me when I return."

Rieker gently squeezed Tiki's hands. "Let's get Johnny well and then we can decide where he lives. Tell me what you've learned."

Tiki quickly brought him up to speed on their search for the flag and the news about the Court Jester being captured. "We've just returned to London to search for the missing MacLeod but Larkin has informed us she's going to return to Faerie to help the jester."

Rieker glanced over at Larkin. "I agree the jester was entertaining, but why would you risk your life for a man who didn't claim allegiance to either court?"

The air seemed to thrum as they waited for Larkin's answer.

"Because," Larkin practically snarled, "he is important … to *me*."

Tiki's breath caught at the turbulent expression in Larkin's eyes. Something wasn't right. What was the faerie hiding?

Rieker half laughed. "That's all you're going to tell us? The jester is *important to you* and you're going to risk your life—to what? Save him?"

"Perhaps the meaning of the word *loyalty*," she spat the word, "has never been properly explained to you, but in my world, it—"

"Come off it, Larkin," Rieker interrupted. "You're not going to save the jester." His lip curled in disgust. "There's something else going on, and in typical fashion, you're not being honest with us."

Larkin's eyes narrowed to deadly slits. "How little you know of my world and yet, for some inexplicable reason, you think you know it all. You—"

Dain stepped between them and raised his hands for them to stop. He turned to Larkin. "I'll go with you."

Tiki choked. "*What?*"

"I said I'll go with Larkin." Dain shrugged. "I can vouch that she knows more about Donegal than anyone outside, and possibly inside, the UnSeelie court. If she says it's more important to save the jester than to find the Fourth Treasure, then I will help her do it."

"Thank you, Dain," Larkin said.

"I don't believe this." Rieker slammed his hands on his hips and turned away, his shoulders rigid with anger.

Tiki didn't know what to think. She shuddered at the idea of the Court Jester being tortured as Larkin and Dain had been, but to try to sneak into the White Tower again or into the Palace of Mirrors while Donegal ruled …

Her skin crawled at the thought. She spoke to Larkin. "At least tell us why the jester is so important?"

The faerie looked away, seeming to fight some internal battle. Finally, the words exploded from her lips.

"Because he saved me." Her turbulent gaze circled the group. "You three should know better than anyone that there is no escape from the White Tower without help. When Donegal captured me, I would have died there if it hadn't been for the jester. *He* is the reason I was able to escape from the White Tower. *He* is the reason I am alive today. And I won't leave him to die by Donegal's hand. Not as long as there is breath in my body."

The room was silent but for the distant sounds of trains coming and going.

"There's more to it than that, isn't there?" Tiki spoke with a quiet surety. "You said the jester had never pledged himself to a sovereign—never claimed a court. Why would he risk his life to help you?"

Rieker nodded, his face unreadable. "Tiki's right. For once, Larkin, tell us all of it."

Dain shifted to stand next to his brother, a frown furrowing his brow. Identical in height, together they were an intimidating presence. "Yes, Larkin, I'd like to know too. We've risked our lives over and over for the Seelie court, for the Macanna, for you. We're about to do it again and battle a war that we all know we'll be lucky to survive. We deserve to know whatever truth you've hidden from us."

Larkin looked from Tiki, to Rieker, and finally to Dain. She pressed her lips together and for a shocking moment, Tiki thought she was trying not to cry. Instead of speaking, Larkin sank into one of the rickety chairs and put her face in her hands.

Tiki exchanged a glance with Rieker. This was a side of Larkin she'd never seen before. Was it an act? Or, for once, was the faerie revealing a true emotion? And if so, what kind of secrets had she been keeping that would evoke such a response?

Dain spoke again. "I've always trusted you, Larkin. Now it's time to trust me. To trust all of us. Tell the truth."

The faerie lifted her head and pushed her golden hair away from her face. In that moment, her skin was like parchment and dark hollows carved the space beneath her cheekbones. *She looks beaten,* Tiki thought.

Larkin's lips twisted in a bitter grin. "I suppose it is somehow suitable that we should return *here* to speak of this." She looked around the room and her nose curled in disgust. "The hovel where I doomed Clara to live when I first left her for you to find."

Tiki had to bite her tongue not to snap a retort that the child had been loved here, but Larkin continued.

"The same place where you and William plotted against me. My hideaway when I escaped from Donegal." Larkin let out a heavy sigh. "It's been a long road. Such a long road." She stared at the floor. When she spoke again, it was as if she were talking to herself. "I never dreamed I might be the only one to survive."

Tiki reached for Rieker's hand and threaded her fingers through his, suddenly afraid of what was coming.

Larkin looked up. "But as Eridanus and Finn saw fit to hide all four of the treasures in the mortal world, I suppose it is only fitting that you should learn the truth of their plan here as well."

Dain sank cross-legged to the floor next to Larkin. "Go on."

Tiki tugged on Rieker's hand, and they also sat, forming a half circle.

In a mercurial mood swing so typical of Larkin, a fleeting smile lit her face, and she reached out to cup Dain's chin. "As you listen, Dain," she said, dropping her hand and taking Rieker's, "and William"—she turned to Tiki—"and Tara, you must always remember we believed it was up to us to change the future." Larkin whispered, "And to do that, we gave up *everything*."

Tiki's stomach twisted and she fought the impulse to tell Larkin to *stop*. She had a terrible feeling she didn't want to know what the faerie was about to reveal.

Larkin folded her hands together and rested them in her lap in a rare moment of repose. "There is so much to tell, I'm not sure where to begin, but I think the most important thing you should know, William and Dain, is that the Court Jester in the Palace of Mirrors is the man you knew as Kieran—"

"*Kieran?*" The name exploded from Rieker's and Dain's lips at the same moment.

She held up her hand and her voice gentled. "And he is your birth father."

Chapter Eighteen

Tiki's gasp echoed like a cannon shot in the silence. It was as if time had become suspended. Then the room exploded in questions.

"Kieran's *alive*?" The hope in Dain's voice was unmistakable.

"Our *birth* father?" Rieker's words were thick with disbelief.

"The *jester*?" Tiki squeaked.

Larkin held her hands up to stop further questions. "I know it's a shock, but let me speak before I change my mind. There's more you need to know."

"Tell us," Dain and Rieker said at the same moment.

"*More*?" Tiki whispered.

"The jester's last name is Winterbourne."

"Kieran told me that was my last name," Dain exclaimed.

Larkin raised her eyebrows. "He must have sensed his life was at risk, then."

"What does it mean?" Rieker asked.

Larkin's face remained impassive. "Winterbourne is an ancient name, from a line of fey who were UnSeelie by birth but left the court long ago to strike their own path."

Tiki looked from Rieker to Dain. "UnSeelie? What are you saying? That William and Dain are—"

Rieker finished her sentence. "*UnSeelie*?"

"Half," Larkin said matter-of-factly. "Breanna was Seelie, Fial was UnSeelie, but he was born to the light."

"Wait." Rieker shook his head as he held his palms out to Larkin. "I don't understand. My father, Will Richmond, was not our birth father?"

"No."

"But before you said—"

"I lied."

"I thought faeries couldn't lie," Tiki said.

"Don't be ridiculous." Larkin snorted. "Yet another convenient mistruth that we use to suit our purposes. You should know by now that we are powerful creatures far beyond the abilities of mortals—"

Rieker interrupted her. "You're telling us our real father is alive?"

Larkin raised her chin a notch so she appeared to be looking down her nose at him. Her eyes were narrowed in a calculating expression. "Yes."

"And you want me to believe that our father is the man we knew as Kieran and also as the Court *Jester*?"

"You've got it all exactly right, William." Larkin clapped. "Bravo."

Rieker's eyes narrowed and one side of his mouth lifted in a sneer. "Why do you think we would believe the madness you spew, Larkin?" He pushed himself to his feet. "I've often questioned your loyalties, but now I question your *sanity*. This time you've gone too far."

Larkin remained unaffected by Rieker's reaction. "You have just confirmed that we have been successful in hiding our true purpose. Think it through, William. It was our goal to bury the truth so deeply, beneath so many layers of lies, that no one would ever suspect the reality of who we were and what we were doing. If they knew or found out—we would be dead—as most of us are." Her lips pressed in a thin line. "We had to do it this way—to keep you and Dain alive."

Dain remained seated and seemed much less shocked by the news. "You mean, we're not half mortal?"

Larkin shook her head. "No. Of course not. You're pure fey, though of mixed blood, to be sure." One corner of her mouth quirked in a taunting smile as she looked at Rieker. "Not a mortal half-breed, after all. Just a fey half-breed."

Rieker's mouth tightened. "You'll have to give me some proof to believe this, Larkin."

"I know it's difficult, William, especially given the mortal upbringing you've suffered. This is difficult for me as well. We've hidden these secrets for so long because our lives depended on it—all of our lives—that even now, when I know I must tell you, I worry that my revelations will put us at even greater risk."

Dain leaned forward, an eager expression on his face. "I've seen the jester loads of times and he's never acted any differently toward me than anyone else. Are you sure—"

"And because of that, you are still alive to speak of it."

"Hmm, he is old enough to be my father," Dain mused.

"Dain," Rieker barked, "are you going to believe what she tells you? Don't you find it a little far-fetched to believe the Court Jester—the clown, the juggler, the *Fool*—is our *father*?"

Dain returned Rieker's glare with a steady look of his own. "I understand your disbelief, William, but anyone born to Faerie knows the term *fool* is not literal. I've seen the man juggle *fire*. He can skewer the highest lord with just the twist of a phrase, and he can create birds out of thin air. He may be a juggler but he knows powerful magic, not to mention he knows the secrets of kings and queens—which probably makes him the most powerful man at court. Let's listen to what she has to say."

"William," Larkin snapped. "Sit down. We don't have much time. If Donegal has imprisoned the jester, then he must suspect him of treachery, which means he might know far more than I suspected. The jester and I are the only ones left alive who know the truth. I will not let Donegal sacrifice him too. I must return to the Otherworld and save him. You lot will have to go on and find the MacLeod's and the flag. That is ours—and your father's—only chance."

Tiki tugged on Rieker's hand. She had a terrible feeling that Larkin was speaking the truth. "Wills," she said. "Let's listen."

Rieker turned to where Tiki still sat on the floor. "You don't mean to tell me—"

"Think about it—who gave us the clue about fate and truth to find the Stone of Tara? Who told us not to fear the water so we would know how to get to Dain when he was imprisoned in the White Tower?" Tiki's voice was beginning to rise. "Who gave us the card that could've led us to the Fourth Treasure if we'd only been smart enough to figure it out—"

Dain reached over and yanked on Rieker's other arm, pulling him to the floor. "Sit down and shut up. We're going to hear what Larkin has to say."

Rieker muttered under his breath as he pulled a crate over and sat on it, his lips pressed in an angry line.

Larkin tilted her head at Dain. "Thank you. I can't possibly tell you all of it now—"

"No, of course not," Rieker interrupted, "because then someone might know as much as you, and you wouldn't be able to yank our strings and force us to dance for you over and over again—"

"Wills—*please*," Tiki implored.

"If you are quite finished, William," Larkin snarled in an icy tone, "I will tell you what you need to know, and then we must be on our way." She stared at Rieker as if she expected him to interrupt again, but he held his tongue.

Larkin took a deep breath. "Now, then. Fial is the jester's true name—your father's name. Fial Lasair Cathall Winterbourne—a man of honor and unbelievable strength." Her eyes became distant. "You should be proud to call him father. His bravery is unmatched by anything the rest of us have done, for you see, your father is the ultimate spy. He has lived between two worlds and belonged to neither for most of his life—all for the sake of a promise made long ago. Those who have known his secrets and his sacrifice have been murdered one by one: Finn, Eridanus, Adasara—even Breanna—until only he and I remain."

Dain leaned closer to Larkin. "Why is he such a threat to Donegal?"

"Because he knows great magic—much more than anything the Winter King can accomplish—and he knows secrets that Donegal doesn't want revealed."

"If he's so powerful, why does he act the fool?" Rieker asked. "Aren't there other positions he could assume for one court or the other?"

"As Dain said, the term is not literal. Fial chose carefully when he became the jester—and he doesn't reveal himself because he has secrets of his own. It's not in his best interest, or that of the courts, to reveal all—which is precisely why we have operated in the shadows and behind glamours all these years—waiting for the right time to overthrow Donegal."

"You mentioned a promise—what was that?" Tiki asked.

"To stop the killing and reunite the courts as one. To live side by side with the mortals in peace. And most importantly—to create a future where one wasn't labeled Seelie or UnSeelie, but simply as fey."

"But what is he?" Dain asked. "Seelie or UnSeelie?"

"Fial is a Winterbourne," Larkin said, "which makes him UnSeelie by birth, but the Winterbournes left the UnSeelie court long ago and created their own autonomous political world. Because of that, their name is rarely spoken here anymore."

"Did they leave because they wanted to be Seelie?" Tiki asked.

"Not exactly. They wanted the right to live and act as they pleased—whether it be in the light or the dark, the Plain of Sunlight or the Plain of Starlight—the Night Garden, the Wychwood Forest, or the hills of Tara." Larkin's lips twisted in a sad smile. "Fial's troubles started when he fell in love with a Seelie girl named Breanna. Her father was an underlord of one of the fifths of Connacht."

Dain interrupted. "What's an underlord?"

"A sort of royalty back in the day—in ancient Ireland, there were five kingdoms called fifths that were ruled by underlords. They, in turn, were ruled by the Seelie king. Breanna's Seelie heritage, and the fact that her father was among the politically elite, made their relationship impossible on many levels. But they were in love and headstrong. They believed they were invincible, so they disobeyed their parents and ran away and married. It wasn't long before Breanna was pregnant"—Larkin lifted her long, elegant fingers and pointed at Dain and Rieker—"with the two of you."

Tiki glanced at Rieker's face. His eyes were hooded, shielding his thoughts, his expression cold and unreachable, reminding her of when they first met, when she'd considered him dangerous.

Larkin smoothed her gown over her knees and continued. "Fial and Breanna did have enough sense to know that children of mixed parents would not be accepted in any part of fey society, so they moved often and hid the truth. Eventually they landed in London. Fial had already begun to use the glamour of Kieran. He knew his family was looking for him, particularly his brother, so he made a pact with Finn and Eridanus: if they helped keep the two of you alive, Fial told them he would commit his life to the promise of rejoining the courts.

"That's why Eridanus sent you to London, William, to live with a mortal family who owed him a favor—and why you, Dain, stayed in the Otherworld. They had to keep you apart. They couldn't take the chance that someone might uncover the truth of your heritage."

Dain squirmed. "So what happened?"

"Shortly after the two of you were sent away, Fial and Breanna were found by Fial's family. Breanna was murdered. They came for Fial next. They carved a letter T—for traitor—across his back, beat him until they believed he was dead, then tied him to a rock and threw him in the river to drown, just to be sure." Larkin's face became fierce. "But Fial survived."

"You're serious?" Dain glanced over at his brother, but Rieker remained expressionless. "How could anyone survive that?"

Larkin's nostrils flared with emotion. "His will was stronger than that of his attackers. But the UnSeelies are a brutal, unrelenting lot. To survive, Fial knew he had to stay dead."

Larkin pushed off the rickety chair and paced to the back of the little room. "But the courts were in disarray.

Finn was helping Eridanus, who had been mortally wounded in battle. As I told you before, Finn, had also been mortally wounded, but didn't die immediately. Instead, he suffered a slow, lingering death, a piece of iron arrowhead lodged in his lung. After his death, rumors swirled that he and Adasara had had a child—an heir to the Seelie throne—so Donegal placed a bounty on Adasara's head and that of the child's, if it existed. Arrangements to hide Tara had barely been made before Adasara was also murdered." Larkin's voice faded away, her face creased with painful memories. "And now, only Fial and I are left."

"It's a sad tale, to be sure." Rieker's voice sounded razor sharp in the shadowed silence of the room. His lips were set in a firm line as he considered Larkin. "But if Kieran, or Fial—whatever name you'd like to use—was UnSeelie, and he was supposedly our father, why did he tell me I was descended from Eridanus?"

Larkin turned from where she stood by the cold box stove. "Kieran was preparing you for your future."

"How does telling me I'm descended from Seelie royalty prepare me for anything?" Rieker spat. "Especially when it's another *lie*."

Tiki considered the expression on Larkin's face. It was a strange mix of pride and sorrow.

"William ..." Larkin's words were deceptively gentle. "I applaud your passion—it speaks well of your ability to face what the future holds for you—for all of you."

"For once, just tell us the truth," Rieker snarled.

Larkin raised her eyebrows. "You want the truth, but then you don't believe me when I tell you. It's one of the reasons I only reveal pieces at a time—"

"*Why*, Larkin?"

"Because you *are* descended from Eridanus," Larkin snapped. "Fial is also the son of a mixed relationship. His father was the child of a Winterbourne lover that Eridanus took centuries ago. Fial himself is a half-breed, though Eridanus never publicly acknowledged any relation to him. Fial was raised in Winterbourne until his mother left to join the UnSeelie court, but the blood of Eridanus runs in his veins, just as it does in yours and Dain's."

Chapter Nineteen

The guard held the torch high above his head to light the rough-hewn stone steps that led down into the rocky depths of Wydryn Tor. Far below the Palace of Mirrors, Donegal followed the flickering flame to a dungeon he had created long ago for precisely this kind of prisoner: someone who could never be allowed to escape; someone who could never be allowed to speak the truth.

At the bottom of the stone stairs, a stern-faced guard stood before a wooden door, an iron-tipped spear clutched in one hand. A horizontal slit at the top of the door allowed the guard to view the prisoner and a small cutout at the bottom of the door allowed what little food and drink that was granted to be slid through the opening.

Donegal motioned to the guard. "Is the prisoner chained?"

"Yes, sire." He lowered his eyes and bowed. "Hands and feet."

"Open the door, then." The Winter King pointed up the stairs into the darkness. "I want total privacy. There is a landing above us some thirty steps. You may wait for me there." He reached for the torch. "Both of you."

The guards hurried to do his bidding, their boots echoing against the stone steps as they climbed up to the landing. Donegal waited until he was sure they were positioned out of earshot before he entered the dim cell and carefully pulled the heavy door closed behind him. He lifted the torch, using the wavering pool of light to locate the prisoner.

The orange glow from the flame glinted off the manacles that bound the jester's wrists and ankles, where he was tucked into one of the corners, crumpled on his side. The light making the metal shimmer as if it were on fire. Donegal stepped closer, illuminating the bloody face of his prisoner.

"Hello, Fial." He nudged the prisoner with the toe of his boot. "Imagine my disbelief when I saw the scar on your back." Donegal spoke with a deadly timbre echoing in his voice. "What an interesting surprise to find the brother I thought I had murdered so very long ago—has actually never left me at all."

Chapter Twenty

"I have a question." Dain broke the silence that had filled the room as they absorbed Larkin's shocking news. "Why did Kieran abandon me? All these years, I haven't known if he was dead or imprisoned—"

A flicker of emotion crossed Larkin's face and for a second, Tiki thought she saw something that looked like sympathy. Then Larkin's face hardened.

"He left you to save your life. Donegal and his followers were asking questions, sniffing around. He must have suspected something. Fial knew the time was approaching when he needed to inform you and William of your true heritage—of the promise.

"He went to London as Kieran and found William, intending to tell him the truth, but it was too risky. Donegal and his inner circle were suspicious, sniffing around too close to William—and to me. Then Donegal murdered William's mortal family and Fial feared the Winter King had somehow found William out. Fial didn't dare reveal the truth then—in fact, he didn't dare have any contact with either of you. So, he gave Kieran up and has lived only as the jester these last few years, communicating with me and biding his time to share the truth with both of you."

"If any of us survive," Rieker said with a hint of bitterness.

"I think I believe you," Dain said. "It all fits."

Tiki glanced from Dain to Rieker. Kieran's sudden appearance in Rieker's life had seemed strange—as well as his knowledge of the Otherworld. What Larkin was describing did make sense. But Tiki had an uneasy feeling that Larkin had not shared everything yet. She feared there were more surprises to come.

Rieker was neutral when he spoke, revealing nothing. "How will you free the jester? The Palace of Mirrors, the White Tower, the Plain of Starlight—wherever they are holding him—those areas are impenetrable. What is your plan?"

"Why is it your concern?" Larkin smirked with familiar arrogance. "Unless you're planning to help me?"

Rieker didn't blink. "Perhaps. I'm not sure how, to be honest."

"It's no different from what you've done the last four years, William—running through the underbelly of London pretending to be a pickpocket." She shrugged. "You dress a certain way, you play a particular part—you become someone else to gain information." Her eyes flicked over to Tiki, and the dare was clearly communicated. "It's simple: to find and free the jester, we must become UnSeelie."

It was too late in the day to call on Leo at Buckingham Palace and retrieve Johnny, so they agreed to spend the night in Charing Cross. Dain and Rieker went out to scout for wood to light the box stove, Larkin muttered something about an "errand," and Tiki was left by herself.

The whistles and gasps of the trains as they came and left the station were a familiar backdrop, and Tiki had the oddest sense she'd gone back in time. Any moment Toots and Shamus would come through the back door or push the plank aside that hung on a nail and tell her what they'd nicked today. Fiona and Clara could be out in the station looking for anything edible that might have been dropped or thrown away. She hadn't forgotten what it was like to be hungry all the time, and afraid—afraid of being caught and sent to a workhouse, afraid of starving to death, afraid they would be separated somehow ...

Thirty minutes later, Tiki pushed her way into Mr. Potts's bookstore, the bell above the door giving a familiar jingle.

"Hallo, Mr. Potts," she called out, peering down one aisle, then another, looking for the old man. She found him at the back of the store, shelving a stack of books.

"Mr. Potts?"

"Eh?" He startled when she called his name. "Sorry, miss. Didn't 'ear yer come in." He squinted at her through the shadows between the stacks. "Is that yer, Tiki? By golly, it is. You look different again." He set the books down and pulled a handkerchief from his back pocket to wipe his nose. "Must be growin' up, I guess." He went past her down the aisle. "Come up front wit' me so I can see yer pretty face."

Tiki obediently followed the old man, noting how thin he had become, his baggy trousers held up by a belt pulled tight.

"How have you been?" she asked as they returned to the front of the store where the light was much better.

"Busy. Yer know—people comin', people goin'." He gave her a wobbly smile and smoothed what little hair he had with a gnarled hand. "What 'ave yer been readin' lately? Yer haven't borrowed a book in a long time."

"I haven't had a lot of time to read, but I will again soon. What do you recommend?"

He reached for a book that was sitting on the corner of his desk, brushing aside papers haphazardly stacked on top. He ran his fingers over the green hardback cover.

"I set this aside for yer—what with the way yer and the young'uns love faerie stories." He peered at her from under his bushy gray eyebrows. "Those faeries can be a nasty lot—thought maybe yer should be aware of their dark side too—so you don't end up like my poor Bridgit."

Tiki's heart sank. Poor Mr. Potts missed his daughter so terribly. How she wished she could help him get over the pain of his loss from when the girl had disappeared from Hyde Park during a terrible storm.

"What's the book about?" she asked gently.

"It's a poem, actually, by an English bloke named John Keats. Called 'La Belle Dame sans Merci'—'The Beautiful Lady without Mercy'—about a faerie called a *leanan sidhe*." He shook the book at her. "Beautiful but vicious, that one."

"How's that?" Tiki asked curiously. "I didn't know you read poetry."

"I'm a bookseller. It's my job to know all kinds of books." He waggled a crooked finger at her. "The poem tells of a lady so beautiful, men are mesmerized by 'er. They willingly trade their lives for the inspiration 'er beauty gives 'em. And then she destroys 'em." He stared hard into Tiki's eyes. "Because as beautiful as she is, it's her nature to destroy."

Tiki tried to mask her surprise at his insightfulness. In some ways, it sounded like he was describing Larkin. She reached for the book and opened the pages. Out loud, she began to read:

> *O what can ail thee, knight-at-arms,*
> *Alone and palely loitering?*
> *The sedge has withered from the lake,*
> *And no birds sing.*
>
> *O what can ail thee, knight-at-arms,*
> *So haggard and so woe-begone?*
> *The squirrel's granary is full,*
> *And the harvest's done.*
>
> *I see a lily on thy brow,*
> *With anguish moist and fever-dew,*
> *And on thy cheeks a fading rose*
> *Fast withereth too.*

> *I met a lady in the meads,*
> *Full beautiful—a faery's child,*

She paused at the words "faery's child." When had Mr. Potts learned so much about faeries?

Tiki resumed reading:

> *Her hair was long, her foot was light,*
> *And her eyes were wild.*

An image of Larkin's exquisite face and blue-green eyes filled her vision.

"Now, now." Mr. Potts made a shooing motion with his hands. "Yer take that wit' yer and read it all."

Tiki smiled at the old man. "You seem awfully worried about faeries for someone who lives in the City. Don't they live out in the country somewhere, like Cauterhaugh Wood where Tam Lin had his adventure?"

"Yer laugh, young lady, but Dickey's brother-in-law works up Bucking'am, yer know, and he's heard the whispers that the royals have some goin's-on with the faerie folk."

Tiki sobered. "What sort of 'goin's-on'?"

He spoke in a gruff whisper. "Somethun' 'bout a stolen ring and a war. He heard enough to scare 'im into believin'." Mr. Potts nodded at the book Tiki held. "The poets and storytellers been writin' 'bout them for hundreds of years. Who are we to say they don't exist? Somethun' took my Bridgit away that day, and my best guess is it were the faeries."

Chapter Twenty-One

It was Tiki and Rieker who went to Buckingham Palace the next day to retrieve Johnny. At Rieker's suggestion, Leo invited them for tea, giving Tiki the opportunity to visit with Fiona, Toots, and Clara.

"Teek, we're havin' so much fun stayin' with Leo," Clara bubbled, her eyes dancing with excitement. "We get to play in the park behind the palace and feed the ducks and there are swans—some are white and some are black—"

"And I've been learning how to train Molly, one of the dogs," Toots exclaimed. "They've even let me help brush down the horses!"

"It seems you lot have been busy." Tiki smiled. It was reassuring to see the children safe and happy, though Fiona looked half-sick with worry. "Perhaps you'll have enough skills to get a job when you come home."

"If it's workin' with the animals, I wouldn't mind a'tall," Toots said with a wide grin. "James told me I'm a natural."

"And how have your travels been?" Leo asked Tiki. "Safe, I presume?"

"Safe enough," Tiki said. "And enlightening, thanks to the gift you sent with Dain. Thank you."

Leo's eyes lit up. "It was helpful, then? You've unlocked its secrets?"

"Rather the other way around," Tiki said with a smile. "The mirror provided an essential bit of information that allowed us to resolve some unanswered questions."

"Really? You were able to figure out its purpose. I knew it was meant for you." Leo was like a puppy wagging its tail. "Are you better able to protect yourselves?"

"There's more work to be done, but we're on the right track."

Leo bent ever so slightly, as if the air had been let out of a balloon. "I so hoped that you'd conquered whoever threatens you there—that you'd be able to return home again soon."

"We'll be back, Leo, don't you worry about that," Rieker said, giving Tiki a meaningful look. "Just not quite yet."

Tiki pulled Fiona aside as they made ready to leave. "You do know where we're taking him?" she asked gently.

Fiona nodded, her angular face drawn. She didn't look like she'd been eating either. "It seems the only way to save him." A light flared in her eyes and she clutched at Tiki's arm. "Can I go too? I could care for him there."

Tiki slowly shook her head. "No, Fi. You'd be putting yourself at risk. Before, Larkin was careful that you were only provided with mortal food and drink, but that can't be done forever, and right now, Larkin is too distracted with other matters to care for you. Let us take him and get him well. After that, we'll figure out what to do."

They arrived at the Plain of Sunlight with Johnny just as the sun was setting behind Wydryn Tor. They stood before the stone entry to the Seelie headquarters and looked toward the border.

"If you ever question why we're doing this"—Larkin pointed to the grisly silhouettes in the distance—"look at those dead bodies impaled on stakes. Donegal has no respect for any of us. He wants to eradicate those who resist him. He will continue to murder until there are no Seelies left. It is only about power for him."

Tiki stood next to Rieker who cradled the wraith-thin Johnny in his arms. The muscles in Rieker's jaw flexed at the view before them, and he cursed under his breath before he ducked his head to follow Larkin through the stone entry into the Seelie headquarters.

Tiki remained alone on the plain. She couldn't tear her eyes away from the seemingly endless row of staked bodies that circled her like some ungodly chain of prison bars. A cool wind whistled across the valley and raised the flesh on her arms, as if Death had blown his cruel breath in her direction. Tiki shivered and turned to follow the others. It didn't seem possible they could survive the Winter King's relentless pursuit.

They delivered Johnny to a nurse, and Larkin called for Toran as soon as they reached the gathering area.

"What have you learned of the Fool?" she demanded. But the guard had no further information on the jester.

"No one knows where he's being held. The last anyone saw of him was when Donegal had him arrested."

"And where was that?"

"In the Great Hall at the palace. Olcán said the jester was entertaining Donegal and his guests, levitating a great ball of white light, when something went wrong and somehow the Winter King was burned."

"On purpose, I'll bet," Dain whispered.

Tiki peered at him out of the corners of her eyes. "What?"

Larkin shushed them. "And then what happened?"

"Olcán said Donegal went crazy. Ordered the jester stripped and flogged on the spot. But when the guards pulled the shirt from his back and were tying the jester's wrists to a wooden pole across his shoulders, the Winter King started choking. Told them to stop and ordered Sullivan and Cruinn to take the jester away."

"Are you sure it was Sullivan and Cruinn?" Larkin asked.

Toran nodded. "That's what Olcán said. And that's the last anyone saw of the man. The next day, Donegal announced the Court Jester was a traitor and that he was going to feed him to the hounds at the full moon."

"We'll go to the White Tower first," Larkin said as they stood in a small antechamber off the gathering room. It reminded Tiki of the room where she'd shed the glamour she'd unconsciously worn since being left in London as a baby. In a strange reversal of that moment, her current appearance looked dramatically different from the beauty revealed that day. Larkin had taken charge of their glamours, explaining that she knew best which types of creatures wouldn't draw unwanted attention in the UnSeelie court.

She had glamoured Tiki to look like a small UnSeelie male. Her nose was large, with a substantial hook to the bridge and white hair held by a band behind her neck. Her eyes were black rather than vibrant green, and her shoulders bore a slight hunch, as though she hid something within the folds of her worn jacket. She'd gone from strikingly beautiful to hideous.

Dain looked like her older brother, and Rieker had metamorphosed from a handsome young aristocrat into a rail-thin man with a pockmarked face. His greasy, black hair was tied behind his head and reached his shoulders. In some ways, he looked like an eerie, younger shadow of Donegal.

"You look dangerous," Tiki said to him as she searched his face for a familiar feature.

"I feel dangerous," Rieker growled. "I'm ready to fight this battle."

The ride from the Plain of Sunlight to the northern part of the Wychwood where the White Tower lay hidden behind a glamour was uneventful. Larkin was surprisingly reclusive during the trip, keeping her distance as they rode, unwilling to answer any additional questions.

The air became bitterly cold the farther north they went, and ice coated the trees as they turned onto the trail that led to the overlook. A mist threaded its fingers through the trees as if to grab them as they rode by.

"It burns when I breathe," Tiki choked as she fought another coughing spasm. "And that smell—"

"It's smoke. There's a fire burning nearby," Larkin said.

"Here." Dain rode close to Tiki and handed her a section of gray cloth that looked like it had been torn from his shirt. "Tie this around your nose and mouth—it should help filter some of the smoke."

Tiki nodded gratefully as she accepted his offering. "Thank you. I thought I'd finally gotten rid of this cough until we started this trip. Maybe it's my new nose." She pointed at her glamoured beak and smiled, revealing sharklike teeth. Then she coughed again and focused on the task of folding the fabric. Once she had the material in a triangle, she tied it over her face, leaving only her eyes exposed.

"You look wicked," Dain teased, pulling back on the reins to keep his horse side by side with hers as Larkin and Rieker rode ahead. "Like a goblin highwayman."

Tiki laughed. "Would I steal your blood or your gold?"

"I'd be happy if you wanted either."

"You'd give up so easily? What happened to the brave knight of court I've come to know?"

"You bewitch me, milady—"

"Be quiet back there and stop your nonsense," Larkin growled in their direction. "We don't need to let the entire Wychwood know of our presence."

Tiki and Dain smiled at each other, but they remained silent as they continued to ride north through the smoky forest.

Larkin and Rieker had already stopped on the overlook when Tiki pulled up next to them. It was hard to read their expressions given their glamours, but even so, the grimness of their features was unsettling as she reached the crest of the rocky outlook. Unsure of what to expect, she looked out over the panorama.

Where before the water had reflected the verdant trees that ringed the lake and the gathering of buildings at the far end with an almost mirrorlike image, now there was nothing to reflect except smoking ruins. The entire north end of the lake had been burned to ash. Funnels of smoke rose into the air from the blackened and charred stumps of the devastated forest. Every tree and bush had been eradicated in a fire that had swept through the area.

"What happened?" Tiki cried.

"It appears to be part of the fire the Winter King used to oust the hobgoblins," Larkin said.

Dain pulled up next to Tiki and let out a snort of disgust. "Only Donegal would destroy the forest that sustains our world."

"I don't see how anything could survive that," Tiki whispered. "Do you think the White Tower is still there?"

"No," Larkin said flatly. "A glamour cannot survive a fire like that. We can only pray that Fial didn't perish along with the forest."

Chapter Twenty-Two

Their ride back through the Wychwood to the Palace of Mirrors passed far too quickly for Tiki's liking. The sun had barely reached its zenith in a hazy, smoke-filled sky the next day when they arrived at the base of the Tor.

They were still hidden among the trees when Larkin pulled to a stop. "We'll need to release the horses here. We can't be seen riding up to the palace."

"Is Donegal here?" Dain asked as they dismounted.

"Yes." Larkin's response was terse. "Word is that Donegal has remained at the palace since the capture of the jester. He's probably afraid to leave. Fial knows far too many of his secrets to be left to the mercy of the guards."

Tiki gave Larkin a sidelong glance. The glamour Larkin had disguised herself with had been a startling choice. Tiki couldn't decide if the mercurial faerie looked more like a witch or a dryad. Her fingers were extended and knobby, like long, skinny branches, and her eyes were little more than black hollows in her face, eerily like a knothole in a tree trunk. But her nose was long and hooked like a witch's, and rust-colored hair the color of dead leaves hung long down her back, a distinct departure from Larkin's normal silky, blond strands.

She reminded Tiki of the Elder Dryad, the volatile creature she'd bargained with that day in the Wychwood when she had been so desperate to find where Donegal's men had taken Rieker.

"If Donegal is here, what will you do?" Rieker asked as he climbed down from his horse. "Surely you don't mean to just walk into court."

"Actually, I do," Larkin said with typical fearlessness. "Donegal captured the jester here at the palace, and I don't think he would risk transporting him to the Plain of Starlight. Fial is too clever not to escape, and Donegal knows it." Her voice dropped. "I think the jester is here, hidden somewhere in the palace."

"But won't the guards want to know who we are?" Dain asked, motioning to Tiki and Rieker.

Larkin let out a dark laugh. "What makes you think Donegal and the UnSeelie court don't know who we are?"

Tiki jerked her horse's head and the beast let out a sharp whinny in protest. "Explain yourself."

Larkin spoke softly, though her sarcasm was still easy to hear. "You do know what I've been these many years, correct?"

Tiki gave a hesitant nod. "A spy."

"And you're not possibly naive enough to think I was able to infiltrate the UnSeelie court successfully for decades by using the same identity throughout that entire time?"

Tiki slowly shook her head.

"Exactly. In this glamour, I'm known as Fachtna among the UnSeelie. A witch from the—"

"*You* are Fachtna?" Dain stared at Larkin with a stricken expression.

She tilted her head at him, looking pleased. "You've heard of me?"

"We've all heard of Fachtna. She's practically a legend—"

"An evil legend, no doubt," Rieker muttered.

"Are the rumors true?" Dain whispered. "Do you make soup with the bones of mortal children?"

Tiki's jaw sagged. "*What*?"

Larkin scoffed. "Dain, you, of all people, know how it works. To make people believe you are UnSeelie, you must be perceived as UnSeelie. I have simply played my part over the years."

A familiar twinge twisted Tiki's stomach as she noted Larkin had not answered the question. Where did the truth stop and start with the enigmatic faerie? Would Tiki ever know?

"That's true," Dain said, "but *Fachtna*? Even I would never have guessed. You would have had to create that cover—" He paused to think.

"Before you were born," Larkin said dryly. "As I've said before, I have committed my life to this court, though at times, I question if the sacrifice has been worth it." She looked up at the outcropping of rock that jutted into black clouds overhead. "When we get inside the palace, we'll split up. That's the only way we'll be able to find the jester. Somebody has to know something."

"If you are this Fachtna, who are we?" Rieker asked.

Larkin's expression was inscrutable. "My servants, of course."

The climb up to the peak of the Tor was less arduous than Tiki expected. Instead of the secret, practically vertical trail that Dain had taken her down when they'd escaped from the Winter King before, this time they followed a well-worn road that wove its way back and forth up the sloping side of the mountain.

The higher they climbed, the darker it became. Black clouds, heavy as though weighted with ink, pushed down on the mountain, encasing the top in a dark mist. Lightning forked in the near distance, followed by the rumbling boom of thunder, causing Tiki's arms to crawl with gooseflesh. The storm seemed an inescapable omen. She tried to push away the sensation that she was marching to her own death.

The Night Garden of the UnSeelie court had grown even more macabre since Tiki's last visit. The brambles and thorns were as razor sharp as ever, but now, it appeared shreds of flesh dangled from their murderous tips, as if scraped from their prey's bones in the plant's hurry to consume their victims. The flowers that flourished among the skeletal branches were glorious and vibrant—reds, oranges, yellows, blues, and greens—glowing and enticingly fragrant, so alluring it took great willpower not to lean close and absorb their magnificence. A lovely melody wafted through the garden, cajoling them to come closer, yet beneath the sweet scent lay a bitter stench of blood and death.

"Of course, you remember the garden sings to its prey," Larkin said over her shoulder as she led the way across broken stones that had once been a path. "Don't touch, don't look, don't smell. The flowers want only for you to become their next meal."

Tiki tried to reconcile the shadowed garden that surrounded her with the sunlit, bountiful sight this same space became when the Seelies were in control of Faerie. There was such a dichotomy between the two images that she couldn't superimpose one over the other. It was impossible to imagine that the space she stood in now could be anything other than evil, dark, and deadly.

She heaved a sigh of relief when they were past the garden and stood before the entry to the Palace of Mirrors. She stopped next to Larkin and stared at the sight before them. Guards lined the entire front of the palace, armed and watching. Bonfires roared on each corner of the building, their flames crackling and throwing sparks into the air like hungry jaws snapping to be fed.

"Donegal is expecting something to happen," Larkin said. "Look there." She pointed to an area where black-suited guards trained in various formations.

"Is he expecting an attack?" Rieker asked.

"It appears that way."

Dain frowned. "From the Macanna?"

"Who else would dare attack him in the palace?" Larkin moved forward. "He knows we're plotting. Let's see what we can find out."

"Stay close to me," Rieker murmured in Tiki's ear as they followed Larkin.

With every step, Tiki's heart reverberated a little harder in her chest, like the strike of a bell clanging from side to side, as she silently counted the guards who stretched from one end of the columned portico to the other. Seventeen. Even if they found the jester, how would they get him out of the building alive?

As they approached, the guards closest to their group dropped their spears to block any passage.

"Halt!" barked the tallest of the four who had taken a defensive position. "Name your business."

Larkin stepped ahead of the others. "Donegal seeks my counsel. Tell him Fachtna has arrived."

One of the guards dashed into the palace while the others remained frozen, blocking their way. Tiki could feel the weight of their eyes boring through her as surely as if their claws had touched her flesh. A flash among the blackness that engulfed the palace caught her eye but as she shifted to look, the flutter of white disappeared amid the smoke.

The runner returned and whispered into the foremost guard's ear. The burly man raised his hand and as one, the spears snapped upright and the guards shifted to the side to allow entrance.

"Donegal awaits your arrival in the Great Hall."

"Come," Larkin said as she swept through the line toward the palace entrance.

The building was intimately familiar to Tiki, having just lived within its walls for the last six months. Yet, in its present state, the space looked distinctly different. What had once been light was now dark. Black had been replaced with white, night had replaced day, evil had replaced goodness. It was as though they strode into the depths of hell.

Larkin went directly to the hall where Donegal liked to command from the golden Dragon Throne. The towering pair of doors lay open, and as before when Tiki had visited the Palace of Mirrors during Donegal's reign, the room was filled with partygoers in an array of opulent dress. Now, however, there were also black-suited soldiers armed with a variety of weapons—somber and menacing.

Larkin paused in the hallway. "We part here. Split up and see what you can learn. The jester will be guarded, so watch for soldiers who appear to have no purpose. And remember"—she held up a finger—"Fial is extremely ingenious. If he is still alive, he will find a way to give us a sign."

Chapter Twenty-Three

The jester lay on his side in the cell, the cold stone absorbing what little warmth remained in his body. There were no windows in his prison, save for the barred viewing slot in the door and the small pass-through for food at the bottom. He'd overheard the guards discussing his fate: to be fed alive to the hounds at the full moon, less than a week away. The cruelty of his punishment didn't surprise him—his brother had always been cruel. That had not changed over the centuries.

Fial considered what he could see of the small cell without moving. It hurt too much to move. They had beaten him unconscious before dragging his limp body to the hidden dungeon. He doubted that word would get to Larkin of his fate, but he had to try, just in case. She was his only hope.

He ground his teeth together against the pain to raise his battered, shaking hands to his mouth, trying to ignore the burn of the iron against his wrists. He started to inhale but his breath caught as a knifelike pain stabbed between his ribs. He tried again, barely opening his mouth and attempting to resist any movement of his rib cage.

When he had sufficient breath gathered, he blew into his dirty, cupped palms and slowly rubbed them together. A snow-white dove emerged from his fingers, one wing broken and dangling at its side. Fial cursed under his breath as the bird attempted flight but awkwardly fell to the floor where it dissolved in a puff of smoke.

The jester's body sagged against the unyielding stones. Every breath hurt. He brought his shaking hands to his mouth again and closed his eyes against the pain. Ever so slowly, he inhaled deeper this time, then blew flame into his fingers. As the fire diminished, a small but perfect white dove perched there.

"Find the dove with the heart of a fox so that she may find me," he whispered.

The bird flew around the room in one great circle before it flapped through the slot in the door and disappeared.

Chapter Twenty-Four

Tiki, Rieker, and Dain watched as Larkin marched into the Great Hall, her glamoured hair fluttering behind her.

"We need to split up too," Dain said. "I'll go on my own since I know the UnSeelie palace best. The two of you need to stick together. If you find something, make the cry of the raven—I should be able to hear you."

Tiki frowned. "Are you sure? I don't like the idea of you being alone."

"Don't worry. I know my way around here," he said, smiling, "but your kind heart is always a pleasant surprise and reminds me that I do have a family now. For that reason, I will take great care." With a nod, he strode away toward a motley contingent of guards who stood near a short stairway that led down to an area where weapons were cleaned and stored. As he approached, Dain raised his hand and called out. Whatever he said made several of them laugh, and they willingly cleared a path for him.

"He seems to be blessed with the tongue of an Irishman," Rieker said, staring after his brother.

"He is charming," Tiki agreed. "I hope he knows what he's doing."

"He lived a double life for many years. He doesn't seem afraid."

"As you should well know," Tiki said in a dry tone, "lack of fear does not equal good sense."

Rieker grinned, his sallow, pockmarked face stretching in a fearsome expression. "Ah, but a good adventure outweighs good sense or fear any day."

Tiki rolled her eyes. "Where do you think we should look?" She peered into the Great Hall. The discordant strains of an out-of-tune fiddle floated out the doors, making her teeth grate. A raw smell permeated the air—a strange combination that reminded her of charred meat and fresh blood. She wrinkled her nose in distaste. "There are a lot of people in there, but an almost equal number of soldiers. I doubt they'll tell us anything."

"I think we need to go explore while Lar—" Rieker caught himself—"*Fachtna* keeps Donegal distracted." He pulled Tiki away from the grand room as the screech and howl of other instruments joined in the cacophony. They walked down a spacious hallway lined with doors on one wall. "What areas of the palace could Donegal keep a prisoner out of sight for days and weeks or even months?"

"I don't know. The palace is large, but I've never seen anything that looks like a prison. The Tor is solid rock—there's nothing below the palace. That's why the kitchens, stables, and housing for the slaves are built to one side."

Rieker nodded. "And the barracks for the soldiers couldn't possibly hide a prisoner."

"No. Definitely not. Considering how many soldiers Donegal has forced into service, I doubt half of them could fit into those buildings." She pointed straight ahead. "As you know, that way leads to the ruler of Faerie's chambers and beyond that are mostly offices and drawing rooms." She pointed the other direction. "The High Chamber of Lords and Ladies is that way." She glanced one way and then the other with a look of dismay. "I'm not sure where to start."

"Where do these go?" Rieker pointed at the long row of doors that stretched down the hallway.

"I know one leads outside to the Night Garden. Dain took me that way when we escaped from Donegal my first visit. I don't know about the others. Do you think one leads to a prison?"

Rieker walked over and yanked the closest door open to view the moonlit shadows of the Night Garden. "Not that one." He walked down the hallway to the next door and pulled it open. Again, the barren, gnarled branches of the Night Garden were lit by a waxing moon and could be seen swaying to the muted music emitted by the flowers. "Not that one." He strode down the hall opening door after door, but they all led to the same place. "Clearly, this hallway won't lead us to where we want to go."

They walked again, their heads bent together. "Did the jester have rooms of his own?" Rieker asked.

"I don't know—it never came up in conversation. I only saw him in the Great Hall or the High Chamber."

Rieker jerked his head up. "What about the High Chamber? Maybe they're keeping the jester hidden there."

Tiki imagined the room where the lords and ladies of the Seelie court met to discuss the business of the realm. Many of the rooms in the palace dripped with gilded opulence—soaring columns and elaborate decoration—but the High Chamber was like stepping into the shaded comfort of a wooded glen. Spongy moss coated the floor and the babbling voice of a nearby brook trickled over stones. Lilting birdsong floated among the branches that stretched overhead. It was as far from the normal sense of the word "room" as one could get. Though Tiki had never explored the chamber beyond the large plank table where she met with the lords and ladies, the wooded space appeared to go on forever.

"You think there could be a prison hidden within the High Chamber?"

Rieker shrugged. "Why not? It seems large enough."

"William, you're brilliant," Tiki murmured. "Do you think there are guards watching the doors."

"Only one way to find out."

Tiki hurried after Rieker as he strode down the hallway to the High Chamber. Squeaks from a flute pierced the air with knifelike stabs as cellos, fiddles, and harps strummed in a frenzied pace. Tiki could just imagine the harried dance that might accompany such music and gave silent thanks she wasn't in the Great Hall with Donegal and his UnSeelie court.

She hurried after Rieker, anxious to hide within the High Chamber. She felt too exposed out in the open passageway. They were barely a third of the way down the immense corridor when an odd sound caught Tiki's ear. She cocked her head, trying to differentiate what she'd heard from the musical din that crashed down the hallway behind them, but it was impossible.

The sound came again, and this time she knew immediately what she'd heard: the low growl of a dog with deadly intent. Tiki jerked around just as two hellhounds, teeth bared and jaws snapping, broke into a gallop, headed directly at them.

Chapter Twenty-Five

Tiki didn't have time to scream. She reacted purely by instinct. She clamped a hand around Rieker's wrist and tugged him across the hallway. She yanked open the nearest door and dove into the space, pulling Rieker along behind her. Using her foot as they fell forward, Tiki slammed the door shut just as the first dog reached them. The door rattled upon impact as the dog crashed into the wood, followed by a loud *yip*.

Instead of falling into the Night Garden as she had expected, they collided much more abruptly with a set of stone steps.

"Umpf!" Tiki cried as her head cracked against the hard surface. Rieker landed next to her, his breath forced out in a sharp exhale.

"Ouch," Rieker said, rubbing his ribs as he pushed off the stairs to stand. He held a hand out for Tiki. "Are you all right?"

Outside the door, the dogs could be heard sniffing and one had begun to howl. Before them, a set of stone steps stretched up in a circle above their heads and disappeared out of sight. A wavering light from above cast enough light to navigate the stairwell.

"Where in bloody hell did those dogs come from?" Rieker said. "And why are they after us?"

"Let's keep moving," Tiki replied, starting up the stairs. "We've got to get out of here." Tiki climbed as fast as she could, keeping one hand on the curving wall.

"Where are we going?"

"I have no idea, but those dogs are Bearach's hellhounds. Dain thinks Donegal has set them after me—they first showed up in Grosvenor Square just after you left for Scotland. They must be able to smell my scent through the glamour. We'll need to divert them somehow."

"That much seems obvious," Rieker muttered as he followed her up the stairs. "Unless you have a spare leg you can offer up in sacrifice."

Tiki smiled despite the tension that crackled inside her. "I'll get back to you about that one." By the time they neared the top of the stairs, her breath came in short gasps. They stepped onto a small landing that led to another door.

"Where do you suppose that goes?" Rieker whispered as he looked around. "And where are we? We opened every one of the doors in that hallway, and they all led to the Night Garden. Where did these stairs come from?"

"I don't know, but we can't go back, so I guess that means there's only one direction for us to go." Tiki stepped forward and put her ear to the door, but she could hear nothing. She wrapped her fingers around the handle and took a deep breath. "I am the queen," she muttered under her breath. "I can protect us …" But she didn't believe it for a second. Not in the palace while Donegal ruled.

With a quick movement, she twisted the handle and tugged on the door, but it was locked. She pulled again, harder this time, but the sturdy wooden portal wouldn't budge.

"Let me try," Rieker said, edging closer. He wrapped his long fingers around the bronze handle and gave a forceful yank. But the door would not yield. Rieker released his grip and stepped back, sizing up the frame that held the door in place. In a smooth motion, he stepped forward and kicked the door open, the wood giving way in a wrenching *crash*.

Tiki jumped in surprise. "All right, then. That's one way to do it."

Rieker raised the thin black eyebrows of his unattractive glamour. "When you can't go back, one must go forward …"

"Funny."

He stepped into the room and stopped.

"What is it?" Tiki crowded close to look around his shoulders. Deep crimson carpet, shot through with what looked like gold stars, reached to the far end of the long room. The carpet was rich and sumptuous, giving the room a luxurious air, but it was the rest of the space that made Tiki's jaw sag in surprise.

Her first impression was of a cathedral, for the walls were covered in a magnificent array of stained glass windows. Even the floor was covered with a million pieces of colored glass artfully arranged in design after design. The craftsmanship was so fine, some windows appeared to be paintings, each meant to tell its own story—some achingly beautiful, others ghastly.

Tiki followed Rieker into the room. "What is this place?"

"I don't know," Rieker said, "but you can be sure it serves some purpose."

"Who could have created all this?" Tiki turned in a slow circle. The room appeared to have been made from colored glass. "It's beautiful in a haunting sort of way."

Rieker walked along the perimeter as Tiki walked down the narrow, carpeted paths between the windows. Black dogs with snarling fangs and red, glowing eyes growled up at her; knights with blades drawn fought to the death while others lay with heads severed; mothers cradled babies crowned by halos; lovers entwined; a young boy on bent knee being knighted by a king; forests, waterfalls, and towers, witches and dryads, demons and mortals. All manner of fey—immortalized in time.

She stopped at one window. Depicted by the fine pieces of cut glass was the image of a queen, her hair neither brown nor blond, her face neither young nor old. She appeared to be carved from pale marble, a golden crown encrusted with jewels upon her head.

"I've seen this one before," Tiki whispered as she got down on her knees to run her fingers over the leaded pieces that formed the queen's face. "This image is on the card the jester gave me."

"And I've seen this before," Rieker said from where he stood in a small alcove.

Tiki hurried over to his side. "What is it?"

Rieker pointed to a fine silver medallion in the shape of a Celtic cross that lay in a box of crushed emerald-green velvet. "Kieran wore that when I knew him in London."

Tiki sucked in her breath. "Do you think these are the jester's rooms?" She turned around to look again at the brilliant mosaic of color. "Do you think he made these windows?"

Rieker turned and followed Tiki's gaze. "Do you think he's really my father?"

Tiki slipped her hand into Rieker's and squeezed gently. "William, whether he is or isn't doesn't change who you are."

He tightened his fingers over hers. "You're right. By now, I know we each create our own path in this life." He looked around the room. "The bigger question is, where do we go from here?"

"I don't know. We don't dare go back the way we came."

"No. We need to find another way out." Rieker released Tiki's hand and walked to the wall, running his fingertips over the stained glass image of a tower with flames shooting from the top. "It's like these images tell a story—"

"Or, knowing the jester, hide a message." Tiki drew a sharp breath and pointed to one of the images on the floor. It was a grotesque picture of a redheaded giant wearing a chain of severed heads around his waist. "I recognize that one too. It's on the—" Her words died in her throat.

"What?" Rieker looked from Tiki to where she pointed. "What is it?"

Tiki hurried to the picture and fell to her knees in front of the colored glass.

"Teek, what are you doing?"

She leaned close until her nose was almost pressed against the glass. "Come look," she cried, motioning him over. He dropped to his knees next to her.

"What is it?"

"I recognize this picture—it's on the ceiling of the Great Hall when the UnSeelies rule. Don't you see? We're on the other side of it—*above* the Great Hall." She sat back on her heels and looked at Rieker. "This room is a spying post."

Chapter Twenty-Six

"The jester's spying post—it makes perfect sense." Rieker looked over at Tiki. "How else would he know everything that went on in the Great Hall?" He pointed. "What about that one? Can we see through that one too?" It didn't take long to realize that the entire row of images on the floor allowed a view of the activities in the huge room below.

"Look, when the angle is right you can see reflections in some of the mirrors," Tiki said. "If someone was wearing a glamour, you'd be able to see it. Perhaps that's how the jester recognized Larkin the first time she brought me here. And there's something else that's been bothering me. When we opened several of those doors in the hall, we saw the Night Garden with the moon in the sky—but there was no moon when we got to the top of the Tor. The palace is encased in black clouds. I think those doors in the hallway are glamoured to look like they lead to the Night Garden with the purpose of hiding the stairs that lead here."

Rieker pushed himself to his feet. "If these are the jester's rooms, there must be another exit." He headed back to the alcove and examined the walls for any kind of opening that might lead them out.

Tiki remained kneeling on the floor, gazing through the stained glass windows. Many of the guests danced with wild abandon, seemingly oblivious to the lack of melody that screeched from the musicians' instruments. Others huddled in small circles talking and swilling blue wine from elegantly curved bottles.

"I can see Larkin," she called. "She's still talking to Donegal." Tiki's gaze wandered from the Winter King and Larkin disguised as Fachtna to look for Dain, though his garments would make him blend in with the crowd. In some places, it was difficult to see through the smoke that belched from the wall-mounted torches, but it appeared the room was still full of guards, armed as if prepared for an attack. What diversion could be created to draw them away from protecting the Winter King long enough that someone might remove him from the throne?

As she stared down into the crowded hall, a flash of white caught her eye. She leaned forward, scanning the room.

There! She saw it again. A small, white dove, oddly out of place in the dark and smoky atmosphere, flew in a wide arc around the room. There was something familiar about the bird, and she searched her memory for where she might have seen it before.

Another flutter of white caught her eye, and this time, she followed the dove's path as it flew to one end of the Great Hall. The bird made a great arc over the Dragon Throne.

She scrambled to her feet. "Rieker!" she cried. "The jester is here—in the palace."

Rieker jerked around. "How do you know?"

"Do you remember Dain said he'd seen the jester create firebirds? I've just seen a snow-white dove in the Great Hall. It has to be a sign from him. We need to follow that bird—it's our only clue."

"What are we going to do about the hounds?" Rieker frowned. "They've got your scent again—you can't go back down there."

"We'll have to deal with them somehow." Tiki looked around the long room but there was nothing obvious they could use to stop the two giant dogs. "Do you think they're still out there?"

"I don't know, but we can't take a chance if they are. We'll never outrun them."

Tiki propped her hands on her hips. "We've got to think of something. We need to follow that dove—it might be our only chance to locate Fial." She hurried to the alcove. "Did you see anything that looked like another way out?"

Rieker followed her. "No."

Tiki ran her fingers over the walls, looking for anything that might be a hidden door. Rieker looked too, but no other exit was obvious. After ten minutes of searching, Tiki dropped her hands. "We need to think like the jester."

"Not likely." Rieker snorted.

"This was a spying room for him, not his personal chambers. If he saw something in the Great Hall that was of interest, he would probably want to be able to get down there quickly." She turned in a slow circle. "But he couldn't just drop into the middle of things, now, could he? He would need to enter unobtrusively."

She walked back down one of the carpeted paths in the middle of the room and stared through the glass into the Great Hall. "He would have to arrive on the perimeter somewhere—" She stopped. "Why would he need two exits when he could just go back down the stairs and cross the hallway? There are thirteen doors in that hallway—maybe the rest of them actually *do* lead to the Night Garden. If someone saw him coming out of the door, they might assume he just stepped in from outside."

Rieker came to stand beside her. "You might be right, but how does that help us? We still need to stop the hounds."

Tiki pointed through the glass. "Look! The dogs have returned to the Great Hall, and they're seated by Donegal now." The two great black hounds sat at attention next to the Dragon Throne, their heads almost level with Donegal's. Even seated, the dogs were huge. Tiki's heart sank. How could they possibly escape from such beasts?

As she considered the room below, she realized that Larkin was no longer in conversation with the Winter King. Tiki searched for Fachtna or the white dove—any kind of answer. She stopped, and her brows pulled down in concentration.

"We don't need to think like the jester—we need to think like you."

"What?"

She grabbed Rieker's hand and pulled him to the door. "I have an idea."

They wedged the splintered door shut and followed the stone steps back down to the spot where they'd entered from the hallway. Tiki reached for the door handle, but Rieker pulled her aside.

"Let me look. The hounds don't care about my scent." He motioned for her to stand back, and slowly, slowly pulled the door open a crack to peer into the hallway. "No dogs that way," he whispered as he pulled the door open farther. He wedged his body close to the crack, so if a dog appeared, it would have to go through him to enter the small space where they stood. He tilted his head to look the other way down the hall. "All clear."

They exited and hurried down the hallway to the next door. With a quick glance over her shoulder, Tiki opened the door. Once again, the alluring sound of the Night Garden sang to them, the gnarled bare branches and brambles swaying in the soft moonlight.

"Wait here," Rieker said. "Don't move until I return."

Tiki slipped inside the door and pulled it almost closed. It would only be a few minutes before Rieker returned with the diversion she'd planned for the dogs. She prayed it would work. They wouldn't be able to accomplish anything here if she was constantly being hunted.

She glanced over her shoulder to make sure she was alone and froze. Instead of the shadowy, bramble-filled garden she'd expected, she was standing in a library. Bookcases crammed to overflowing lined the walls of the round room. Above her head, a circular walkway bisected the room, allowing access to a second story of books. A couch and several chairs centered around an ornately carved wooden table created an intimate reading area. The room had an air of elegance and sophistication that seemed alien to anything Donegal could create. Who, then, came to this spot?

Tiki walked over to the nearest bookcase and ran her fingers along the spines, some leather, some cloth, some with glittering gold letters, others stamped in black block letters. In many ways, the room reminded her of Mr. Potts's bookstore. But it also reminded her of the Octagonal Library in Buckingham Palace where Leo had dropped the ring of the truce that fateful night while she hid under the desk.

She wound her way around the room and over to the carved table where a small stack of books waited. The top one had a bookmark protruding from its pages. Curious, Tiki picked it up and turned it over to read the title. She dropped the book as though her fingers had been burned. It landed on the table with a thunk, the title gleaming up at her: *Oliver Twist.* She reached for the next book, intuitively knowing what the title would say: *The Count of Monte Cristo*. Beneath that was a thin book: *The Field of Boliauns.*

Why would someone in Faerie be reading the very books she had purchased for Rieker and Clara? *Who* would be reading them? How did they know? Unsettled, she backed away from the table. Had someone from the Otherworld been spying on them all this time?

"Teek," Rieker called in a harsh whisper through a crack in the door. "Are you ready?"

Tiki ran back to the door, pulling off her jacket as she went. There would be another time to investigate this room. She slipped into the hallway.

"Yes, I'm ready. You've got what we need?"

Rieker held up two bags that sagged with the weight of their contents.

Tiki curled her nose. Fresh blood. "Yes, I can smell your success."

"Let's hurry before someone wants to know what we're doing." As if in response to his words, a pair of leprechauns exited the Great Hall headed in their direction. Matching gold buckles adorned their long shoes and belts, shooting reflections from the torch light.

"Keep walking," Tiki whispered. Louder, she said, "I agree. The goblins have done an excellent job of protecting the border. It's no surprise Donegal has called for them to join in this war …"

The leprechauns barely glanced at them as they walked by, deep in their own conversation. It sounded to Tiki like they were discussing a stockpile of gold.

"It's too valuable. We can't take a chance it could be found."

"Agreed. I told him to bury it deep in the earth where it can't be seen," the first one said. "No one will find it that way."

"But how will *we* find it again?" His companion responded. "If the spot is marked, then someone else might see the …"

Their conversation faded as they moved farther down the hallway.

Tiki and Rieker had almost reached the wide entrance to the Great Hall before they stopped. Rieker glanced over his shoulder. "They're gone." They hurried back to the door to the spying post. Tiki opened it and Rieker dropped the two bags he carried in front of the opening. One by one, he turned the bags upside down and two raw pieces of meat slid out in a puddle of blood.

Tiki shuddered. "What are those? They look like some creature's *legs*—"

"I didn't ask when I took them. Honestly, I don't want to know. I just hope those hounds want to eat them more than they want to eat you."

Tiki reached down and with a grimace, picked up the meat in each hand. She nodded at Rieker. "I'm ready."

Rieker's jaw was set in a grim line. "All right." He ran back to the opening that led to the Great Hall. Though Tiki couldn't hear him over the din coming from the party, she knew he was whistling for the hounds. In his hands he held her jacket. If her plan worked, the scent would be enough to lure the dogs to him and then the bloody meat would be enough of a diversion to distract them. *If* her plan worked.

It seemed only a split second before Rieker was sprinting back in her direction. Tiki sucked in a deep breath and tightened her grip on the meat as the two dogs skidded out of the Great Hall to race after Rieker. When he was a doorway away from where Tiki stood, he threw her jacket back at the hounds and slid to a stop at her side.

"Give me one of those," he said, reaching for the meat. The dogs paused long enough to sniff the jacket before they turned their glazed red eyes on Rieker and Tiki.

"Here goes," Tiki whispered. One of the dogs lifted her snout and sniffed the air, her eyes locked on Tiki. "Let's hope they're hungry."

With a wild bark, they both dropped their heads and took a giant leap at Tiki and Rieker. Tiki shook the meat she held, green blood splattering the floor.

"Ready—now!" Rieker cried. As one, they threw the bloody meat into the room and ducked behind the door. The dogs never broke stride. They raced into the room and dove onto the meat in a wild frenzy of snarling growls as Tiki and Rieker pushed the door shut behind them.

Chapter Twenty-Seven

Time ceased to have meaning for the jester. There was no natural light to discern morning from night, no schedule by which to measure the passage of days. He faded in and out of consciousness, awakening mostly from the excruciating pain of his battered body, only to wish he could lapse back into oblivion again to escape the agony.

But a terrible sense of urgency kept him awake, prodding him to act—but how? He stared at the slatted bars that covered the small window in the wooden door—what stood between him and freedom? He raised his cupped hands to his lips and breathed flame into his fingers, then rubbed his hands together. When he opened his palms, another small white dove flew free and circled the room.

"What are yer doin' in there?" the guard shouted through the barred window. "There'll be no magic in here—"

The guard yanked open the door and was across the room in three steps, grabbing the jester by the neck with a meaty paw. "NO MAGIC—you hear me, Fool?" He stretched his arm across his chest and swung the back of his fist into the prisoner's head. A loud crunch sounded in the small room as the jester's nose was shattered.

Brilliant lights exploded in front of Fial's eyes, followed by a curtain of red pain. He flew backwards and hit the wall before everything went black.

Behind the guard, the small white dove flew out the open door.

Chapter Twenty-Eight

Rieker used Tiki's jacket to wipe the blood from the floor. They then hid the coat in a large pot near one of the columns lining the hallway before they hurried to the High Chamber. Tiki's face fell as they rounded the corner and she spotted two soldiers standing in front of the entrance.

"Guards," she whispered as they backed up and hid behind one of the giant fluted columns. "I forgot. They've been there every time I've attended a meeting."

Rieker leaned around the column to assess the situation. "What's in that room that needs to be guarded?" he mused. "It's nothing but a woodland." He jerked back sharply when one of the guards glanced down the hallway in their direction.

"I don't know, but we won't get in there until we figure out a way to get rid of those guards."

The festivities were in full swing in the Great Hall as Tiki and Rieker entered. No one spared them a second glance. They'd decided there would be a better time to try to gain access to the High Chamber, perhaps when Larkin or Dain could help them distract the guards.

"The dove is pure white—it should be easy to spot," Tiki said as she scanned the ceiling. Do you think Donegal would recognize it as the jester's magic?"

"I doubt the jester conjured anything white for Donegal. Everything about his world seems black and evil. Where might Fachtna be?" Rieker mused, searching from one face to another.

"I was watching her when the dove flew by. I think she saw it too." Tiki searched the paintings that filled the ceiling, looking for a flash of white. She paused at the image of the Jack-in-Irons. From this distance, the stained glass looked like another painting, its bleak colors and somber content not revealing the secret room above. Tiki followed the line of paintings—were other secrets hidden in that ceiling not revealed to the casual glance?

A flash of white flickered in the corner of her eye, and she jerked her head to the left just in time to see a snow-white dove collide with a column, then disintegrate in a puff of smoke.

"Oh no," she cried. "It's gone."

"If the jester sent one, he'll send another."

"I hope so. I don't know how else we're going to locate him."

Rieker steered Tiki to the opposite end of the room from where Donegal presided. "There's Dain." Rieker's brother was drinking wine and chatting with a strange creature that looked to be a faun.

Dain glanced in their direction, then raised his cup to the man-goat before walking to join them. "I've been looking for you two. Anything?" He glanced hopefully from one to the other.

"No. You?"

"No. I've found nothing and no one even willing to talk about the jester. Everyone is afraid to speak of him."

"We did see something that we think might be a clue."

"What's that?"

Tiki told him about the bird.

"Yes, I've seen the jester create those doves before during the summer months. If he's sending a message like that, he must believe Larkin will come for him."

"That's a good point," Rieker said. "Who else would dare attempt to rescue one of Donegal's prisoners?"

Dain glanced over his shoulder toward the Dragon Throne. "It's risky to stay in the Great Hall where the mirrors may reveal we are wearing glamours. Let's go outside and see if there is anything to be found there. Perhaps they've converted the *zagishire*?"

Tiki frowned and was about to give a sharp answer when she realized Dain was serious. Only Donegal would think to change a hospital to a prison. "We also thought we might check the High Chamber, but it's being guarded."

"Come." Dain headed for the door. "Let's discuss this outside."

It was a relief to leave the cloying black smoke, the nauseating smells, and the chaotic music of the Great

Hall, even though the weather outside had deteriorated and rain fell in a cloudlike mist that seemed to cover everything with water droplets. The clouds that had settled on the Tor were even denser now, making the world feel small and claustrophobic.

They walked through the line of soldiers who guarded the palace and followed the path away from the grand building to the small, thatch-roofed structure that served as a hospital. It was at the *zagishire* that Johnny had spent most of his time being cared for by Fiona after his *liche* attack.

"Where do you suppose Fachtna could be?" Rieker asked again. "I'm beginning to—"

"Worry?" A familiar voice spoke behind them. Larkin in her glamour as Fachtna followed them on the trail. With her skin glamoured dark and woody, and her hair the color of a dead leaf, she blended so completely with her surroundings, she was almost invisible. "How sweet of you. And here I thought you didn't love me anymore." She used one of her long, branch-like fingers to stroke Rieker's cheek, but he jerked away with a scowl.

"I've been to see Fintan McPhee," she said as she joined their group.

"My uncle? Why have you gone to see him?" Dain asked.

"Long ago, Fial saved Fintan's son from being drowned by a river hag, and Fintan promised he would do anything to help him. The favor Fial asked was to swear Kieran was his brother, thereby giving Fial a way to legitimize this alter ego and to make it that much more difficult for Donegal to track him down. The two men have remained close, and I thought if anyone might have heard from Fial or had news of his imprisonment, it would be Fintan."

"But?" Dain seemed to know already what Larkin was going to tell them. "What did he say?"

Larkin shook her head. "He's heard nothing."

They arrived at the *zagishire*, but one glance told them the building was vacant. No light shone from any window, no smoke billowed from a chimney to indicate a fire burned within, and the door hung ajar, swinging back and forth with the wind.

"I saw a white dove in the Great Hall," Tiki said as they gathered in a circle, "before it dissolved into ashes. Only the jester can create birds like that—isn't that true?"

The dark hollows that were Fachtna's eyes turned to Tiki. "I saw it too. If the bird is of Fial's creation, then it must have a way to get out of wherever he is being held. Those birds can't go through solid walls or doors—they would destroy themselves."

"So, he must be alive and he must be here," Dain said hopefully. "But where could they have him hidden?"

Rieker spoke up. "Tiki and I thought perhaps Donegal might be holding him in the High Chamber."

Larkin shook her head, the rust-colored strands shifting with the movement. "The chamber only gives the illusion of being endless. Fial is far too clever to be hidden in a place like that. He would escape before they shut the door."

Tiki wanted to stamp her foot. "But where, then?"

"Donegal knows the jester too well. He has put him in a prison of some sort to contain him and any threat he might pose."

"But where could the jester be?" Tiki finally asked. "You and Dain know the palace better than any of us. Where could they possibly hide him?"

Larkin crossed her arms. "I don't know. Donegal could have the entrance to the prison glamoured. That would make it difficult to spot."

"The doors that open off the hallway outside the Great Hall are glamoured. They look like they open onto the Night Garden but they don't. Or at least some of them don't," Tiki said.

The faerie swung around to stare at Tiki with her hollowed-out eyes. "And what rooms did you find?"

Like usual with Larkin, Tiki sensed the faerie sought more information than revealed in the the question.

"We found the jester's spying post above the Great Hall," Rieker said, "but only one entrance and exit. Could he be hidden within that room?"

A frown creased Larkin's weathered face. "I'm surprised you were able to find that room. Fial had concealed those entrances with powerful magic. You should have been diverted to the Night Garden."

"Well, we weren't," Rieker said. "Perhaps there is an advantage to being the true Seelie queen."

Larkin gave a derisive snort. "And being Fial's son couldn't hurt either."

Rieker remained silent.

"What about the other doors in that hallway?" Dain asked. "Where do they lead?"

Larkin flicked her wrist as if to dismiss his question. "A variety of places. None are designed to hide a prisoner."

Tension filled the air as they sought answers that eluded them.

"We've less than five days to the full moon," Larkin said. "Donegal is planning to use Fial's death as the catalyst to start the final push to claim the Seelie court. We've got to stop him."

Dain slapped his knee in frustration. "He's valuable—where would you hide something of value here?"

The leprechauns had talked of hiding something of value. Tiki caught her breath. "I know where he is."

Larkin, Rieker, and Dain swiveled to look at her.

"You do?" Dain said doubtfully.

"Teek, what is it?" Rieker asked.

"Spare us the drama, guttersnipe, and just tell us," Larkin muttered.

Tiki looked at Dain. "Didn't you say the Tor used to have a waterfall? That the mountain is riddled with caves?"

Dain nodded. "Yes, but—"

"'Bury it deep in the earth where it can't be seen,'" Tiki quoted. "'No one will find it that way.'"

"What are you talking about?" Rieker asked.

"I think you're right." Larkin nodded, her rough voice tinged with excitement. "That makes perfect sense."

Tiki smiled. "Donegal has hidden the jester in a cave beneath the Palace of Mirrors."

Chapter Twenty-Nine

"He's got to be close enough that one of his doves can fly into the Great Hall." Larkin began to pace, a trait that somehow made Fachtna look familiar to Tiki. "Think, Dain. Where could Donegal have access to a cave beneath the palace?"

"From the Night Garden?" Dain didn't sound convinced of his own suggestion.

"If the stories we've heard are true, then Donegal arrested him in the Great Hall—" Rieker started.

"And had Sullivan and Cruinn take him somewhere," Larkin finished. "They couldn't have taken him too far without making a huge scene. Sullivan and Cruinn are part of Donegal's inner circle—they probably know the palace as well as the Winter King does."

Dain snapped his fingers. "As did Bearach."

Larkin stopped pacing. "Bearach? What has he got to do with it? He's dead."

"Yes, but he was my ... keeper after Donegal arrested me for being a spy. I've tried to block my memories of that time, but Bearach was the one who beat me—and took pleasure in doing it." Dain's eyes were shadowed with painful memories. "He liked to threaten me too. He often spoke of a 'dungeon'—a place where he would leave me to starve to death alone in the dark."

Tiki put her hand on Dain's rough sleeve. "I'm so sorry. That must have been awful."

Rieker gripped his brother's shoulders and squeezed.

"And?" Larkin snapped. "What of this dungeon? Did he say where it was? Did you see it?"

Dain slid his hand over Tiki's, his fingers surprisingly warm, and gave her a black-toothed smile that looked more like a leer with his glamour. "I didn't see it but I think I know where it is."

"Where?" The question echoed in the wintry air.

"The queen's rooms."

"The royal chambers?" Larkin asked.

"Bearach made several comments that led me to believe this place he was threatening me with was close to where Donegal stayed in the palace. He said only the Winter King would know where I was, and Bearach assured me over and over that he would never save me."

Larkin paced again. "But where in the royal chambers could there be access to a cave? Do you suppose the entrance is hidden somehow?" She was mumbling to herself more than talking. "Perhaps behind a bookcase or wall panel? If that's the case, we may never find it …"

"Remember," Rieker said, "it has to have an opening for the doves to get through."

"Good point." Larkin turned and paced the other way. "How big of an opening …"

Tiki closed her eyes and envisioned the opulent royal chambers where the ruler of Faerie lived during their reign. There were four chambers: the sitting room, a place for the ruler to rest in privacy; the drawing room, where they met with their subjects and two rooms in the bedchambers. Where and how anyone could have created or found access to a cave with an opening into one of the rooms wasn't obvious. She mentally started at the grand entrance to the chambers and walked through each of the rooms ...

Her eyes flew open.

"The fireplace in the sitting room! It's tall enough for a man to walk into without bowing his head. There must be access through the fireplace."

"That is brilliant, Teek," Rieker said, "and makes perfect sense. It's not a place where an opening would be obvious."

Larkin nodded. "It's worth checking."

Fachtna marched in the direction of the royal chambers as if she owned the palace. Her three servants hurried behind, shoulders hunched and eyes lowered, fearful she might turn and strike. The guard in front of the bedchamber doors straightened when he saw the witch and her retinue approach. He lowered his speared staff to block their way, his impassive face giving away no emotion. His voice was like gravel crunching underfoot.

"There is no entry allowed here." He turned from Fachtna to measure the three young men behind her when Larkin struck. Her branch-like fingers were just a blur as she stabbed at the guard's throat. Blood spurted from his neck and his eyes bulged in surprise. A terrible gurgling erupted as he tried to breathe, blood-tinged foam gathering at the corners of his mouth as he sagged to the floor.

Dain jumped around the twitching body and opened the door, peering into the room.

"Clear in here," he whispered as he grabbed the guard by the shoulders. Rieker clutched the dead man's feet and together they hauled him through the doorway. Larkin shoved Tiki into the room, then used the hem of her long dress to wipe the floor clean. She glanced over her shoulder to check the hallway, then slipped into the royal chambers and quietly locked the door.

"Put him over there"—she pointed to a corner—"and bring his spear. I'll check the other rooms and see if there are any more." They spread out and quickly searched the four chambers, but they were vacant. Larkin held a finger to her mouth as they gathered in front of the fireplace in the sitting room. She spoke in a whisper. "If this is the entrance to the prison, you can be sure that Donegal will have Fial guarded. It's probably a stairwell that leads to a cell—one way in and one way out." She looked around the circle. "Which means there's only one way to save him."

A cold chill ran down Tiki's arms as Dain and Rieker nodded, their expressions equally determined.

Larkin held up the razor-sharp blade she had used to kill the guard. "What other weapons do we have?" One by one, they pulled knives and daggers from hidden locations inside their garments. Dain lifted a whip with one hand.

"It will have to do," she said. "I'm a fair hand at throwing knives. Dain, be ready with your whip. You two"—she pointed at Tiki and Rieker—"prepare yourselves. We can't have a moment of hesitation."

They each nodded.

"Good." She turned to the fireplace. "Let's see what we can find."

Dain lifted the metal grate that held the skeletal remains of burnt wood and quietly moved it to one side as Larkin entered the massive fireplace. She ran her fingers along the soot-blackened walls, feeling and looking for an opening.

It only took a few moments to find the hole, tucked back behind the front column of stones, invisible to someone standing in the room. Larkin raised her hand for silence as she disappeared through the rocky opening.

Tiki bit her lip as she struggled to keep her breathing even. She tightened her grip on the knife, as if that might still her shaking fingers. The blackness of the tunnel was complete, and she slid one hand along the rough wall to keep her balance as she blindly followed Larkin, Dain, and Rieker down the crude stone steps.

They cautiously wound downward. As they went lower into the mountain of rock, a feeble strand of watery light from some point below became visible—enough to pierce the smothering darkness.

They went down and down, the air becoming cooler with each step. Someone's foot kicked a loose pebble and the sound of the stone ricocheting against the rock echoed like cannon fire. Larkin stopped abruptly and Tiki held her breath, straining to hear any movement from below.

After what felt like an eternity, Larkin resumed her slow descent.

The guard came boiling around a bend in the narrow passageway, straight for them like a wraith from a graveyard. Tiki screamed as the huge man lunged at Larkin, the longsword in his hand pointed at her heart.

Larkin spun away as the blade ripped through her garments. The guard jerked his arm back in preparation to strike again. Rieker and Dain both dove at the man. The guard's neck jerked to one side, the gruesome sound of snapping bone echoing in the dim hallway. The noise was mixed with a guttural cry of pain—the last sound the man would ever make. The angle of the man's head as he slumped to the ground confirmed he was no longer a threat.

"Leave him," Larkin whispered as she continued down the steps.

"Who goes there?"

Larkin jerked to a stop and held her hand up in a signal to halt. She put a finger to her lips as she eased, ever so slowly, down the next few stairs. Not far ahead, there was a sharp turn and she squatted down very low before she peered around the corner. Behind her, Rieker clutched the spear he'd taken from the fallen guard, the iron-tipped blade at the ready. Dain held two daggers in one hand and his whip in the other, his jaw set in grim determination.

"Declare yourself!" The voice was rough but there was an undercurrent of uncertainty evident in his words.

Without turning, Larkin held up one finger—to indicate one guard. The faerie pointed to the right, then fanned two fingers to the left. Rieker and Dain seemed to understand her sign language without any problem and moved to Larkin's left.

At her signal, they both jumped down the remaining stairs and disappeared around the corner, yelling as they went. A split second later, Larkin disappeared too. Tiki hurried down the steps and around the corner, her knife clutched in her hand, afraid to go with them and afraid to be left behind.

The guard charged Rieker and Dain, his spear lowered with deadly intent. Too late, he realized there was a third threat coming at him from a different angle. He whirled to face Larkin and was skewered by three blades. The recognition of what had happened lit his face, only to fade and disappear like a snuffed candle. He'd barely hit the floor before Rieker, Dain, and Larkin pulled their blades free. Blood spurted from his multiple wounds and gathered around the man's body.

"Are you all right?" Rieker moved next to Tiki, his tall frame blocking the view of the dead man, his long fingers on her shoulder.

"Yes." Tiki swallowed, hoping to settle her queasy stomach. "I've seen as bad on the streets of London." Fights weren't uncommon, especially among the thieves who populated London's underbelly. More than once, she'd seen a knife fight end up with one of the participants dead. The image of MacGregor flickered before her eyes. A meaty fellow with shoulders like a bull under his worn jacket, she had always suspected the man had beaten Fiona's mother to death. Tiki had seen him put his hand to many of the women who worked as seamstresses for him, which often was worse than a knife fight.

"Fial!" Larkin stood on tiptoes, peering through a small barred window in a stout wooden door. They hurried over to her.

"Is he in there?"

"Yes. I can see him in the corner." She grabbed the handle and tugged on the door, but it was locked. She whirled and hurried to where the guard lay in a pool of blood. Larkin didn't flinch as she patted the man's jacket, her fingers turning bloody as she searched for the keys to open the door.

It only took a moment before she pulled a ring with a large key from the man's belt, the metal jangling with the movement. She hurried back to the door and slid the jagged teeth into the keyhole. There was a loud *thunk* as the metal bolt relaxed its grip, and Larkin pushed the door open, the hinges creaking in protest. She hurried to the jester's side where he lay crumpled on the floor.

Tiki took a deep breath and followed the others into the cell. She couldn't help but glance over her shoulder to make sure no one was hiding, waiting to slam the door shut and lock them in this dungeon for all eternity.

"Fial." Larkin leaned over and put her lips close to the man's ear. She shook his arm. "Fial—can you hear me?"

There was no response from the battered body.

Tiki leaned over Larkin's shoulder to get a better look at the jester, and a cold chill filled her. His face was bruised and bloody, both eyes swollen shut. What makeup he'd worn had long ago been rubbed or beaten off. Blood had run from his nose and mouth and dried in a thin crust, encircling his lips and leaving trails from both nostrils—as if he wore ghastly makeup for some mad masquerade.

Dain squatted next to Larkin, taking the older man's head in his hands. "Kieran," Dain whispered with anguish. "Kieran—stay with us."

Rieker remained silent.

"Is anything broken?" Larkin asked, sliding her hands over his arms and legs. "We've got to move him—one way or the other. Every second we stay here, we are a second closer to being captured by Donegal."

Larkin snapped her fingers at Rieker and pointed. "Grab his ankles. Dain, you lift his shoulders. I'll steady his head. Tara, hold on to me—*now*. We're taking him back to the Plain of Sunlight."

They scrambled to do her bidding. Once they were in position, Larkin whispered the words to transport them, and the black walls of the dungeon faded from view.

Chapter Thirty

Three days had passed since they'd returned to the Plain of Sunlight with the jester. He had yet to open his eyes. He rested in a private room, and Larkin made sure someone was with him at all times, but his wounds were grave, and those who tended him whispered that he'd given up the will to live.

Larkin checked on him several times every day, closing the door each time to visit in private. The rest of the time, she and Dain were busy evaluating the troops and strategically planning for the war they seemed sure Donegal would bring to them. To Tiki's dismay, Rieker had enthusiastically joined in, leaving her feeling displaced and useless. She knew nothing of war. The best place for her seemed to be hidden away with the jester.

On the fourth day, Tiki sat in a chair next to Fial's bed as the sun sank below the horizon. In her hands, she held the Faerie Queen's Mirror. Upon her return to the Plain of Sunlight, she had retrieved the mirror from where she had hung it on the drawing room wall without mentioning her decision to reclaim the piece to Larkin. She had removed the camouflage, and with growing familiarity ran her fingers over the intricate designs of the frame. What was its origins—its purpose?

The age of the piece was evident in many ways—by the blue-green patina that clung to the ancient gold, by the archaic design that seemed to tell a story of timeless power.

She ran her fingers over the detailed shape at the bottom of the frame of a man's head wearing a crown of ram's horns—was the resemblance to Donegal coincidental or intentional? Without meaning to, she tilted the frame and the ever-changing swirl of color that filled its center—fire and water, earth and air, light and dark—shifted. A brilliant flash emitted from the glass and then in the center, perfectly reflected, was Tiki's face.

It wasn't the first time she'd seen her image there. When she'd removed the glamour disguising the glass, she'd been startled to see her reflection—a beautiful stranger who stared back at her. After that she'd taken great care not to hold it in front of her face, uneasy for reasons she couldn't—or wouldn't—define. But now, as she sat alone in the small room with the jester asleep beside her, there was no one to see her, no one to judge what meaning the mirror might hold for her.

She considered her reflection with an objective eye. Instead of the glamour she'd grown up knowing—that of an attractive girl who'd been dirty and dressed like a boy for the last few years—she could see her true self: raven-feather black hair hung around a face that one would not easily forget. Her skin was the finest porcelain, fragile and flawless, yet the contours of her face were sharp and vivid, as though evidence of an underlying strength.

But it was her eyes that made her face so memorable—they were lit like the emerald glow of a newly unfurled leaf, translucent yet mesmerizing. She was beautiful, yes, but she looked confident in a way that could only be gained through power and wisdom.

"Who are you?" Tiki whispered to her reflection, for she certainly didn't feel the confidence that her appearance portrayed.

"The Faerie Queen."

The voice was a rasp, like a rusted blade being drawn against aged metal. Tiki dropped the mirror to her lap and glanced around, uncertain who had spoken, but the room was empty. Her eyes landed on Fial, unmoving in the bed. His eyes were closed. The swelling that had distorted his face had gone down significantly, now that he was receiving proper care, and he looked more like the man she had come to know as the jester, sans the decorative swirls of paint that had adorned his face.

"Fial?" Tiki whispered. She leaned over him and smoothed a lock of hair from his brow, searching for any sign that he had regained consciousness. She took one of his hands in her own as she studied his face. "Can you open your eyes?"

The man lay mutely, his chest rising and falling, his mouth slightly open. There was no indication he was conscious of Tiki next to his bed—no indication he was conscious at all.

"Fial?" Tiki said uncertainly. She laid a hand on his shoulder. "Can you hear me?"

"Has he moved?" Rieker spoke from the doorway.

Tiki jumped and jerked her head to glance over her shoulder. "Rieker, you scared me. I didn't hear you open the door." She turned back to Fial. "I'm not sure—I think he spoke, yet I didn't see him open his eyes, and he hasn't regained consciousness. I'm not sure what to make of it."

Rieker's words echoed with hope. "What did he say?"

Tiki hesitated. "I'm not sure." She lifted the mirror and sank back down into the chair.

Rieker pointed to the mirror as he pulled another chair close and sat next to her. "Why is that here? I thought you left it in Larkin's chambers."

"I was curious." She tried not to sound defensive. "There's something mysterious about this mirror—I can't quite figure it out."

Rieker looked back at their sleeping patient. "What do you make of everything Larkin has told us?" His expression hid whatever emotions he was feeling. "Do you believe her?"

Tiki slid her hand into Rieker's, enjoying the warmth of his fingers and the fact that he was no longer glamoured to look like an UnSeelie. She studied his familiar features—the angle of his nose, the cut of his jaw, the quiet strength that emanated from him. "It has a ring of truth to it, wouldn't you agree?"

He let out a long sigh. "Yes, it does. I'm afraid my life is getting more complicated rather than less."

Tiki held up the mirror. "Look into this—what do you see?"

Rieker gave her a questioning look before he grasped the mirror and held it up in front of his face. He searched the glass as Tiki leaned over to see what was reflected. Instead of his image, the glass was shadowed, depicting what looked like mountains in a snowstorm.

"I see winter." He shrugged and lowered the mirror. "What do you see?"

"Myself."

As if in answer to Rieker's question, a gravelly voice spoke. "The Faerie Queen."

Tiki and Rieker both turned to the bed. This time Fial's eyes, black as a bottomless well, were open. He glanced around the room once, then came back to them.

"Where am I?"

Tiki stood and clasped his hand. "The Plain of Sunlight." Rieker stood next to her.

Fial looked from Tiki to Rieker, where he lingered. "Larkin found me, then." He spoke slowly, as if each word was painful.

"Yes." Tiki nodded. "Dain and William helped find you too."

"And Tiki," Rieker added.

The jester exhaled slowly and closed his eyes. Tiki wondered if he'd fallen asleep when he spoke again.

"That means we have arrived at the endgame."

Chapter Thirty-One

"What do you mean, he's *gone*?" The shocked disbelief in Donegal's voice didn't hide the fury behind his words, and the guard delivering the message trembled where he knelt before the Dragon Throne. He shook as if he could already feel the cool whisper of the blade against his neck.

"The guards have been murdered and the prisoner is gone, my lord."

Donegal jumped to his feet with a roar of rage. "That is IMPOSSIBLE! Who could have known—" He stopped mid-sentence. "Larkin," he snarled, "and that miserable little wretch of a queen." He thumped the gold staff he held against the stone floor in anger. "They think they can steal from the Winter King?" He looked around wildly. "Where are Sullivan and Cruinn? Get me Scáthach!" His words echoed around the Great Hall. "THE JESTER WILL BE THE LAST THING THOSE TWO EVER TAKE FROM ME."

Chapter Thirty-Two

Upon hearing of Fial's awakening, Larkin rushed to his side and shooed everyone from the room. Several hours passed as she remained behind closed doors with him.

"What do you think they're talking about?" Tiki asked again, unable to hide her annoyance. "And why does it have to be in secret?" They sat in the antechamber of her rooms, Rieker stretched out on a couch, Dain standing with his arm braced against the fireplace, and Tiki tucked into an overstuffed chair between the two. "It makes you wonder if she isn't plotting with him to ensure their stories match up."

Rieker raised his eyebrows. "I thought you believed Larkin?"

Tiki pushed herself from the chair and wrapped her arms around her waist. "One moment I do, then the next I don't know what I believe anymore. Living in this world is like standing on a shifting sea of sand." She looked at Rieker. "I want to go home. I miss Clara and Toots, and I'm worried about Fiona, and I haven't heard a word about Shamus or the Bosworths since we left." She turned away to hide the tears that welled in her eyes. "I'm not *doing* anything here—I'm not needed. Larkin insisted that I come, and yet—"

"She doesn't want your help." Dain turned from where he had been staring into the flames. He stood tall and straight, his sun-kissed locks brushed back from his handsome face. "She needs you and the power you hold, but she doesn't want you here to threaten her own power."

"Yes. Exactly," Tiki cried. "I don't know what she thinks she needs from me—she does everything without me."

Rieker sat up. "We came back to save the jester, and we've done that." He looked over at Tiki. "The Seelie court and UnSeelie court have been at war for centuries—who's to say it won't go on for another century?" He ran a hand through his hair. "Maybe it's time to return to London and get on with our lives."

Tiki sucked her breath in with a small sob. "Could we?"

Rieker shifted to his brother. "You're welcome to come with us. You'll always have a place in our home."

Dain stood silent, his eyes distant, his jaw set. "I appreciate your offer, but I can't go now. I've unfinished business with Kieran—I mean, Fial." A smile softened the hard cast of his expression. "I'm sure you do too, but perhaps not with the same urgency I feel."

"I have questions, certainly—but they can wait." Rieker reached for Tiki's hand. "Fial gave me up long ago, and my allegiance is not to him but to those who have cared for me these last few years."

"I understand," Dain said.

"You'll visit us?" Tiki asked, coming to stand before Dain. "Often?"

"Most certainly." The corner of his mouth lifted in a grin, but sadness shadowed his blue eyes as he took her hand. "Now that I've found you both, you'll never be away from my thoughts for long."

Tiki and Rieker visited Johnny's room before they departed. The young boy was sitting up in bed, juggling three small oranges for a pretty nurse when they entered.

The young girl's mouth sagged in surprise as she recognized Tiki. She dropped into a low curtsy and dipped her head. "Blessings and long life, Majesty." She scooped up her skirts and hurried from the room, throwing a last look at the group over her shoulder.

"Tiki!" Johnny cried when he spied her small form, the oranges falling to the bed, forgotten. He threw the covers aside and slid from the bed to run barefoot across the room and wrap his stick-thin arms around her. "I've been hoping to see you. Have you heard from Fiona? Is she well? And Clara and Toots? Are they still at the palace?"

Before Tiki could answer, Johnny stuck his hand out toward Rieker. "And Mr. Rieker, it's a pleasure to see you again, sir, though a bit of a surprise"—he motioned to the room—"given that we're here and all." A cough rumbled deep in his chest and his shoulders shook with the effort of clearing his throat.

"Back in bed with you, right now," Tiki said, turning Johnny around. "I can see that you're feeling better, and certainly improving your juggling skills, but you're not quite well enough to be running in circles, now, are you?"

Johnny crawled back among the blankets looking crestfallen. "But I am better and making progress every day. And I don't feel sick to my stomach at all anymore."

"That is wonderful news," Tiki said, perching on the side of the mattress. "Keep resting and gaining strength, and you'll be up and about in no time."

"And then do you think Fiona can come visit me?"

"It's possible," Tiki hedged, not wanting to dash the boy's hopes while he was recovering. "We're off to see Fi right now, so I will give her your best and tell her you're just as incorrigible as ever."

"Incorrigible? Does that mean handsome and charming?" Johnny's eyes sparkled and for a second, Tiki saw the persuasive young man she had first met in London.

She pretended to tweak his nose, feeling lighter. "Something like that."

They arrived in London in the evening, in a shadowed park close to Westminster Abbey, just as Big Ben tolled the eight o'clock hour.

Tiki took a deep breath, inhaling the smell that was London. She held her arms out and twirled once. "We're back." Rieker caught her as she tilted. "Do you think it's too late to call on Leo?"

"No." Rieker grinned. "I've called on Leo at much more disgraceful hours." They hailed a hansom cab and twenty minutes later, they were ringing the back bell at Buckingham Palace.

"Lord William Richmond and Miss Tara Dunbar MacLochlan to see Prince Leopold," Rieker said to the footman who answered the door.

"Very good, sir." The man tucked his head in a neat bow. "One moment, please."

Tiki couldn't stand still, shifting her weight from one foot to the other and then back again. She clutched and unclutched Rieker's hand, fighting the urge to jump up and down.

"Take a deep breath, Teek," Rieker said with a low laugh, "before you wrench my fingers from my hand."

"Oh." Tiki jerked her hand free, her cheeks warming. "Sorry about that."

"This way, sir and miss."

Tiki hadn't heard the approach of the footman and she jumped to attention. As he led the way through the winding corridors, the smell of fresh-roasted meat permeated the hallway. Tiki's mouth watered. It seemed like forever since she'd sat down to one of Mrs. Bosworth's hearty English dinners. It was when they reached the third floor that Tiki heard a familiar shriek. Somewhere up ahead, a door was yanked open and voices that had been muted suddenly became clear.

"Tiki's here!" The pitter-patter of feet echoed down the hallway.

Tiki couldn't stand it any longer. She peered around the footman's shoulder and there at the other end of the hallway were Clara, Toots, and Fiona.

"There she is!" Toots shouted and pointed. The three children raced toward them.

Tiki didn't hesitate. She yanked her skirts up and ran as fast as her feet would carry her to her family.

The footman jumped to the side as Tiki zoomed past him. Behind him, Rieker chuckled.

They collided in the middle of the corridor, hugging, laughing, calling out each other's names as they fell into a giggling heap.

"You're back! Where have you been? How have you been? Have you seen Johnny? Are you well?" The questions floated in the air above their heads like jumbled birdcalls.

"And Rieker's here too!" Toots jumped up and ran to where Rieker stood a step back from their joyful celebration. Rieker bent down and caught Toots in his arms, hugging him tight and twirling him around.

"William!" Clara shrieked, sounding like a younger version of Tiki, which caused Tiki and Rieker to break out in laughter all over again. "Twirl me too." She bounded from where she had her arms wrapped around Tiki's neck and threw herself at Rieker. He scooped her up and held her at shoulder height as he spun in a circle.

"Whhhheeeeeee!" Clara cried as she held her arms out like a bird. Fiona clapped her hands and laughed while Toots danced an impromptu jig.

Behind them, a deeper laughter joined theirs. Tiki swiveled to see who had joined them. Queen Victoria and Prince Leo stood watching with broad smiles. Leo gave Rieker a sharp salute, then held his hand out to Tiki and pulled her from the floor.

"Welcome home, Wills and Tara." He bent and kissed Tiki's hand, which reminded Tiki of her first dance with the young prince. He lifted his head and smiled into her eyes, as if he were remembering too. "So nice to have you back where you belong."

Chapter Thirty-Three

Tiki and Rieker stayed at Buckingham Palace for two days while Rieker arranged for a townhome somewhere other than Grosvenor Square.

"We can't take the chance." Rieker had been adamant, and Tiki agreed. They'd been found there more than once—it was time to start somewhere new. "I've found a nice place up in Hampstead that should do just fine."

After stewing for hours trying to figure out how to ask the question delicately, Tiki found a rare moment of privacy with Rieker at breakfast the morning they were to move.

"It has four bedrooms and a good-sized drawing room with an excellent study for my office. I think Mrs. Bosworth will be happy with the kitchen—"

"The house in Hampstead sounds lovely, but how will we explain our living situation?" she blurted.

Rieker put down his fork. He cocked his head at her, and his expression turned serious. "It does seem that perhaps it's time to fix that problem, wouldn't you agree?"

Tiki gave a hesitant nod, not sure of his meaning.

"I didn't plan to do this over toast and jam, but lately it's been hard to find a 'right' time." He smiled at her. "I am, however, convinced more than ever that this is the best decision I'll ever make in my life." To her surprise, he slid off his chair and got on one knee. He took her hand in his. "Would you, Tara Dunbar MacLochlan, most beautiful queen of the Seelie court and love of my life, do me the honor of becoming my wife?"

Though she had hoped Rieker would one day propose, he came from such a different world than she, it seemed an unbridgeable gap at times. But now, she thought of the peace and security she would enjoy, knowing she would wake up by his side every day—

"Teek? My knee is starting to hurt …"

"Yes!" She laughed and threw her arms around his neck. "Yes, yes, yes—a thousand times, YES!"

He took her in his arms and kissed her.

"Why are you kissing already this morning?" Clara walked into the room, holding Doggie. "Isn't that for nighttime?"

Tiki laughed as they separated and planted a kiss on the little girl's forehead. "Do I only kiss you at nighttime?"

"No, but I've only seen you kiss Wills at night." Clara crawled onto a chair and positioned her dog next to a glass of milk that waited for her. "But that's all right." She smiled at them. "I like it when you kiss."

"I don't. Blech." Toots came into the room, followed by Fiona who was yawning and rubbing the sleep from her eyes. "Why would anyone want to press their lips together and share spit?" He grabbed a biscuit from a nearby bowl and took a bite. "Disgusting, if you ask me."

"No one asked you," Fiona said as she sat in the chair next to Tiki. "Why are you kissing so early in the morning?" She looked at their intertwined fingers. "And holding hands?"

Tiki smiled and looked at Rieker. "I forgot what it's like to live with this lot—no privacy—ever."

Rieker swallowed his bite of toast. "We're kissing because we're happy."

"That's nice," Clara said, pretending to let her stuffed dog drink from her glass. "Doggie and I are happy too."

"Tiki has just agreed to marry me." He squeezed Tiki's fingers and grinned at her, his gray eyes clear of the shadows that so often lingered there.

Three heads shifted to look at Tiki and Rieker. Then everyone started talking at once.

"Does that mean you're gettin' a fancy dress, Teek?" Clara cried, her eyes glowing with excitement. "And Fi can do your hair!"

"Married!" Toots scratched his head. "Aren't you already married?"

Fiona clapped her hands. "It's about time!"

Tiki laughed, feeling as though she were floating. "We haven't picked a date yet or—"

"What's this I hear of marriage?" Leo stood in the doorway, a startled look on his face.

"Good lord, who left the barn door open? Is the Queen of England going to join us this morning too?"

Rieker laughed. "Tiki has agreed to marry me. I will die a happy man now."

Tiki frowned and squeezed Rieker's fingers. "Don't say that."

"My most hearty congratulations." Leo pulled out a chair and sat down at the table. Behind him, liveried servants magically appeared and moved soundlessly serving the meal. "And when will we celebrate this great event?"

"I'm not sure." Rieker looked at Tiki. "In the summer, I would think—"

"Yes, in the summer." Tiki nodded. "When the sun is out and the flowers are blooming—"

"And the palace is at its best. Perfect. You shall have the wedding here." Leo raised his cup of tea at them. "It will be the event of the season."

"And I," Fiona said with a breathless smile, "will *finally* attend a ball."

The move to the Hampstead house was simple as they barely had more than the clothes on their backs. "I don't think we dare take the chance to even visit Grosvenor Square," Rieker said. "If Donegal has someone watching the place, then we've lost our advantage. Better to make do with what we've got and move on."

He secured a carriage and driver, and though the children had been sad to say goodbye to Leo and the palace, they were excited to be reunited with Tiki and Rieker and to be moving to their new home.

"Maybe we can get a horse and a dog," Toots had suggested.

"We have a dog," Clara said, holding up her pink stuffed doggie.

"A real dog, birdbrain," Toots said, pretending to knock on Clara's head.

"Doggie's going to bite you if you do that again," Clara threatened.

"Hush, you two," Fiona scolded, frowning at them. "Or I might bite you both."

Tiki smiled, soaking it all in. She was home.

They had been in their new home for barely a week when a terrible storm descended upon London. Trees thrashed as though whipped by unseen hands, while the wind shrieked around the corners of the house. Day turned to night, and the lamplighters set about their rounds midday rather than evening.

The sky was layered with threatening black clouds that formed great swirls of darkness—as if stirred by some greater force. The skies pressed down on London until it seemed the City would crumble from the oppressive weight.

Tiki found Rieker out on the porch, staring up at the sky with a worried frown.

"It's him, isn't it?"

Rieker slid an arm around her shoulders and pulled her close. "It has to be. Even though it's December, I've never seen the sky look like that before, have you?"

Tiki shook her head, a cold knot of worry forming in her chest. "No."

"If we're seeing a storm like this in London, you can imagine what it must be like in the Otherworld." As if to prove his statement, hail pelted the ground. The wind shifted in their direction and a few pellets struck Tiki on the arm as if thrown at her, stinging her skin.

"Ow," she said, stepping back.

Rieker pulled the door open and motioned for Tiki to go inside. "No need for you to be out here."

She retreated indoors, wishing she could ignore what the elements were telling her, but she couldn't stop thinking of Dain, the jester—even of Larkin.

It was late when a knock sounded at the door. The children had long gone to bed, and the fire in the drawing room where Tiki and Rieker sat had turned to orange-glowing coals. There was no one who would be calling on them at this location, especially at this time of night and given the storm that still blew outside.

"We know Larkin would never bother knocking," Rieker said as he pushed himself off the couch. "Let's see who it is."

"Is that supposed to be reassuring?" Tiki whispered as she followed him to the door. The lamps had been turned down for the night, and they cast just enough light to illuminate the long hallway.

"Maybe you should wait here," Rieker said as they reached the foyer.

"No. I want to know who it is."

The knock came again. More insistent this time.

Tiki followed Rieker to the door, her heart pounding harder with each step. She stood slightly behind him, her fingers nervously tugging at the back of his vest. It was one thing when she and Rieker had to defend themselves, and something entirely different when the children were here, unprotected.

Rieker gripped the brass handle and pulled the door open.

A man stood on the doorstep. He wore brown slacks, a white shirt with a brown coat and vest, a bowler hat clutched to his chest. Though tall, his shoulders slumped as though under a heavy weight, and exhaustion lined his face. Before he could speak, a name burst from Rieker's lips.

"Kieran! What are you doing here?"

Chapter Thirty-Four

Before the man could respond, Rieker retracted his outburst. "I ... I beg your pardon, sir," he stuttered. "You remind me of someone I used to know."

"You do know me, William," the man said gently. "You know me as Kieran tonight, but you also know me as the jester or, as some would call me, the Fool. Eventually, I hope you will know me as Fial."

"Kieran?" Tiki said, coming to stand next to Rieker. "But I thought—"

The man raised his eyebrows. "May I come in? It would be better if I remain unseen."

"Yes, yes, of course." Rieker pulled the door open and swung his arm wide to invite the man in. "My apologies."

The man stepped over the threshold and nodded his thanks. As tall as Rieker, his clothes hung on him, emphasizing his frail frame. Yet, even so, there was something so familiar about him, Tiki felt instantly at ease.

Rieker led them back to the drawing room, and Tiki peered at the man curiously, seeing him without makeup or artifice for the first time. "I'm so glad you're feeling better," she said.

"Yes, thank you." The man nodded. He moved slowly, as if still in great pain. "Better every day, I'd say."

"Sit here, by the fire." Rieker indicated an overstuffed chair positioned close to the warmth of the flames. "Can I get you something to drink?"

The man waved off Rieker's offer and braced his hands on the arms of the chair as he slowly lowered himself onto the soft cushion. He let out a small sigh of relief as he relaxed into the chair.

"We saw the storm today. You've brought us news, I take it?" Rieker asked, perching on the edge of the nearby sofa. Tiki sank down onto the cushion next to him, watching their visitor with a mix of fascination and fear.

Fial nodded. "Not good, I'm afraid."

His hair was swept away from his face, revealing handsome features that were not too dissimilar to Rieker's and Dain's. Tiki wondered where one glamour stopped and another began.

"Tell us."

"When Donegal learned of my escape, he attacked the Plain of Sunlight." Fial sighed. "There are many dead and things are getting worse by the day. The Wychwood continues to burn, and the winds are not blowing in our favor." His eyes shifted to Tiki. "We need the Faerie Flag."

"And we need answers." Rieker's tone was crisp. Tiki glanced at him in surprise. It was as if a mask had dropped over his face and London's best pickpocket sat next to her now, coolly appraising the man before them.

Fial inclined his head. "I understand. I suspect that's why Larkin asked me to come."

"Larkin?" Tiki echoed. "But how did she know where to find us?"

In a move reminiscent of the jester, he gave an eloquent shrug. "I believe her daughter lives with you?"

Tiki's heart pinged at the word "daughter." It still hurt to think Larkin had some claim to beautiful little Clara. But with Kieran's comment came a sudden clarity that as long as Clara was with her, Larkin would somehow always be able to find them.

"The first thing I want to know"—Rieker's gaze was locked on the older man—"is who you are to me?"

Their visitor crossed his legs and steepled his long fingers together, gazing at the fire. "A fair question. What wise man doesn't seek the answer to his origins?" Fial'a black eyes were unreadable, making Tiki wonder at the secrets he knew. "And your past has been unusually complicated. I apologize for that."

"So, you're saying you're my—"

"Father. Yes, William. You and Dain are my sons."

Rieker sank back against the couch. "Larkin told us the truth?"

Fial's lips curved in a pensive smile. "She usually does, but in a twisted sort of way that leaves one unsure. Part of her charm, wouldn't you agree?"

"Hardly." Rieker scowled. "She said something about being a Winterbourne—"

The older man nodded. "It's true. You, Dain, myself—we all have Winterbourne blood. Just as we have Seelie blood and probably five other kinds of blood if you go back far enough. It doesn't change who we are. It shouldn't change our choices in life." He looked down and smoothed the fabric of his trousers with thin fingers. "The truth of the matter is, the Winterbournes broke away from the UnSeelies long ago. They returned to Ireland and created their own courts—fought their own battles, primarily with Somerled. But still, to some, the name Winterbourne will always be synonymous with UnSeelie."

Fial raised his head to consider his son.

"I remember other nights when you allowed me to warm myself by your fire, William. Hidden beneath bridges and within burnt-out buildings. You didn't know who I was—*what* I was—or if I had one kind of blood or another." Fial held out his hand. "You only saw a man in need. And you reached out and helped me. That is the measure by which we should be judged. It was for that goal that Finn and Adasara gave their lives. It is for that freedom that Larkin and I sacrificed those we loved most—our children—to fight for a future we believed in, at a most painful cost."

Tiki looked down. The thought of sending Clara off to live with strangers made her stomach roil uncomfortably. Would she make a similar sacrifice in an attempt to change the world? She doubted it.

"But I kept an eye on you boys as you grew up, and I was pleased with what I saw." Fial smiled gently at Rieker. "You've become young men I am proud to know." He turned to Tiki. "As have you, my young queen. And now the time has come that I must ask you both to help protect a world you've barely even known." He tilted his head to consider their reaction. "Hardly fair for either of you, is it?"

"You may ask, Fial." Rieker's face remained blank, giving away nothing. "But in the end, it's my choice whether I choose to help you, so I wouldn't say 'fair' has anything to do with it."

Fial nodded. "Well said, William. A strong man chooses his own path in this life. Will you help us?"

"I assume the help you want involves finding the Faerie Flag, but it isn't my help you need. There's only one person in this world—or the Otherworld—who is meant to find that flag." He reached for Tiki's hand. "It's Tara, not me."

Fial smiled gently. "You're right, but as the jester would say, 'The body closest to the light casts the largest shadow.'"

Tiki frowned. "Now I am quite sure you're the jester. There's no one else I know who speaks in riddles."

Their guest chuckled. "Perhaps the riddle will become the rhyme. I ask you, William, because I believe you have the most influence with Tara. Together I believe you are meant to find the Faerie Flag." His expression sobered. "Will you help us?"

Tiki reached for Rieker's hand and gave a slow nod. "Tomorrow we shall set out for Lombard Street in search of the Fourth Treasure."

They left the next morning headed for Richmond, where the Bosworths and Shamus were tending to

Rieker's estate. The drive took less than three hours, but along the way, the City gave way to scenic vistas and country roads. The sky overhead cleared from the threatening blackness that consumed London the farther they drove. The change in scenery gave Tiki the feeling they'd traveled far away from London, and part of her desperately wished they could just keep going.

The driver had barely halted the carriage when Toots and Fiona jumped down and raced for the front door of the house.

"Wait for me!" Clara called as she sprinted after them, her short little legs struggling to keep up. Though she had grown in the last year, she was still thin as a water reed and barely reached to Tiki's elbow.

Mrs. Bosworth's scream could be heard all the way outside.

Tiki laughed and smiled at Rieker. "The children have found Mrs. B." She hurried after them, anxious to see Shamus as well as the Bosworths. She found them in the kitchen seated around a big wooden table. Clara was sitting on the housekeeper's lap while Fiona, Shamus, and Toots were so busy talking, they kept interrupting each other.

"Tiki!" Shamus's thin face lit up, and he jumped from his chair to hug her.

Tiki laughed in surprise. "Shamus, if you keep acting like that, I'm going to think you missed us."

"I have," the young man admitted, a sheepish grin on his face. "More than I ever thought I would. I guess I got used to you lot chattering and talking and making noise all the time."

"And Toots still *toots* all the time," Clara cried, then pinched her nose. "If you know what I mean. I bet you didn't miss that."

"Well, maybe not *that* part"—Shamus smiled—"but it's not been the same without you."

"And I've missed you little dears something dreadful," Mrs. Bosworth chimed in. "I hardly know what to do with myself all day long."

Shamus laughed. "Don't believe a word of it. Mrs. Bosworth doesn't rest." They continued to chatter happily and Tiki listened with a deep sense of satisfaction. This was her family. This was where she belonged. She would go find the Faerie Flag and deliver it to Larkin so she could solve the problems in the Otherworld, but as soon as possible, Tiki was going to return here, so her family could be together once again.

It was early evening when Tiki and Rieker sat alone with Shamus in the den, a fire burning in the nearby grate as they filled him in on the details of the war.

"I've not seen anything that would make me suspicious since we got here," Shamus said. "I'm sure the children will be safe." He stared down at the carved wooden figure of a four-leaf clover that he held, his fingers smoothing the curves and angles. "I worry about you both, though." He looked up. "How much longer do you think this will go on?"

Rieker exchanged a glance with Tiki before he answered. "It's hard to say, Shamus. When we leave this time, we're going to try to stop it once and for all."

Chapter Thirty-Five

The sun had barely stretched its fingers over the tops of the buildings on Lombard Street when Tiki and Rieker stood at one end and surveyed the road.

"The driver in Dunvegan said Mr. MacLeod was a bank clerk here, but the whole bloody street is full of banks," Tiki said. "How are we going to find him?"

"We're going to visit these banks one by one and ask." Rieker motioned to the building nearest them. "Starting with that one." The gold plate on the side of the building read Alexander, Cunliffes and Co. He held his arm out for Tiki and together they climbed the stone steps and entered the building.

They pushed through the oversized doors, and the first thing that struck Tiki was the silence. It was as if they were inside a vault. Behind a raised counter, tellers sat at their windows, scribbling notes with somber faces.

"Excuse me"—Rieker stepped up to one of the windows—"is there a Mr. MacLeod in your employ?"

The older man narrowed his eyes, his eyebrows pulling together like two bushy caterpillars. "MacLeod, you say? Never heard of him."

The next bank was Barclay, Bevan and Co. The teller there had never heard of MacLeod either. Nor had the tellers at Barnett, Hoare and Co., Bosenquet and

Co., Fuller and Co., Glyn and Co., or Roberts and Co. Soon the names blurred together along with the faces.

It was when they entered Martin and Co. at No. 68 Lombard Street that they found the answer they sought.

The teller didn't bat an eye. "Norman MacLeod? That's him over there—behind number three. Best hurry, he's about to take tea, I believe." He flicked his thumb to the right and went back to the pile of paper he was carefully stamping. Tiki gave a hopeful look to Rieker as they hurried through the great expanse of the lobby to window number three.

As they drew closer, Tiki peered at the man curiously. He looked to be past middle age. The top of his head had gone bald, but great gray muttonchops covered the sides of his face. Bags formed half circles below his eyes, magnified by the silver-rimmed glasses that perched on the tip of his nose. His shoulders slumped as though he'd been beaten down by life. He hardly looked like a man who might hold the Fourth Treasure of the faerie world.

"Excuse me, sir." Rieker held his hat in his hands as he approached the window. "We're looking for Mr. MacLeod of Dunvegan, Scotland?"

The old man raised his head. "Pray tell why two young people such as ye'selves be seekin' a poor soul such as he?"

"We've come on good authority that Mr. MacLeod has—"

"Been seeking word of Dunvegan," Tiki interrupted, fearful that Rieker was going to ask straightaway for the flag. That would never do.

Especially with this crusty old gent. "We have just recently come from Dunvegan." She nodded at Rieker. "William's father visited the castle as a boy and had told such glorious stories of the place, we had to see it for ourselves. Are you Mr. MacLeod?"

The man tilted his head to peer through his glasses more closely at the two of them. "What was your father's name, lad?" he asked Rieker.

"Fial Winterbourne," Tiki said quickly. "Do you remember him, by chance?"

"Winterbourne?" The old man shook his head. "Nah. Been gone nigh on twenty years now. The Potato Famine drove us from our home. Don't remember anyone by the name Winterbourne, though." He shuffled some papers to the side. "Do you have a deposit you wanted to make today? Banking business I could help you with?"

"No," Rieker said. "We came to talk to you about Dunvegan. I'm with the *London News*, you see, and we're running a series of articles about historical sites."

Tiki glanced at him from the corner of her eye as Rieker kept talking.

"Dunvegan was one of the places we've chosen to cover. I've always been curious about the place. It was quite a disappointment to find the castle had been vacated, and we thought maybe you could answer a few questions for us."

"Questions?" the old man said brusquely. "Don' know what kind of answers I might have." He slid a little wooden sign that said Closed in red letters in front of his work area. "I'm off for tea break. You can join me if you care to."

"Yes, we'd like that," Tiki replied. They walked along the teller line until Mr. MacLeod emerged at the far end. He was shorter than he'd appeared from his window—barely reaching to Rieker's shoulder.

"It's just through here. We've got a small sitting area for the staff. It'll be all right if you come in for a few minutes. No one else will be there this time of day." He led them into a small room that held little more than a round table and four chairs. One wall had a small counter with a burner and a kettle. He raised the kettle in their direction. "Care for a cup?"

"That would be delightful, thank you." Tiki nodded.

"So, what is it you want to know of Dunvegan? The current structure was built in 1266—the oldest castle in Northern Scotland." Pride was evident as he pulled a chair out, the legs screeching against the floor. His shoulders slumped as he sat down and a sad smile lit his face. "I am the twenty-fifth chief of a castle I cannae afford to live in. Not a very glorious or interesting tale to share, I'm afraid."

"But someday you'll return," Tiki said gently.

Mr. MacLeod looked away. "Not in this lifetime."

Rieker took up the conversation. "One of the stories we were told was of a great treasure the MacLeods have had for centuries—"

"A treasure?" The old man snorted. "If there were a treasure, I'd surely still be in Scotland." The kettle began to sing and MacLeod shuffled from the table.

"A flag of sorts—said to be connected to the faeries …"

The man paused as he reached for the kettle and glanced back over his shoulder. His eyes shifted from Tiki to Rieker and back again with an air of suspicion. "How do you know about *Am Bratach Sith*?"

"William's father told us," Tiki said. "Said it was one of the clan's most prized possessions. Rory Campbell mentioned it too."

"Ah, you met Rory, did you?" He ran his hands over his side whiskers.

"Did you bring it to London with you?" Rieker looked hopeful. "I know my editor would jump at the chance to run an illustration with the story."

"Bring it to London." MacLeod snorted again. He pulled the kettle from the stove and the teapot immediately ceased its shrill whistling. "There are some things—sacred things—that are not meant to be put within the reach of the pickpockets and thieves that populate every corner of this godforsaken city." He returned to the table and placed the steaming cup in front of Tiki.

"Thank you." She wrapped her fingers around the cup, enjoying the warmth. "You've left *Am Bratach Sith* at Dunvegan, then?" She tried to speak as naturally as she could—as if the topic weren't of paramount importance.

"London is not the place for something as precious as *Am Bratach Sith*, but that's not to say I left it unprotected in Dunvegan either."

"Sounds like quite a mystery. Can you tell us the story of how the flag arrived there?" Rieker asked. "I suspect the truth of the tale is one that only the MacLeods know."

MacLeod took a cautious sip of his tea, then settled back in his chair. "I'm sure Rory told you the story as it is a favorite tale of his. But regardless, it was a gift."

Even though she had heard the caretaker's version, Tiki had to bite her tongue to stay still and let the man tell the tale how he would.

"It was my ancestor—one of the first chiefs of Clan MacLeod. He fell in love with a lass who couldn't stay with him. When she left, she gave him a gift."

"She was a faerie?" Tiki asked.

Instead of answering, MacLeod lifted his cup again. When he finished, he let out a long, satisfied sigh and nodded. "Aye, that's right, little lass. They say she was a faerie." He peered at Tiki over the rims of his silver glasses. "Do ye believe in faeries?"

Tiki nodded.

"Hmmmm, an' I see that ye do." He smoothed his whiskers again. "The gift she left behind was a flag meant to protect the bearer. On two separate occasions, we have unfurled her gift and been given the strength to prevail against our enemies. Legend says the flag will save us one more time."

"But you've kept the flag's location a secret?" Rieker asked. "For over twenty years?"

"The flag is safe, and those within our clan who need to know are aware of its location. That's all that matters." The older man spoke with confidence. "I will tell you this—the silk lies within an iron chest below the sign of MacLeod and awaits our return. *Am Bratach Sith* is in a place protected by those who gave us the flag in the first place. Only those who know where to look could find our treasure."

After thanking the man for his time, they left Mr. MacLeod and ventured back out onto the streets of London again.

"We can't possibly expect to find the flag without any idea where to look," Tiki said as they walked down Lombard Street to where they'd left their carriage. "And Rory Campbell certainly isn't going to reveal where it's hidden—if he even knows."

Rieker turned to her in surprise. "Didn't you hear what the man said?"

"What I heard was nothing of substance," Tiki replied. "He wasn't about to reveal the flag's location to us."

"'The silk lies within an iron chest below the sign of MacLeod and awaits our return.' The only place that old man would return to would be the castle of his ancestors. I'd bet a thousand quid that the flag is at Dunvegan." Rieker practically skipped beside her. "And who is more perfectly suited than the two of us to find a faerie treasure? We've done it twice already—three times, if you count the ring." Rieker grinned at her. "Why, Teek, you're like a faerie treasure magnet! You'll probably step foot into Dunvegan and the flag will display itself."

Tiki rolled her eyes. "You're a bit too much of a believer." But she did agree. The card the jester had given her definitely held a picture of Dunvegan. There had to be a reason.

Rieker threw his arm around her shoulders and gave her a squeeze. "You've got to believe, little lassie," he said in a thick brogue. "Perhaps the good folk will smile down upon ye and grace ye wit' the answer."

"Please, William O'Blarney, spare me your witless prattle. You know as well as I that we won't be finding any buried treasure at Castle Dunvegan without better clues than what we've been given."

Rieker's eyes sparkled with mischief. "We'll never know until we try."

Chapter Thirty-Six

A small woman hurried along the shadowed corridors of Buckingham Palace, her white hair bright in the dim light. The heels of her shoes tapped intermittently against the marble floors when not muffled by the lush rugs spread along the hallway. She slowed as she approached a tall pair of doors and grabbed one of the ornate golden handles with both hands to tug the door open.

Light spilled out into the hallway along with the low murmur of conversation as the door slowly swung outward. The voices paused as the occupants of the room turned to see who had joined them.

"Mamie!" Both young men rose from their chairs at the same time. The dark-haired one came around his seat with his arms extended. "You never cease to amaze me. I've only returned in the last thirty minutes and already you know I'm here."

"Arthur," Mamie said, lifting her cheek for the young prince to kiss. "I'm so glad you've returned safely from your trip." She squeezed his fingers. "We need you here—now more than ever."

"Mamie?" Leo stepped near, concern etched on his face. "What is it?"

"It's Donegal—the Winter King," she whispered. Her bright blue eyes were wide with fear.

"What of him? Is there news? Has he been seen in London?"

"Worse, I'm afraid. He's been seen here—at the palace. Looking for the little girl—the one named Clara."

Chapter Thirty-Seven

"But I don't want to go to bed yet," Clara said in a petulant voice. She crossed her arms and frowned at their housekeeper. "Why do I always have to go first?"

"Because it's your bedtime, little darlin', and yer still growin'," Mrs. Bosworth replied as she lowered the light on the gas lamps in the parlor. "Can you be a big girl and go up on yer own?"

"I don't want to go up alone."

Mrs. Bosworth brushed a stray strand of gray hair from her face with the back of her hand. "Fiona, would you be a dear and take the little 'un up to bed for me? I swear, I'm asleep on my feet tonight." She shook her head. "Don' know what's wrong with me."

Fiona jumped up and dropped her stitching on a side table. She held out her hand to Clara. "Come along, you little monkey, and save me from any more fancywork tonight. I've already poked my fingers too many times with that bloody needle."

"Why do you do it, anyway?" Toots asked from where he was stretched on the floor playing checkers with Shamus.

"All ladies know how to do fancywork."

Toots laughed. "Since when do you care about being a lady? You used to only care about picking the pockets of ladies."

Fiona laughed shrilly and gave Toots a sharp kick in the leg. "You're so silly, Toots."

"Ow!" he cried, reaching to rub his leg while Fi tilted her head at Mrs. Bosworth's back. "Oh. Right."

Clara stamped her foot. "But I don't *want*—"

Fiona didn't wait to hear what the child was going to say. Instead, she leaned down and threw a shrieking Clara over her shoulder. She twirled in a big circle. "Maybe if I make you dizzy enough, you'll stop talking."

"Twirl me again, Fi!" Clara giggled as they went.

"Good thing you're light as a feather, Clara, or I'd have to dump you halfway up the stairs."

"Twirl me again at the top, Fi," Clara cried from where she hung upside down over the older girl's shoulder. "We'll have to teach Leo this game!"

Once they were on the landing, Fiona twirled Clara around and around, the hardwood floor squeaking in that spot as if laughing along. Fiona walked through the door to the bedroom she shared with Clara and twirled one more time before she dumped the little girl on the bed, the feather duster letting out a small *whoosh* as Clara landed. Fiona giggled and fell onto the bed next to her. "You've made me dizzy as well."

"It wasn't my fault." Clara laughed, kicking her feet in the air.

"Hurry up and get your bedclothes on. I'll tuck you in and kiss you good night."

Clara sobered. "What about my bedtime story? Tiki always tells us one."

Fiona tweaked the little girl's nose. "All right, I'll tell you a short one. But be quick about it. I want to go downstairs and beat the boys in checkers."

It was several hours later when a squeak on the landing woke Clara. Someone had just walked up the stairs. She watched as the crack of light under the doorway grew to a long V before a shadow filled the entrance.

"Fi? Did you beat the boys?" she asked in a sleepy voice.

When there was no answer, she sat up, rubbing her eyes with her fists. The shadow had moved from the doorway and now stood leaning over her bed.

Clara screamed as a man with silver hair yanked her upright. He wound a cloth through her little mouth and tied it tight behind her neck, cutting off her screams. With three quick movements, he tied her hands and feet and scooped her from the bed. When he spoke, his words were low and rumbling, like a thundercloud.

"Donegal's been looking for you, little girl."

Chapter Thirty-Eight

They returned to Dunvegan at night, hoping that Rory Campbell had retired for the evening. They stood just outside the castle entry, listening for any noises that would suggest the older man was about.

Convinced they were alone, they walked through the arched entry, Tiki glanced across the windows of the caretaker's apartment, but all was dark.

"It looks like he's gone to bed." She scanned the vacant area. "Now what?"

"We know the flag is in an iron chest."

"Helpful," Tiki said sarcastically. "*Where* would perhaps be more helpful."

Rieker smiled as he whispered in her ear. "Demanding little wench, aren't you?"

"Only when necessary."

"You're a faerie, Teek—where would you hide a faerie treasure in your castle?"

"*If* I had a castle," Tiki said drily, "I would hide it …" She paused as a thought struck her. "In a faeric tower."

"That's a good idea." Rieker looked up at the battlements that capped the towers of the castle. "Do they have one?"

"They do," Tiki said. "Don't you remember? Rory told us the first time we visited. He mentioned it when we were talking about the treasure. He said, 'Why else would we have a faerie tower?'"

They walked up and down more stairs than Tiki cared to count.

"Why don't they make it obvious which tower is the bloody faerie tower?" Rieker grumbled as they descended from yet another tower that had yielded no treasure.

"A true faerie would probably recognize it," Tiki said, concentrating on the steep stone stairs.

"Wait. Teek. Stop." Rieker motioned for Tiki to climb back up to where he waited. "It's worth a try—you can see most of the battlements from here—which would you pick to be built for the fey?"

Tiki scanned the castle that stretched before them, not exactly sure what she was searching for but trying to recognize intuitively something that would feel familiar. "That one." She pointed. "The one with the sawtooth stairs on each side. Let's go there."

It was a winding path they followed to reach the steeply pitched faerie tower. The four floors were connected by a circular stair that opened onto a rectangular room at the top. The small stone room had a soaring ceiling with wooden arches that supported the peaks and was lit by a beautiful, arch-topped stained glass window. In the center of the window was a design and the motto, "Hold Fast."

"Oh, how lovely," Tiki said as they entered the quiet space. "It almost feels like a cathedral."

"I get the sense we have entered hallowed ground here." Rieker pointed to a stone table positioned beneath the leaded glass at the end of the room. "That looks like an offering table." He looked over at Tiki. "Perhaps this is where the MacLeods come to kneel before the Faerie Flag and acknowledge powers greater than their own."

Tiki walked slowly toward the table, Rieker by her side. A thrumming hummed in her veins, and she knew they were exactly where they were supposed to be. They stopped before the display and Rieker pointed to a wooden bowl centered on the table. "Do you suppose that holds the flag somehow?"

"Perhaps." Tiki slid her hands over the bowl and whispered the words to remove any glamour that might be cast. The ripe smell of clover filled the air, but the bowl remained unchanged. "Where else could it be hidden?"

The sun was low on the horizon the next day when they arrived back at the house in Hampstead. Tiki's shoulders sagged with exhaustion as she walked into the front parlor to light the fire. They had spent hours looking for the Faerie Flag without success. They had searched every inch of the faerie tower. The treasure was simply not there.

Someone spoke from a chair in the corner of the room.

"What did you learn?"

Tiki whirled in surprise. "Larkin—will you ever arrive at the front door like a normal guest?"

The blond faerie shrugged. "Where's the fun in that?" She sat forward. "Did you find MacLeod?"

"We did. He works on Lombard Street just like the driver told us." Tiki went back to the business of lighting the fire they'd previously laid in the grate. "He acknowledged the flag existed—called it *Am Bratach Sith*—but wasn't about to tell us where the clan had hidden it."

"But you think it's at Dunvegan?"

Tiki blew gently on one corner of the pile of wood and paper, encouraging the flames to grow. The fire took hold, the paper crackling as it burned. The wood popped as the sap melted on the bark. "Yes."

She pushed herself off the floor and sat in a nearby chair. "Tell me what's happening in the Otherworld. Fial made it sound like the situation was dire. Have you rallied the Macanna? Are you fighting back?"

"Donegal's army outnumbers ours five to one," Larkin said flatly. "When are you planning to go to Scotland? We need the flag."

Something twisted in Tiki's chest, and she couldn't suppress the desire to test Larkin. "Will you come to Dunvegan and help us look?"

Larkin stared into the flames. "No."

"Why not?" Tiki frowned. "How do you expect William and me—who know practically nothing of the Otherworld—to find one small flag hidden somewhere in an immense castle that requires some special faerie logic? It could take us years!"

"I hope not, because we don't have years."

There was something in the faerie's expression that sent a chill through Tiki's heart. "Something's happened, hasn't it?"

Larkin stared at her without answering.

"Larkin?" Tiki's breath quickened. "Tell me."

The faerie pressed her lips together and inhaled before she spoke. "Donegal has Clara."

It was as if someone had taken Tiki's heart and clamped it in a cold vise. Her skin turned to gooseflesh and for a second, she couldn't draw a deep breath. "That's not true!"

Larkin answered in a whisper. "It's true."

Tiki jumped to her feet. "Why are you sitting there talking? Tell me everything you know *right now*. I will not allow that monster to harm Clara."

Larkin put her hands to her face and rubbed her forehead. Her words came out muffled. "The last I heard, he has her at the Palace of Mirrors—"

"How did he get her? She was with the Bosworths in Richmond—"

"I don't know," Larkin snapped. "He was at Buckingham looking for her too. I got to Richmond too late. She was already gone."

Tiki raced for the door.

"Where are you going?" Larkin called after her. "You need to find the flag—"

"I've got to tell Wills!"

Tiki was looking over her shoulder at Larkin and didn't see Rieker coming through the door. He caught her by the shoulders before she ran into him.

"Tell Wills what?"

"Donegal has Clara!" Tiki cried. "We've got to go back!"

Larkin stood. "Dain and Fial are already on their way to see what they can learn. I came to tell you."

"Why would he take her? She's just a little girl."

"It's a trap, of course," Larkin said. "To lure you to the palace."

"Well, it has worked."

"We need the Fourth Treasure to battle him."

Tiki's words were as sharp as needles. "I'm not wasting any more time searching for a treasure that may never be found. I'm returning to the Otherworld now to save Clara—whether you come with me or not."

Chapter Thirty-Nine

They arrived in the forest outside the stonecutter's cabin deep in the Wychwood Forest where Dain had hidden Tiki so long ago. Smoke hung low, like a cloud, and the air was sharp with the smell of fire. Tiki wore tight-fitting black clothes that emphasized her petite size. Her black hair was braided down her back and she was dressed to blend with the shadows that gathered among the trees. Larkin and Rieker were dressed in a similar fashion.

Larkin motioned at an impenetrable thicket of brambles. "Dain told me of this abandoned cottage long ago. It will serve our purpose." She flicked her wrist and the brambles and thicket magically parted, revealing a small stone structure.

A flood of memories played before Tiki's eyes—Dain glamoured as the scarred, lonely Sean ó'Broin, helping her escape from Donegal, neither of them realizing who the other was and that their fates were inextricably woven together. So many secrets revealed over the last year—and yet, so many more still held. She didn't want to think of the risk that both Dain and Fial were taking to return to the palace now. But there wasn't a choice—for any of them.

Larkin led the way to the cottage. Rieker motioned for Tiki to follow when a gust of wind rattled the leaves in a way that made them chatter like voices speaking. Tiki turned, her senses alert.

"You've returned."

Tiki searched the shadows until she spotted a familiar face. Formed within the bark of an immense tree, two dark eyes watched her without blinking. Tiki nodded. "I've returned. And I haven't forgotten our bargain. Now I'm looking for a child that Donegal has taken from me."

The Elder Dryad stood very near. The treelike woman blended with the forest so seamlessly, Tiki hadn't noticed her or the thorny plum and oak tree dryads who stood behind her.

"I know nothing of the child. We are running out of time. The Winter King will burn us to death if he's not stopped."

Tiki nodded, her jaw set with determination. "Make your way to the top of the Tor. I will keep my promise."

Larkin turned on her as soon as they were inside the stonecutter's cabin. "You've made a pact with the Elder Dryad?" The faerie's voice echoed with disbelief.

"I needed her help to find Rieker when Bearach captured him," Tiki said. "I didn't have a choice."

"The thorny plum, the oak, and the elder are a deadly combination," Larkin muttered. "Do you have any idea what you're taking on …"

"Yes, so I've heard—but perhaps more so for Donegal than for us."

"One can only hope, but she is the least of our worries right now." Larkin stood before the fire she had conjured in the small stone fireplace. "We need to split up and enter the palace separately."

Tiki came to stand next to the blond faerie. "Do you know where Clara is? Tell me."

Larkin shook her head before she spoke. "She's in the palace, I can't say beyond that."

"But she's alive?" Tiki faltered.

"I believe she's alive. She's worth more to Donegal alive than dead."

"Where are Fial and Dain?" Rieker asked.

"Dain was headed to the palace when I left. He was going to try to locate where Clara is being held. I don't know where Fial is, nor would I expect to. He never gives away too much, though you can be sure he understands the seriousness of the situation." Larkin paced. "We have to think like Donegal. He has taken Clara to lure Tara back to the palace—that much is obvious. How do we turn this into an advantage?"

"I don't care if we turn this to our advantage." Tiki's voice was shrill. "I just want Clara back safely." She stood in front of Larkin. "Where are the Macanna? Who is commanding them?"

"Most have fled from the Plain of Sunlight since the last attack. They've scattered throughout the Wychwood recovering from their wounds and waiting for our direction."

"But there must be someone in command?"

"We have five generals who direct the different factions."

"And who directs the generals?" Rieker asked.

"I am going to command them," Tiki said firmly. "We need to have them bring their armies, in whatever shape they may be in, to the Tor. Have them stay hidden, but be prepared to storm the palace when we give the sign."

Rieker nodded. "What are you thinking, Teek?"

"Once we get inside the palace and find Clara, we'll have to create a diversion to draw Donegal outside. I suspect the diversion will have to be me. I'll need some support for what I plan to do."

"And what is that exactly?" Larkin asked.

"The Elder Dryad told me that she, the thorny plum, and the oak were witches who Donegal had trapped within the trees long ago. For them to leave, someone with powers equal or greater to their own had to stay." Tiki raised her chin. "We made a bargain. I promised to deliver Donegal to the Elder Dryad. She will pull him into the tree and be able to step free."

Rieker scowled. "Donegal is not one to be easily tricked. Your plan sounds too dangerous to me."

"We don't have a better one, and we have to do something." Tiki looked over at Larkin. "Can you send word to our generals? Have them make their way to the Tor."

"Yes." Larkin seemed distracted. "It won't hurt to have reinforcements closer to the palace. We can worry about the exact details of how we roust Donegal once we have freed Clara, but first, we need to get back inside the palace and find her. Then we need to figure out how to get back out again *before* we hand Donegal to the Elder Dryad." She propped her hands on her hips. "Any ideas?"

"Actually, I do have one," Tiki said. Her plan involved much more than just setting the Elder Dryad free, but she didn't fully trust Larkin—even now. She doubted she ever would.

"Tell us," Larkin said.

"It's winter. The UnSeelies control Faerie now, which means any UnSeelie can enter the palace—giants, Jacks-in-Irons, hellhounds, sprites, selkies, brownies—or redcaps." She gave them a significant look. "Ailléna is a redcap. Perhaps she'll spy for us and help us find where Clara is being held."

It was only a few short moments before Larkin had glamoured herself in preparation to go to the far side of the Tor, where the homeless faeries congregated on the barren rock cliff.

"Three strangers arriving to the camp would be no different from blaring our arrival from the loudest horn," Larkin said. "The news of one stranger will travel fast enough. I know best how to blend in. Wait here. I'll be back."

Before Tiki could protest, she was gone.

"I am not going to wait here," Tiki stormed, pacing across the small room. "What if Clara needs *me*?"

"Larkin knows this world, Teek. Let's give her a little time. Where did you leave the Cup of Plenty and the Faerie Queen's Mirror? Maybe they could provide us with some answers."

Tiki jerked to a stop. "You're right. I left them both at the Plain of Sunlight. We need to get them now."

They arrived outside the stone opening that led to the underground chambers of the Plain of Sunlight, but the area was as foreign as another world. The meadows that had graced the plain were black and smoking—what remained of the trees was now nothing more than black spikes of burnt wood.

"What has he done?" Tiki cried, turning in a full circle, unable to comprehend the destruction.

"While the Macanna were fighting on the Tor, Donegal must have sent other troops here. He will kill everything to control this world," Rieker said, his jaw set in a grim expression. "Then he'll move on to London."

They entered through the open doorway and climbed down into the Seelie headquarters, only to find the space was eerily empty—as if they'd entered a long-forgotten tomb.

"Where is everyone?" Tiki whispered.

"They've gone—either to fight or simply to survive. Those who are still alive are probably hiding." Rieker's voice was thick with unspoken emotion. "It's clearly not safe here any longer. Let's gather what we came for and leave."

Many of the rooms looked like they'd been ransacked. Tiki's heart began to pound harder and harder, until finally, she raced down the last hallway to Larkin's hidden chambers. Her footsteps echoed in the empty space until it sounded like she was being followed—or chased. After all this—would the cup be gone?

They slipped behind the wall of greenery and entered Larkin's chambers. Tiki caught her breath. The room was untouched—it still looked just like the drawing room in Grosvenor Square. For a split second, she imagined she heard Toots laughing and Clara's playful shriek as she ran after him. Fiona seemed to be murmuring nearby and she could have sworn she heard Shamus snore.

"William—" Tiki swayed and reached out for him.

"Steady, Teek." He caught her arm and pulled her close. "Stay focused. Let's gather what we came for and return to the Wychwood. Clara needs us."

They brought the Cup of Plenty and the Faerie Queen's Mirror back to the stonecutter's cottage. On impulse, Tiki took the ring from the chain around her neck and held it in her fingers so they could see the fire in its depths. But rather than the flickering flame that had warmed the ring before, now there was barely a glow, and the metal had grown cool.

"What does it mean?" Tiki asked, afraid to take her eyes from the ring for fear the flames would extinguish entirely.

"It means Donegal is getting stronger. We're running out of time."

Three hours passed and the shadows within the Wychwood grew ever longer as Tiki and Rieker waited in the stonecutter's cottage. Tiki finally couldn't stand it. She jumped to her feet.

"I'm going up there. I can glamour myself just as well as Larkin."

"Teek, I know how you feel, but do you think it's wise?"

"I can't sit here—knowing little Clara is being held by that monster—" Tiki's voice broke. "I've got to do something." With a wave of her hand, the fresh scent of clover filled the room as she transformed. A heartbeat later, she held out long, clawed hands, then carefully felt a face where fang-like teeth jutted from her lower jaw and a strongly hooked nose stretched past her lips. On her head she wore a red cap that appeared to have been dipped in blood.

"God save the Queen," Rieker gasped. "What have you done?"

"William, don't you recognize me?" Tiki smiled, causing Rieker to flinch away from her. "I'm Ailléna's long-lost sister."

They arrived in the garden near the homeless camp—Tiki glamoured to look similar to the little redcap they'd come to know, Rieker glamoured as a slightly bigger, male version.

"I feel like I'm trapped in the skin of a dwarf," Rieker whispered as he stretched his arms and did several deep-knee bends. "I keep trying to stretch it"—he flexed his arms, his shoulders hunched—"but I think that just makes it feel tighter ..."

"A redcap is half the size of a grown man—by your standards, you *are* a dwarf," Tiki replied. She swung her arms, trying to ignore her own sense of constraint. "Come along." She grabbed his oversized hand and pulled him behind her. "We'll get used to it as we walk."

"I doubt that," Rieker grumbled, but he followed behind her.

They took the winding trail that led through the gardens. Lush foliage had changed to brambles and thorns when the UnSeelies had claimed the Palace of Mirrors for winter. It wasn't long before even the brambles turned to scrabbly bushes and eventually gave way to the barren rock upon which the homeless camp existed. Unlike before, when the Tor had been covered with a teeming mass of homeless faeries, now there were fewer than twenty—and of those, most looked too weak to walk.

"Ailléna's not here," Tiki cried in dismay as she surveyed the group.

"Donegal has forced even the homeless into this war," Rieker said, his lips pressed together in distaste. "They are scattered throughout the Wychwood and on both the Plain of Starlight and the Plain of Sunlight. She could be anywhere."

"Then why didn't Larkin return to the stonecutter's cottage and tell us?" Tiki said. "It would only have taken her a few moments to realize that Ailléna was gone."

Rieker shook his head. "I can't say, Teek."

Frustration welled in Tiki's throat and she fought the urge to cry. Instead, she gritted her teeth and inhaled sharply through her long beak of a nose.

"We don't need Ailléna *or* Larkin to enter the palace. We know the palace as well as either of them." She turned and pulled Rieker back the way they had just come. "We'll go find Clara on our own."

Chapter Forty

Disguised in their redcap glamours, Tiki and Rieker were barely given a second glance as they entered the Palace of Mirrors through the side door near the kitchens.

"Where are the platters I sent you to fetch?" A harried-looking faerie, holding what looked like the blade of a battle-ax, yelled as they strode through the halls empty-handed.

"We're on our way to get them," Tiki called, walking faster.

"You're headed the wrong way"—he jabbed the cleaver in the air—"the kitchen's *that* way!"

"Be right back," Tiki called as they rushed around a corner. She had only visited the kitchens a few times during her reign in the summer months, and the rabbit warren of halls were a confusing maze. She glanced through one doorway to see several servants standing over hot fires stirring large pots. One glanced up as they passed, and Tiki had a fleeting sense of familiarity. Was the girl someone she'd seen in the Great Hall during the summer months?

She didn't have time to ponder the question as they passed another door that opened into a room full of bottled wine. Light, dark, red, white, green, and blue— the bottles were every size, shape, and color, as were their contents. A tall man with a long, thin neck, reminding Tiki of a giraffe she'd once seen at the London Zoo, stood counting the bottles and making notes on a long piece of parchment. He frowned in their direction and Tiki immediately backed out of the room.

"Let's head toward the noise," Rieker said as they continued down the corridor. "That's got to be coming from the Great Hall."

"Maybe we should go in the opposite direction. It's doubtful Donegal has Clara in there." She pointed to a group of faeries clustered at one end of the passageway. "Let's see what we can find out from the servants."

The faeries were a mix of creatures: two old, weathered gnomes, a black-haired pooka, a bogey, a banshee, and a hag who stood on the fringe. The group barely glanced at them as they approached.

"Heard Donegal's got another prisoner," Tiki said, making her voice scratchy like Ailléna's. "Do you know where he's keeping this one?"

"We're all prisoners," the bogey croaked. The goblin had the face of a dog and the body of a man. "Can't tell one from the other." Several of them laughed.

The hag cast a dark look at Tiki. A hideous creature, her face was wrinkled with sunken eyes and a nose and chin jutting in equal proportion. "Donegal doesn't reveal the location of his prisons—everyone knows that."

Tiki returned her pointed stare. "I heard he took a child this time—a mortal girl."

"What would he do with one of those?" the banshee shrieked. "They're useless."

"Unless he wants to bargain with her," the pooka said slyly.

Tiki looked around. "I heard he has her in the palace. Hasn't anyone seen her?"

"Why do you want to know, redcap? It's none of your business," the hag growled.

Tiki grinned, emphasizing the fang-tipped bottom teeth that jutted above her upper jaw. "Because she's valuable. Donegal's not the only one who wants her."

"Valuable," the bogey croaked. "Who'd be mad enough to steal from Donegal? Is it Larkin?" There was a rush of hushed conversation among the group.

"It doesn't matter who it is," Tiki replied. "That's my business and not yours, but if you help me find her, I'll pay you."

"With what? Blood?" The hag let out a dry laugh. "That's the only currency a redcap deals in."

"I'll pay you with whatever you want," Tiki interrupted. "But only if I get the girl unharmed." She looked around. "It's too bad the jester isn't here—he would know where to find her."

The banshee shrieked, rattling Tiki's nerves even further. "Donegal banned the jester from court."

"The jester is dead," one of the gnomes said, his sizable brow twisting in a frown. "Donegal fed him to the hounds."

"No, he didn't," Tiki snapped.

"He did." The gnome jerked his head up and down. "On the full moon."

"Did you see the execution?" Rieker spoke for the first time.

"No, but we heard those beasts howling half the night." The gnome shivered. "It's somethin' awful to listen to—but not as bad as the screams of their prey."

Tiki took a step back. The gnomes didn't know what they were talking about. She'd seen the jester since the full moon. They'd saved him—even if she didn't know exactly where he was now. "Spread the word—I want to know where the girl is. If you can't find me, wait by the—" She thought fast, trying to remember a spot where her reflection wouldn't be seen in the magical mirrors that lined the hall. "Wait for me by the fountain at the far end of the Great Hall."

The UnSeelie creatures dispersed in different directions, the pooka slinking off down the shadowy hallway, the gnomes headed into the Great Hall waddling on their short, bowed legs, and the banshee shrieking as she went back to the kitchens. The hag was the last to leave, her pointed face reminding Tiki of the Elder Dryad.

"Since when does a redcap give orders in the palace? Somethin' doesn't smell right, goblin." She pointed her long nose into the air and inhaled sharply. "Not right a'tall."

"Then don't help us," Tiki snapped. "And don't get paid."

"You must have a death wish if you think you can steal from Donegal."

Tiki fought the urge to growl at the faerie. "Donegal must have a death wish if he thinks he can steal the girl."

The hag let out a disbelieving laugh. "Fight the Winter King over a mortal child? You've gone daft, redcap. Best run back to the border before Donegal feeds *you* to the hounds."

It was only a matter of moments before Tiki and Rieker were alone in the hallway.

"You don't think Donegal caught Fial again, do you?" Tiki asked.

"Pray that he didn't. Let's check the hall and see what's happening there," Rieker said. "If Fial and Dain are here, I'd like to know where they are. Maybe they've learned something."

"And let's not forget Larkin," Tiki whispered. "What is she up to?"

They stopped under one of the arched entrances to the Great Hall, careful to stay far away from the reflection of the magical mirrors that would reveal their true selves beneath their glamours. Tiki's gaze went immediately to the golden Dragon Throne, but the seat was vacant. Donegal was nowhere to be seen.

"That's odd," she said. "He's not here."

"I'd bet he's in the palace somewhere," Rieker replied. "Plotting."

As before, the hall was full of UnSeelie fey dancing and drinking—cavorting as if life was nothing more than a party. Out-of-tune instruments screeched and groaned, creating a cacophony that the group seemed to mistake for music.

"If he didn't bring her here—where would he take her?"

Rieker shook his head. "It's impossible to say. Is there anyone out there who looks like the jester or Dain?"

Tiki imagined the colorful clothes and makeup of the Court Jester, his floppy, three-point hat jingling with each prancing step. Where was he and how was he glamoured now? Given the secrets Fial knew, would he be foolish enough—or brave enough—to return to the Palace of Mirrors and face Donegal?

And where was Dain? Larkin seemed sure he was back in the palace but disguised as whom? He was skilled at living undercover within the UnSeelie world—he could be any of the myriad creatures before them.

Tiki let out a quiet groan of frustration. "No one looks familiar. We have no clues—how are we possibly going to find her?"

"Like we just did," Rieker said with a determined tone. "We're going to ask the fey who are here one by one and see if anyone knows anything—see if anyone will *sell* the information."

"Do you think we should disguise ourselves as something other than redcaps? The hag had a point. Redcaps are only interested in blood—"

"Mortal blood at that," Rieker interrupted. "All the more reason why we would want the girl. The problem I see is that they all want something different—if we tell them we can give them each what they want, then it becomes obvious we aren't what we seem. Already the hag is questioning who we are."

"I know." A shadow flickered behind one of the stained glass windows on the ceiling that looked like paintings. Tiki clutched Rieker's wrist with her clawed hand as she stared at the spot. "Look."

Rieker tilted his head. "What do you see?"

"I saw a shadow move—I think there's someone in the jester's rooms."

They were halfway there when a blare of trumpets cut into the noise of the Great Hall, drawing everyone's attention. A contingent of soldiers entered with bladed weapons glistening from their shoulders and waists. Some even had knives strapped to their legs. Donegal entered behind the wave of armored men, his silky black robe rippling like dark waves of water as he moved.

"YOUR ATTENTION!" he shouted. "I BRING YOU THE PRIZE THAT WILL LURE THE SEELIE QUEEN TO HER DEATH!"

A buzz of excited whispers exploded among the crowd as heads leaned close and fingers pointed to something behind the Winter King.

"AS THE SEELIES HAVE TAKEN FROM ME— I HAVE TAKEN FROM THEM."

"What is it?" Tiki asked, standing on tiptoes to try to see over the crowd.

"I'm so bloody short in this glamour, I can't tell," Rieker growled, "but with an entrance like that, it can't be good."

"THIS MORTAL CHILD IS THE SEELIE QUEEN'S WEAKNESS."

"Oh no," Tiki cried.

Donegal turned and pointed at the open doors through which he had just entered. Two servants rolled in a platform that supported a giant hook. Hanging from the hook was what looked like an enormous golden net weighted down by a captive held within. The net trap swung gently with the movement of the rolling device, and small fingers gripped the golden strands from the inside. In one of the larger gaps above the fingers, a small, frightened face peered out.

"IF ANYONE IS LOOKING FOR THE MORTAL CHILD OR ASKING WHERE TO FIND HER—I WANT THEM ARRESTED IMMEDIATELY." Donegal turned in a circle, his words echoing throughout the silent hall. "YOU MUST ALL BE ALERT. THIS IS OUR OPPORTUNITY—THE SEELIE QUEEN WILL BE AMONG US SOON!"

Chapter Forty-One

"Just as you predicted." The jester was expressionless as he stood in the room above the Great Hall and watched Donegal make his entrance. Fial's hair was combed back from a face unadorned with artifice or makeup. Though wrinkles creased the skin around his eyes, the architecture of his face was similar to that of Dain and William. The bruises were fading from the beating at the hands of Donegal's guards, but the angle of his nose appeared to be permanently skewed.

Larkin stood next to him, her fingers threaded through his. Her blond hair hung in a simple plait down her back, her exquisite features relaxed and unguarded for once.

"A well-planted suggestion by Fachtna convinced him the child was the bait he needed to draw the Seelie queen to him."

"And so the endgame begins."

"Yes."

"How long have we worked for this moment?"

"Too long, my love," Larkin said. A long sigh passed her lips. "I fear I have grown tired of the lies—weary of the battle. The lives of our children seem too great a sacrifice now."

"Indeed. But if not ours—then whose? There was no one else to stop the evil. And had we not lied—had we not partnered with Finn and Eridanus—Tara and our children would have been butchered long ago."

Larkin wiped a single tear from her cheek. "True," she whispered. "But it's been so very much to give." She hesitated. "Perhaps we should have run instead—"

The jester turned to face her. "Breanna, this is not like you. Where is the arrogance I love so much? We must look forward, not backward, my dear." He turned to her and ran a gentle hand along her cheek. "We chose this path because it was what we *had* to do—and look what we have achieved: we are alive—our children are still alive. Our sons are smart, honest, and loyal. They are together again and committed to each other. William will marry Tara, the true-born Seelie queen—the daughter of your best friend, Adasara. They love each other and together they will take the Seelie court into the future in the way we have fought for and dreamed of—without prejudice or fear. We are accomplishing everything we planned so long ago."

"*If* they survive, Fial. If we survive." Larkin's face was bleak. "Addie is dead, along with Finn and Eridanus. And so many more. Are we really winning?"

"Bree—never forget the reason we started the lies so long ago. It was what we *had* to do. Finn and Eridanus knew of the coming evil. They planned with their underlords for decades in anticipation of what the future would bring. When Finn fell in love with Adasara, he *asked* for our help. In my heart, I believe he knew what the future held for all of us. You and Adasara began the charade of being sisters for exactly this purpose—so no one would ever suspect Larkin was the diversion, the one who pretended she wanted to be queen—until Tara was old enough and ready to find the Four Treasures, ready to claim the Seelie throne." Emotion was thick in his voice. "*Think* where we would be if we hadn't fought back. We would all be dead, and Donegal would rule Faerie."

"I know, I know." Larkin closed her eyes and leaned her head against his shoulder. "But I'm tired of playing this part. Of never being completely honest, of forcing Tara to dislike me at every turn so she will choose to help the Seelie cause, to believe she is the only one who cares enough to fight for them." A small sob rose from her chest. "I've played it for so long—how different am I from Larkin? I feel that I've become her."

"Then you know beneath the arrogance and anger, she has a heart of gold. You have played her brilliantly, Breanna, and you have made Tara strong in a way she would never have been if you hadn't forced her to choose. Adasara would be so proud of both of you. You're just tired and worried. Stay the course a little longer, and we will be free. I promise you."

"And what of Dain?" Larkin raised her head. "Fial, I fear he has fallen in love with Tara as well." Her eyes glistened with tears, one leaving a trail down her cheek.

The jester smiled and ran a gentle finger beneath her eye. "Dain only thinks he loves Tara because he has yet to meet his own true love. He will find her one day, my dear, he will."

"And our baby? What of Clara?" Another tear ran down Larkin's cheek as she choked out a sob. "I've missed so much with her. She loves Tara now, not me. If nothing else, she must survive—be protected. I couldn't stand it if—" Her voice broke on a sob.

Fial cupped her face with both hands. "Breanna, you must be strong for just a while longer. We have been forced to live a lie for too long—you as Larkin and me as the Court Jester. But we are almost done. We have accomplished the impossible—we have kept the true-born queen alive until she reached an age where she could claim the throne. She is strong enough now to battle my brother, and through your cleverness and sacrifice, she has come to desire the same result as us, something that would never have happened if she had only been told of her destiny. We are so close. Don't give up now. We can win this war. *Finally.* Then we will once again find the life we gave up so long ago."

Chapter Forty-Two

As Donegal made his announcement, Rieker moved lightning fast and wrapped his long arms around Tiki's waist to stop her from running to Clara.

"Let me go!" she cried. "I have to protect her."

"*Think*," he whispered harshly. "You are glamoured as a redcap. We can't help her right now." Tiki continued to struggle and Rieker tightened his grip. "We are outnumbered," he growled low in her ear, "with no weapons. If we die, then Clara is left to face Donegal alone."

Tiki stopped struggling. Around them the crowd buzzed with excitement over the new captive.

"Why would the Seelie queen care about a *mortal* child?" one woman whispered.

"Who cares? As long as we can get rid of her once and for all," replied her companion. "She's too powerful—to make the Stone of Tara cry out—that hasn't happened in centuries. Best to be rid of her."

"What do you suppose the mortal girl tastes like?" muttered another who looked like something that had climbed from a swamp.

"What will you do with the child?" a brave soul called to Donegal as the Winter King made his way through the crowded, rectangular-shaped room to the Dragon Throne.

"SHE WILL BE HELD HERE, ON DISPLAY IN THE GREAT HALL NEXT TO MY THRONE UNTIL THE SEELIE QUEEN IS *DEAD*."

"Listen to me," Rieker whispered in Tiki's ear. "We know where she is. We know she's alive. Take a deep breath and let's think."

Tiki dropped her hands but Rieker didn't release his grip. She glanced over her shoulder at him. "You can let go now."

"Do you promise you won't do anything foolish?"

"Yes."

Rieker dropped his hands but didn't step back. "The first thing we need to do is change these glamours. Every UnSeelie we spoke to in that hallway will be looking for us, not to mention anyone they told to meet the redcaps at that fountain if they had news."

"I'm not taking my eyes off Clara." Tiki's tone brooked no argument. "Let's get closer." She latched on to Rieker's bony wrist and pulled him forward, winding through the crowd.

"The hag will be the first to come looking for us," he warned. "If we are found here, in the midst of this many UnSeelie fey, we will not be able to defend ourselves."

Tiki led him across the room, working through the crowd to stand among the fringes. The net that held Clara had been positioned at the foot of the steps that led to the golden seat. They were close enough that Tiki could see the little girl's pale blond hair as she sat hunched in a small ball within the golden web.

Clara's head jerked in their direction and her blue eyes settled on Tiki. She stared for the longest time before looking at Rieker.

"She must be so frightened," Tiki murmured to Rieker. "What must she be thinking, looking upon horrible creatures like us—bloody redcaps—in a place like this?" Tiki longed to run to the child, to cut her free, to hold her close and tell her she would protect her, but Rieker was right. They needed a plan. They needed to make sure they could get out alive and end this war with Donegal once and for all.

"There they are!" The hag's voice rose above the hum of conversation that filled the room. Tiki whirled, a new fear filling her.

"We've got to get out of here." Rieker tugged Tiki sideways and pulled her toward the door.

"But—" Tiki cried.

"As soon as we're in the hallway, change glamours," he hissed.

"Stop them!" the hag screeched. "Those redcaps—they were asking about the mortal child!"

Tiki and Rieker dashed into a back hallway, ignoring the startled looks of the fey they passed.

"Where are you going in such a hurry?" a soldier called after them.

"Just remembered an appointment," Rieker called over his shoulder. "Not to worry."

"STOP THEM!" the hag shrieked.

In a delayed reaction, the soldier yelled after them. "You two—HALT!"

Rieker sprinted to the nearby door and yanked it open, pulling Tiki through behind him. He pushed the door shut as quietly as he could and slid the dead bolt home trying not to make any noise.

"Change your glamour. Something inconspicuous." Together, he and Tiki whispered the necessary words and moved their hands from forehead to knees as the smell of fresh clover filled the air. In an instant Rieker had changed into one of the myriad soldiers who guarded the Great Hall, wearing the same black tunic, a silver, curved sword at his side.

Tiki, on the other hand, had become a beautiful woman with long hair the fiery red of a flame. She was elegant and seductive, alluring and dangerous.

Rieker's eyes widened. "*That's* inconspicuous?"

"I am a *leanan sidhe*—'La Belle Dame sans Merci' of Keats's poem—the muse of mortals and knights who are destined to die young." Her eyes grew flint hard. "I don't want to be inconspicuous. I want Donegal's attention on me the entire time you are freeing Clara."

They wasted little time in the room. The walls that stretched high above their heads were hung with banner upon banner of silk—some decorated with crowned lions baring the talons of eagles, other banners bore pictures of ravens that flew before the full moon. Some were elaborate wings that appeared to be dripping blood while others carried harps and five-pointed stars.

"What are those?" Tiki pointed. "They remind me of the flag that the jester used to anoint you as a lord in the High Chamber."

Rieker glanced up. "I don't care if they're the bloody Union Jack. It doesn't have anything to do with us." He pulled the door open and they strolled back into the hallway as if he were one of the myriad guards patrolling the palace. The corridor was crowded as guards and guests both hurried up and down the long hallway looking for the redcaps.

"Keep an eye out there," a guard dressed in an identical outfit shouted at Rieker as he hurried past. Rieker snapped off a salute and followed Tiki around one of the towering columns back into the Great Hall. The room was still crowded as news had spread of Donegal's captive.

Heads turned as Tiki entered. She lifted her chin, feigning confidence. She didn't know how she was going to free Clara and stop Donegal, but she would die trying.

The Winter King's inner circle—Sullivan, Cruinn, and Scáthach—had appeared and were huddled around the throne. Donegal was deep in conversation with them as Tiki and Rieker drew near the golden net that held Clara. Two guards were posted on either side of the giant platform that held the child, their faces stone-like, long, spear-tipped staffs clutched in one hand, the other resting on the hilt of their longswords. The guard closest to Tiki glanced at her as she approached.

It was all Tiki could do not to cry out when she recognized Dain's blue eyes. His face remained expressionless, though, and she realized he couldn't see through her glamour as she could see through his.

While Dain looked at her, Tiki fingered the chain that hung around her neck and pulled the Ring of *Ériu* free. Recognition flickered in his eyes. He gave a slight nod of his head. Convinced he understood her message, Tiki tucked the ring safely back under her garments and nudged Rieker. At his questioning glance, she nodded at Dain and mouthed his name. Rieker's glanced at his glamoured brother and the two cautiously eyed each other.

Tiki started to turn to the net trap when a low growl rumbled from behind Donegal's throne.

Chapter Forty-Three

Tiki turned as the first hound charged. Jaws snapping, fanged teeth bared, the giant black dog exploded from behind Donegal's throne headed straight for Tiki. Screams ripped the air as people rushed to get out of the way.

She didn't have time to think—only react. Fire flew from her fingertips. The dog dropped dead at Tiki's feet, a tendril of smoke curling from the black, charred hole in its chest. Tiki braced herself, expecting the second dog to charge next, but the black hound remained partially hidden behind the throne, her eyes intent upon Tiki.

"What is the meaning of this?" Donegal roared, staring at the dead dog in disbelief.

Of Donegal's three generals, Sullivan was the biggest. He had immense shoulders, a square head, and a nose that spread across his face like a mushroom. He was the first to move.

"Name yourself," he growled, making Tiki wonder if he could communicate with the hellhounds in their own language. More guards gathered, weapons at the ready.

Tiki looked down her nose at the man. "Is this how you treat your visitors to court?" She snapped her fingers at the other dog. "Take that one away too, before he decides to attack the king."

"How dare you—" Sullivan started at Tiki, but Donegal stopped him.

"Sullivan," Donegal barked. "Mind your manners." The Winter King slid to the edge of his seat, his beady black eyes locked on Tiki. "Who are you?"

With a careless gesture, Tiki flicked a flame-red strand of hair over her shoulder. "I am Simone, of course. I've come from London to watch the capture of the Seelie queen." She looked around, then raised an eyebrow at Donegal. "Unless I've missed the fun? Have you murdered her already?"

"If only I had," Donegal murmured, sliding from the throne. He approached Tiki, keeping the damaged side of his face turned away, curiosity burning in his bottomless eyes. "I've not had the pleasure of your acquaintance, madam. Pray tell me your history. If you are here at this time of year, then you must have UnSeelie blood, yet you say you've traveled from London? Any fey who crosses over to the mortal world is braver than most."

"Much braver," Tiki agreed as she forced herself to smile at the horribly disfigured man, "but I enjoy the risk."

Donegal threw his head back and laughed. "You remind me of an old friend. Or perhaps I should call Larkin my adversary. Regardless, she amuses me. I sense you might too."

The guards who surrounded the Winter King watched the exchange with undisguised interest.

"How fascinating." Tiki's mind raced as she swept her gown to the side and walked away from the golden net that held Clara. Could she draw Donegal and his guards far enough away that Rieker could cut Clara free without being noticed?

Donegal fell into step beside her. "Tell me about yourself."

"It's not obvious when you gaze upon my face?" Tiki cocked her head in a pose. "It seems I inspire certain mortals. I am the muse to whom they will gladly pledge their lives in exchange for the artistic brilliance my love brings"—she grinned, revealing fanged teeth—"short though it may be."

"Ah, I see." Donegal nodded with sudden understanding. "Your price is steep."

Tiki resumed walking, leading him away from the net that held Clara. "As is anything of value."

"Why have I not seen you at court before?" Donegal walked with her, his guards trailing in a wave, keeping a discreet distance. "I surely would have remembered someone as lovely and remarkable as you."

Tiki crossed her arms and feigned a pout. "I have been here before, but you only had eyes for your friend, Larkin."

Donegal tilted his head back and laughed. "What you say is true. Larkin can be mesmerizing."

Tiki made a scoffing noise. "She may be beautiful, but I'm still not sure if she claims to be Seelie or UnSeelie. The only thing I do know is that she seems inordinately fond of the color gold."

Donegal again laughed out loud. "That's because she thinks she should be queen."

A few instruments plucked discordant notes until music of sorts flowed through the room again. Tiki led Donegal out through the grand doors of the palace and stopped on the steps overlooking the Night Garden. As darkness had descended, the glow of the beautiful luminescent blooms lit the night with color. She stopped in a place where they could still be seen by the occupants of the Great Hall so Rieker and Dain would know Donegal's location. She desperately wanted to look over her shoulder and check on Clara, but she didn't dare.

"Tell me the truth," Tiki said, in an effort to keep the UnSeelie king distracted. "What breed is Larkin? Seelie or UnSeelie?"

Donegal clasped his hands behind his back and looked out over the twisted maze of brambles and thorns. A storm brewed overhead, the murky clouds swirling as though being stirred from above. With his black robe and black hair, the Winter King blended with the night. The only spot of color was the gold circlet that sat upon his head, reflecting the flames of nearby torches.

His voice was thoughtful when he spoke. "Larkin is as mercurial as a flicker of moonlight, as clever as the Court Fool, and as untrustworthy as a mortal. For a long time, I believed she was committed to the UnSeelie court—partly from her love of power, partly from jealousy of her sister, and in a large part due to her anger at Finn and Eridanus."

Tiki glanced at Donegal from the corner of her eyes. He spoke as if he knew Larkin so well. Did he? What exactly was their relationship?

Donegal shook his head. "But none of it matters anymore. Her sister is long dead, and if Larkin were truly UnSeelie, then we would have destroyed the Seelie court and ruled Faerie together." He heaved a sigh. "But instead, now she taunts me and spies on my court with my *brother*, of all people." He scowled. "I should have killed her when I had the chance."

Tiki drew the folds of her gown close over her chest, chilled. "Why didn't you?"

"That's a good question." He reached out and snatched Tiki's arm, his grip like a vise. "But a better question is, how does a *leanan sidhe* throw a lightning bolt strong enough to kill a hellhound?" He brought his face so close to hers, Tiki could smell his putrid breath and see the pockmarks on his skin. She tried not to look at the side of his face where the skin had melted when the *liche* had burned to death, but it was hard not to stare at the twisted and mangled flesh.

Behind them, a ripple went through the guards as they reacted to his movement and gripped their weapons tighter. Several moved in their direction.

Tiki stepped back and tried to pull her arm free. "You're hurting me."

Instead of releasing her, Donegal tightened his grip, examining Tiki's features as though trying to see through a shrouded window. "I know of only one person who can control the weather like that—and I won't lose you this time," he said.

"GUARDS!" he shouted. "SEIZE HER!"

Tiki tried again to yank her arm away but Donegal's fingers were firmly clamped around her thin wrist. The guards rushed at them, weapons drawn, faces set to attack. Tiki exhaled and visualized her destination. A heartbeat before the first blade pierced her skin—with Donegal still clutching her wrist—the Palace of Mirrors shimmered from view.

But they didn't arrive at the destination that Tiki had envisioned. Instead, when the world shimmered back into view, they were still standing outside the Palace of Mirrors—only a short distance from the guards who had been ordered to seize her.

"I am the UnSeelie KING," Donegal roared in Tiki's face. "You will not transport me against my wishes."

"And I am the queen of the Seelie court"—Tiki hissed—"you will not steal from me." With a smooth sweep of her hand, she removed her glamour and pulled a knife from inside the folds at her waist where it was tucked. She stabbed directly at Donegal's face, but he ducked at the last second. The blade struck him in the shoulder, slipping through his garment and into his skin with surprising ease.

Donegal growled in pain but did not release his hold on her. He shook Tiki until her head felt like it might topple from her neck. He cupped his hand and blew into his curved fingers, pushing his burning palm at her face.

Tiki slapped his hand away as Donegal's guards rushed them.

"GUARDS!" His shout echoed across the landscape like the rumble of thunder. "KILL HER!"

"MACANNA!" Tiki yelled, praying the Seelie forces had come to the Tor as she had requested. "ATTACK!" She was reaching for the thunderclouds that hung low overhead when another shout echoed even more loudly.

"STOP!"

In a stormy burst of wind, Larkin stood between the armed soldiers and where Donegal held Tiki. Nebulous and ethereal in the black garments she still wore, she seemed to waver with the weather. Her arms were raised, as if she would physically stop the attack with her bare hands. "YOU WILL NOT HARM THE SEELIE QUEEN."

The guards slid to a stop, looking from Donegal to Larkin with indecision.

"Larkin." Donegal's voice became deceptively soft. "You do not belong here now. Leave this matter to me or face the consequences."

Larkin faced him. "Don't threaten me. I know your secret, Donegal—you don't belong on the throne any more than I do."

Donegal's face contorted with such rage, Tiki feared his eyes might pop from his head. "LIAR! I AM THE WINTER KING! I AM MEANT TO RULE ALL OF FAERIE!"

"You're not a king—the *Cloch na Teamhrach* did not cry out for you—you're not even pure UnSeelie. I know the secret you've tried to keep all these years,

Donegal. You've got Seelie blood running in your veins. You're a half-breed."

"LIAR! YOU'RE LYING! KILL THEM BOTH!"

In a burst of strength she didn't know she had, Tiki jerked her arm free. As the contact broke between her and Donegal, he darted away with blinding speed. She whirled, prepared to strike again, and froze.

Sullivan held Larkin from behind, one hand around her neck forcing her head back, the other clutching a curved iron dagger tight against her exposed throat. Donegal stood poised on one side while guards surrounded them with their spears pointed in Larkin's direction. Sullivan glared at Tiki with hatred in his eyes. "One death for another."

"Now what will you do, Seelie Queen?" Donegal sneered. "Will you sacrifice the life of another to save your own?"

"No—wait!" Tiki cried. "That was a *dog* that died. You can't possibly mean to—"

"Larkin is a SPY!" Donegal screamed. "A TRAITOR! A LIAR! I should have done this long ago!"

Larkin's lips barely moved but Tiki heard the faerie as if she'd shouted. "Save Clara."

Donegal waved his arm at Sullivan. "I'm done with Larkin. KILL HER!"

Like drawing a bow across the strings of a fiddle, Sullivan pulled the blade across Larkin's throat.

Chapter Forty-Four

Larkin slumped in Sullivan's meaty arms and her eyes went dark—like the light of the sun blocked behind a black cloud.

For a second, Tiki couldn't move. Was it possible? Had that monster really killed Larkin?

Even Donegal seemed stunned at what he had done and stared unmoving at Larkin's still body.

In the next moment, chaos erupted around them—Macanna exploded from the forest and attacked the UnSeelie soldiers. Cries and shouts rent the air as blades flashed and blood spilled.

As reality sank in, Tiki screamed until it was as if the very air shrieked with her pain and rage. She didn't remember moving but found she stood over Larkin's dead body, as if to protect her from further harm. She searched the crowd for Rieker or Dain, Toran, *anyone* who could help her—but she was alone.

In her agony, Tiki reached for the skies and pulled the storm down on top of them. The wind howled and gusted like a wild animal, blowing the UnSeelie soldiers back from Larkin's body and encircling Tiki in a whirlwind. Fury like she'd never known filled her, and Tiki struck, shooting a bolt of pure white light directly at Donegal.

He moved at the last second, but only enough to dodge the full brunt of the attack. The shot spun him around and knocked him to his knees, black smoke rising from his thigh. It was from that position, as Tiki drew back to strike again, that he disappeared.

She aimed instead for Sullivan who swerved through the crowd of fighting soldiers, hiding among those in battle. Tiki caught sight of him and attacked. The bolt struck him on the shoulder as he dove behind a large column. With a cry of rage, she thrust her hands above her head and lightning forked the sky until it looked like the heavens would split into a million pieces. Thunder shook the ground, making it difficult to stand. Screams of fear mingled with the cacophony until the world was a swirl of chaos.

As the soldiers battled around her, Fial appeared and raced to where Tiki stood guarding Larkin's body. He fell to his knees next to Larkin, pulling her onto his lap, his hands cupping her face.

"Breanna," he pleaded, "wake up. Bree—wake up, my love—I'm here." He gave her a shake as if to wake her and her head fell back, revealing the terrible gash across her neck.

Tears ran down Tiki's face as she bent and put her hand on his shoulder. He looked up at her, as if just realizing she was there, the anguish on his face so raw, Tiki wanted to look away, but she couldn't.

"What has he done?" Fial whispered. He looked back down at Larkin, limp in his arms. "What has my brother done?"

He pulled Larkin to his chest, hugging her tight, one hand supporting her head as he rested his cheek against her golden hair. A low cry rose from his chest, getting louder and louder until he tipped his head back and a howl of pure pain split the night.

"BREANNNNNNAAAAA!"

Her name echoed among the trees to the sky and carried on the wind until the entire world resonated with his torment. It was then that the skies opened and sheets of rain began to fall, and the heavens cried with him.

Donegal arrived inside the Great Hall. A wisp of smoke rose from the hole in his thigh, as if the inside of his leg was on fire.

"Bar the doors!" he cried to the few guards who remained within the hall as he limped toward the Dragon Throne. "Where are they?" he growled as Sullivan joined him. His *tánaiste* was also bleeding from his shoulder, his arm hanging limp at this side. Outside, the sounds of the fighting rang out.

"There." Sullivan pointed. Cruinn and Scáthach, along with six guards, stood in the shadows behind the Dragon Throne. "They've captured the Seelie queen's companions—just as we planned."

"You found them," Donegal said as he drew close to the prisoners. Rieker and Dain, still dressed as Donegal's guards, stood on small, precariously balanced platforms, their arms cinched behind their backs and nooses tight around their necks. Should the platforms they stood upon be kicked free, or should they slip, they would hang before anyone could cut them down.

"Aye, they were trying to cut through the ropes to free the girl, just as you knew they would," Cruinn said, "but we stopped them before they finished their work." He motioned to the golden net that hung nearby, weighted with Clara's small body. "The mortal girl is still our prisoner—our bait."

Donegal drew near and peered into their faces. "Remove your glamours," he snapped, "before I slice your throats to see what you really look like." He grabbed a dagger from a sheath on Cruinn's belt and pushed the knife point into the soft spot below Dain's ear until blood dribbled down his neck. Then he turned to Rieker. "Do it now or your comrade dies."

Rieker only hesitated for a moment before whispering the words that would remove his glamour. Donegal took a step back as the vision of the redcap melted away to be replaced with Rieker's handsome features and strong, tall body. He sneered at the Winter King with no sign of fear.

"As I suspected," Donegal said. He turned to Dain and flicked his knife in his direction. "Now you."

Dain didn't move.

"Not only will I kill him," Donegal said, motioning to Rieker, "but I will kill the child as well, and you can watch."

Dain's glamour melted away, replaced with his true features.

"*You*," Donegal spat. "I locked you in the White Tower as a spy for a reason. You should have died there or in the forest, hunted as the Seven-Year King. If it weren't for Larkin and that ridiculous excuse of a queen, you would have been dead long ago." His lips pulled back from his teeth, the whites of his eyes showing like a wild animal. "But it's Larkin who is dead, and she will never save you again."

Chapter Forty-Five

Tiki's last glimpse of Larkin was of the faerie in Fial's arms. With her golden hair hanging long over the jester's arm, she had looked like a princess—or a queen. Her head had been tucked against his shoulder like a sleeping child, hiding the ghastly wound to her neck, and at last, there in his arms, her exquisite face had been at peace.

Amid the chaos of the fighting, it was apparent the UnSeelie soldiers greatly outnumbered the Macanna. Tiki's eyes swept the dead and wounded that littered the Night Garden.

What had it been for?

Donegal and Sullivan had both escaped, and Larkin was dead. Tiki could only pray that Rieker, Dain, and Clara were still alive.

"Majesty." Fingers gripped her arm and Tiki whirled, prepared to strike. "You must leave the battlefield. Come with me." Toran peered anxiously into her face. "Quickly, please. We are being defeated."

Tiki knew without looking further that he was right. "Brave Macanna," she called out, her voice echoing over the Tor. "RETREAT!"

As quickly as they had emerged from the forest, the Macanna melted away and disappeared.

She promised Toran she would return to the Plain of Sunlight soon and transported amid his protests. She traveled to the stonecutter's cottage on the slim chance that Rieker and Dain might be there with Clara, but the room was empty and cold, a few dead leaves resting on the hearth. She only stayed long enough to collect the Cup of Plenty and the Faerie Queen's Mirror before she transported to the one place she felt safe.

Tiki had no idea how long she sat huddled in the dim corner of the abandoned clockmaker's shop in Charing Cross. She lit no candles. Time had ceased to exist. Wrapped in her cloak and shaking uncontrollably, she clutched her knees and leaned her head against the wall, wishing for sleep to take away a reality she didn't know how to deal with anymore.

She didn't know where to find Rieker or Dain—didn't know if they had escaped with Clara from the Palace of Mirrors. She didn't dare visit Shamus, Fi, Toots, and the Bosworths for fear she would be followed. Larkin was dead, and Fial had disappeared. Even Johnny and Toran were hiding somewhere in the Otherworld.

She was utterly alone.

Tiki drifted in and out of consciousness as the tears flowed, seemingly without end. She was drowning in a terrible grief that pulled her down until it was as if she was trying to breathe underwater. Those last moments with Donegal and Larkin replayed over and over in her head—what could she have done differently? How could she have saved Larkin? But she hadn't known Larkin was even in the palace—hadn't known she would step in and try to save her.

Fial's face haunted what little sleep Tiki did find, and after the shaking and the tears stopped, the things he'd said began to reverberate in her head like the pounding of a kettledrum. To find the jester was in love with Larkin wasn't that much of a shock—the fact that Larkin had insisted on trying to save him had been immensely revealing. But in the end, when he'd called her *Breanna*—

Tiki rubbed her eyes with the heels of her hands. Even in death, Larkin was an enigma. The only Breanna Tiki had ever heard mentioned was Lady Breanna of Connacht—Dain and William's *mother*—

A seed of doubt sprouted in her mind. Larkin had said that Breanna was murdered, but what if she hadn't been? What if Breanna had simply ceased to exist as she was forced to assume a new persona—just as Fial had become Kieran and later the jester.

Tiki's thoughts raced, one after the other. What was it Fial had said—that he and Larkin had sacrificed those they loved most—*their children* … Dain and William were Fial's sons and Clara was Larkin's daughter … what if …

She imagined Dain's handsome face, his blond hair and blue eyes, not like Fial's at all, but exactly like Larkin's. *And* Clara's.

Tiki's breath caught in her throat. Larkin had never said who Clara's father was—was it possible? Could it be Fial? Were William and Dain Clara's *brothers*?

The more Tiki considered the idea, the more it made perfect sense. Had Larkin hidden Clara in London for the same reason they'd split up and hidden the boys? For fear that Donegal would hunt them down and kill them for their mixed blood?

What has my brother done?

Fial's anguished question played over and over in Tiki's ears, followed by Donegal's voice:

Now she taunts me and spies on my court with my brother.

Pieces of the puzzle slowly clicked into place. Breanna and Fial had fallen in love—a forbidden love because of their different heritages—and Fial's family had tried to kill them because of it. Fial was a Winterbourne—an UnSeelie—Donegal's brother. It had been the Winter King who had been hunting them. Larkin and Fial had been spies in what was, for them, the most dangerous place in the world. All for a promise made to Eridanus, Finn, and Adasara. A promise that couldn't be fulfilled without Tiki's help.

Tiki pushed herself to her feet and paced to the back of the small room. It was as if Larkin whispered in her ear:

He has lived between two worlds and belonged to neither for most of his life—all for the sake of a promise made long ago. Those who have known his secrets and his sacrifice have been murdered one by one: Finn,

Eridanus, Adasara—even Breanna—until only he and I remain.

And what was the promise? Tiki had asked.

To stop the killing and reunite the courts as one. To live side by side with the mortals in peace. And most importantly—to create a future where one wasn't labeled Seelie or UnSeelie, but simply as fey.

Tiki stopped next to the makeshift table—a plank that sat upon an overturned fruit crate—and fingered the Luck of Edenhall. Her hand slid over to the mirror and raised the ornately framed glass. Her reflection looked back, thinner than she remembered, but just as striking and beautiful—just as powerful.

Who are you? she had asked the mirror, and Fial, on his sickbed, had answered: *The Faerie Queen.*

"And so you are," she whispered to her reflection.

It was late when she transported to Dunvegan Castle. She was dressed to blend with the shadows as she looked around the now-familiar courtyard, looking for any sign of Rory Campbell. A light shone from the caretaker's apartment and some of the tension released from Tiki's shoulders.

She hurried toward the Faerie Tower, instinct guiding her. She was a faerie queen. Surely she, if anyone, would be able to find a faerie treasure. Her feet made a light slapping sound on the stone steps as she climbed to the tower built for the lost wife of the MacLeod ancestor.

She mentally recounted their conversation with Norman MacLeod. What clues had the man let slip when she and Rieker spoke to him in London?

The flag is safe and those within our clan who need to know, are aware of its location. That's all that matters. But I will tell you this—the silk lies within an iron chest below the sign of MacLeod and awaits our return. Am Bratach Sith *is in a place protected by those who gave us the flag in the first place. Only those who know where to look could find our treasure.*

The cathedral within the Faerie Tower had seemed to be the perfect place to hide a faerie treasure—had they simply missed the hiding spot? Tiki pulled open the plank door and once again was struck by the serenity of the room. Moonlight shone through the large stained glass window at the far end of the hall, illuminating the room.

Tiki walked slowly to the offering table, running her hands along the long expanse of wood, searching for clues. She tried to unglamour the bowl once again with no success. She walked up and down the small rectangular room looking for what she had missed.

Where was it? Was the flag hidden somewhere else in Dunvegan? But Rory had intimated they'd built the faerie tower specifically for this prize.

The moon rose higher in the night sky as Tiki continued to search. Desperation churned in her stomach. She didn't have time—Clara and Rieker and Dain were missing. They were waiting for her to save them, but she couldn't do it without the Faerie Flag.

Tiki stood at the offering table and searched once more for a clue. *Anything.* But there was nothing. With a growl of frustration, she banged her fists on the table. "Where are you?" she shouted. But her plea was only met with silence.

Tiki whirled around intending to stomp to the door and exit when she froze. The moonlight streaming through the window cast the design of the leaded glass in clear silhouette on the stone floor before her. There in the middle was the crest and motto of Clan MacLeod: a bull's head between two flags and the words "Hold Fast."

Within an iron chest below the sign of MacLeod.

If she hadn't been standing in that spot at that exact moment, she would never have seen the shadows cast by the moon.

Tiki rushed to the area where the motto glowed upon the floor and fell to her knees. Slipping her fingers between the cracks of the stone, she searched for any loose spot where she might find purchase. It only took a moment when her fingers found the cleverly hollowed-out section where she could jiggle the stone enough to get a grip. With both hands, she hefted the piece of flooring and set it next to where she kneeled.

Her breath caught in her throat. There, hidden in a small hole in the floor, rested an iron chest.

Very carefully, Tiki lifted the chest free, the metal hot against her skin, as she set it next to her on the floor. Its surface was carved with the Celtic knot of Clan MacLeod. Ever so gently, she lifted the lid of the small chest and laid it back flat against the floor. Inside the red, velvet-lined chest was a folded piece of delicate golden fabric with knots of red stitched into its surface.

Her fingers trembled as she lifted the silk free. She'd found the Fourth Treasure—The Faerie Flag of Dunvegan.

Chapter Forty-Six

Tiki went first to Charing Cross and retrieved the Cup of Plenty where she had glamoured it as a plain green vase. The Faerie Flag was neatly tucked deep within her bodice, hidden beneath her clothes. The Ring of *Ériu* hung from her neck. The Stone of Tara had cried out her name for all to hear. She had recovered the Four Treasures of Faerie. And now she was prepared to call upon whatever powers the Four Treasures might offer to a true-born queen to save her family and crush Donegal forever.

She did not allow herself to waver with worry. She needed to focus on how she was going to save them. With great care, she set out the still-furled Faerie Flag, the Cup of Plenty, and the Ring of *Ériu* on the makeshift table within their hideaway. For good measure, she added the Faerie Queen's Mirror to the mix and waited.

Nothing happened.

She rearranged their order and sat back, her looking from one item to the other, unsure of what to expect but certain that *something* would happen.

It didn't.

"Bloody hell." She ground her teeth as she tried stacking the treasures on top of each other by putting the flag and the ring into the cup and then putting the cup on top of the mirror.

Nothing.

After searching for so long to locate the Four Treasures, it had never occurred to her that she wouldn't know what to *do* with them once she found them.

One hour stretched painfully into another as she examined each piece, searching for answers, yet the treasures yielded no secrets. She looked into the depths of the ring where the fire still burned, albeit feebly, but no knowledge was conveyed. She lit a fire below the ring and tried to smoke a secret free—but nothing was revealed. She didn't dare wave the flag and possibly use its last bit of magic, but the silk alone appeared to only be a section of fabric. She stared into the Faerie Queen's Mirror but only her reflection looked back, providing no answers.

In desperation, Tiki picked up the small glass vase. She couldn't continue to waste time here. She needed to be looking for Clara and Rieker and Dain. She turned the cup this way and that, the candlelight reflecting off the colors.

"The Luck of Edenhall," she mused out loud. "As *Corn na bhFuíoll,* the Cup of Plenty, you are said to offer healing, inspiration, wisdom, and sustenance. Johnny was healed by drinking from you. We received inspiration by looking into your depths. The starving fey need sustenance, which is why I think we smell food when they're around you."

She turned the glass in her hands. "But I need wisdom."

Tiki stared at the fragile goblet. "As the true-born queen, I ask you: How do I find the wisdom you might offer?" She slowly turned the vase, the greens and blues and browns of the glass glittering in the light. What did she need to do?

Movement close to the rim caught her eye. She squinted at the space below the fragile twist of gold where lines of small scroll now swirled around the cup. Tiki pulled the glass closer to read the script.

"'As the Stone of Tara represents earth,'" she read, whispering, "'the Ring of *Ériu* represents fire, the Faerie Flag represents air, and the Cup of Plenty represents water. The Four Treasures embody the Four Elements, the essentials of Faerie life. As you command the Four Treasures, earth, air, fire, and water are also yours to command.'" There was a signature below the words—could those letters read "Eridanus"?

Tiki's heart skipped a beat. It was as if the past had whispered in her ear and Eridanus had spoken directly to her.

Black thunderclouds were still gathered in the distance at the top of the Tor when Tiki returned to the Plain of Sunlight. The bodies of the Seelie guards who had been impaled upon the stakes had been pulled down, but what remained was utter devastation. She remembered the first time she'd visited the plain with Larkin—it had been a sunlit meadow dotted with wildflowers. The soothing sounds of a nearby river had been background music to the lilting songbirds who trilled and called to one another. The place had been the very essence of summer.

Look around, Larkin had said at the time. *Memorize this spot—because for now, this is the safest place we've got. Make sure you can visualize it. You may need to find your way back on your own at some point.*

A chill raised the flesh on Tiki's arms. The faerie's words seemed oddly prophetic now—though, under no circumstances would Tiki have ever imagined that the meadow she'd seen that day could ever look like this. Now the fields were burnt and dotted with charred stubs of tree trunks. No sounds could be heard—not even the gurgle of the river couldn't be heard. It was like a ghastly graveyard.

With a heavy heart, she slipped through the rock archway that led down into the Seelie headquarters, unsure how many, if any, of the Macanna and Seelie soldiers had returned.

"Majesty!"

Tiki whirled to find Toran bowing before her. He raised his head revealing a terrible gash across his forehead and two hideous black eyes. Seemingly oblivious to his wounds, he clasped his hands in joy. "We didn't know where to look—I didn't know what had become of you! Please allow me to guard you from this moment forward."

"Toran," Tiki gasped. "You're wounded."

He ducked his head in embarrassment. "It's nothing, Your Grace, especially given what some have suffered."

Tiki nodded. "True, but I'm so pleased to find you, especially, are all right. Where are the Macanna? Are there any left?"

"A few, but we've lost many."

Tiki bit her lip to fight back tears as she imagined those strong warriors she'd met with Larkin. It was hard to believe anything could stop them.

"Some have returned here," Toran continued. "Others hide in the Wychwood in small groups. Donegal's troops are everywhere—searching for anything Seelie. They kill before they ask questions. We've all been waiting for your return to lead us against this great evil."

Tiki nodded. "And that is exactly what I plan to do. Send word—I want as many troops as we can gather. We are going to create an army who will win this war."

"An army?" Toran's voice raised with hope. "How? Has Larkin found some new volunteers?"

His words hit with an unexpected bite, and for a moment, Tiki couldn't think of a reply, nor did she think she could manage one. Instead, she motioned for Toran to follow her and continued down to the hall where the Macanna had gathered in the past. She straightened her shoulders as she finally spoke over her shoulder. "No, it's my army. Get word to our generals—I want them here as soon as possible."

As news of the queen's return spread, more Seelie fey arrived at the Plain of Sunlight. Each day, as arrivals straggled into the stronghold, Tiki met with each newcomer and asked for word of Rieker and Dain, of the small blond girl who Donegal had captured, but no one had news. At the end of the day, she went outside and walked a short distance over a small hill where she wouldn't be seen, and she practiced.

The first time she stood tall and held out her arms. "I speak to you, Air, as the breath and wind of all things living, to heed my command: breathe a chill onto the ground before me until the earth in that spot is coated in frost."

A gust of wind had ruffled through the leaves of nearby trees. When the breeze hit her, Tiki shivered at the intensity of the chill. In a blink, the wind was gone, but the ground at her feet had turned white and was crusted in ice.

At night, she cried herself to sleep, worrying about Clara, Rieker, Dain, and the others. In her heart, she was certain that if they were free, they would have found her. Which could only mean one thing: Donegal had them.

The next day she practiced with fire. "I speak to you, Fire, as the element that can both create and destroy, to heed my command: burn these sticks at my feet until they are nothing but ash." There was a *pop* and a flame began to crackle at the bottom of the small stack of tree limbs Tiki had propped together. As she watched, the flames hungrily consumed the wood, orange tongues shimmering and dancing before her.

She thought of Larkin and Fial frequently. The questions that had always surrounded Larkin continued to swirl, even in death. The worst part—Tiki had the unsettling sense that she'd been horribly wrong about the faerie. She was coming to believe that Larkin had been forced to play her part so convincingly that no one would've ever guessed at the truth of her identity or of those she loved. If Larkin was Breanna, then she had made the ultimate sacrifice in letting others raise her children.

The third day was the easiest when she commanded Water to fall from the sky, and a rainstorm fell in a torrent around her.

The remainder of the generals, MacKenzie, Burns, Connelly, Keegan, and Finnegan, arrived on the fourth day.

"Have them gather in the hall," Tiki told Toran. "I'll join you shortly." She hurried outside and moved quickly to the stand of trees that had been unaffected by the fires. She stood in the dappled shadows beneath their limbs and took a deep breath.

"I speak to you, Earth, as the element that provides strength and life to all manner of plants and animals that live on and within you. I command that you bring to me an army of one."

At her words, a breeze fluttered through the branches above, causing the leaves to chatter, as if speaking a language all their own. A single leaf blew free from its anchor and drifted to the ground. The second the leaf touched the ground, it transformed into a warrior. Bare-chested and brown-skinned, he wore leaf-patterned trousers. He was tall and thin, like the tree from which he had sprouted, with a sinewy strength that rippled in his muscles when he moved.

He bowed. "My queen, I am yours to command."

Tiki exhaled slowly. She had found the Four Treasures, and now she could command them.

"Come with me."

Tiki stood on the steps that led into the common room. Filled with plank tables, great wooden rounds of candles hung from the ceiling, making the room as bright as a summer's day. Never in her wildest dreams would she ever have imagined she might be standing here alone planning to lead these men and women in war. But that was exactly what she intended to do.

"I will be brief."

The room went silent.

"For those of you who don't know me, I am Tara MacLochlan, true-born queen of the Seelie court. I have been so named by *Cloch na Teamhrach*, the Stone of Tara, and I claim my rightful place to lead and rule. We are gathered here today to put an end to the tyranny of the UnSeelie king and the indiscriminate killing that is occurring in Donegal's quest for power. He is not a true-born king, he has not been named by *Cloch na Teamhrach*, and he will be tried and punished for the deaths he has caused."

Cheers went up in the room.

"We have suffered losses and face an army that greatly outnumbers ours—but when the day comes and the battle begins, I promise you that we will have the strength to prevail. For now, work together to gather enough food in the forest so we can be prepared to attack and reclaim Faerie."

"Where's Larkin?" a man called from the back. "She's been our leader all the while you've been gone. We need her too." Tiki pressed her lips together. Given all the times she had loathed Larkin so thoroughly that she'd plotted to never see her again, Tiki was shocked at the loss she felt at the faerie's death. As happened so often now, memories of Larkin whispered in Tiki's ear, *Ah, guttersnipe, you'll come to love me one day.*

Tiki shook her head, trying to shake the faerie's words away. She opened her mouth to speak, but no words came out.

The crowd remained silent, watching her.

"I'm sorry to tell you that—" Tiki swallowed and blinked rapidly. "I'm sorry to say that Larkin was murdered by Sullivan—one of Donegal's *tánaiste.*"

A collective gasp filled the air, followed by cries of dismay. "Murdered? No! It's not true!" "It can't be—nothing can hurt Larkin."

Tiki took a deep breath, hoping she could keep her tears from falling. "One more reason why we cannot let a madman like Donegal ruin our world any longer. Gather your strength—for we attack soon."

Chapter Forty-Seven

Fial stood alone on a windswept cliff overlooking the sea. In his hands, he held a bag woven from grass that sagged under the weight of its contents. He stared out over the shifting water, watching the whitecaps frolic and chase each other until the clouds parted and a shaft of white light illuminated a patch of sea. He tipped the bag and the gusting breeze lifted the ashes, making them fly on the wind.

"To our freedom, my love," he whispered. The contents of the bag, which had moments before been heavy in his hands, were suddenly weightless as they spread in a thousand different directions and disappeared. "We will be together again soon."

It started as a whisper—a rumor: Donegal hadn't killed the jester. The Fool had escaped from the Winter King.

The whispers grew.

The jester had been seen near the *zagishire*—dressed in his colorful finery. He had awed a passerby with his magic, creating a bird of fire out of thin air and had only whispered one word: "*Revolution*."

The gossips said he had juggled seven deadly knives before the slaves in the kitchen without cutting himself or dropping a single blade. The only word he'd spoken: "*Revolution*."

The hobgoblins, forced to join the ranks of the UnSeelie soldiers, raised a cup to him and the Seelie queen. "*Revolution*," they whispered.

Chapter Forty-Eight

"The jester is alive"—Donegal sat in the High Chamber surrounded by his generals—"and spreading discontent. The Seelie queen still lives. We can't wait any longer. Larkin has been the driving force behind the Seelie court since O'Riagáin's death, and perhaps before. Without her," he said as he slashed his hand through the air, "they are *nothing*.

"This new queen—Tara MacLochlan—will be easy to defeat. We hold her two most valued soldiers and the mortal child to whom she has some perverse attachment. In her attempt to save them, she will fall into our trap and we will *murder* her. But in the meantime, we attack."

Sullivan leaned forward, intent upon his king. "Where should we start?"

"I want the jester found *now*. He can't be far because I hear the whispers that he has been sighted near the palace—performing magic and speaking of *revolution*." Donegal spat on the ground. "He has always been a problem. This time when we catch him, we will kill him on the spot, do you understand?"

Cruinn, Sullivan, and Scáthach nodded together.

"I want his head on a platter as proof of his death. Whoever can bring me that prize will be well rewarded."

There were murmurs of approval among the men.

"Assign who you must to find the Fool. I want a second group to find the queen." He pointed a clawed nail at each of them. "One of you will be in charge of her arrest. The rest will be sent on patrols—with the single goal of eradicating any Seelie creature they happen upon. Send your men to the Plain of Sunlight to lie in wait. The queen will be gathering her troops there. Send them to the northern borders to enlist any redcaps who haven't joined us. If the hobgoblins resist, kill them. I am done playing games. This world is mine to rule, and I will rule as I please!"

Soldiers poured in waves from the barracks Donegal had built within the forest bordering the Tor. They were a mix of fey—some rode, some walked, some slithered—but they all traveled with the same intent: to finish the battle and defeat the Seelie court.

Chapter Forty-Nine

The moon had crested and begun its downward descent, only occasionally shooting an arrow of light through the clouds that hovered over London. The knock sounded loudly upon the wooden door of the cottage situated at the edge of the lake in St. James's Park. The visitor cringed as the noise echoed in the stillness.

"Macha," she whispered to the closed door, as if her words would magically transport through the wood. She tapped again—ever so lightly. "Open up—it's me." She glanced nervously over her shoulder as she counted seven long heartbeats waiting for the door to open.

Finally, the brass knob twisted and the door swung inward. A petite older woman with hair the color of fresh-fallen snow peered around its edge.

"A'ine," the woman gasped, her crooked fingers covering her open mouth. "Have you done it?"

"Yes. Through Fial's powerful magic, everyone believes Larkin is dead."

"Come in, then, and get out of sight." Macha clutched at her visitor's hand and pulled her into the cottage. She poked her head out and quickly glanced up and down the pathway before she ducked back inside and bolted the door.

Chapter Fifty

It had been a week since Larkin's death. A week since Tiki had last seen Rieker, Dain, and Clara. The Macanna who'd survived and returned to the Plain of Sunlight were battered and thin. Some were healing from wounds inflicted in the fight, but the generals had promised Tiki that with rest and regular meals, the bulk of them would soon be fit enough again to fight. And all of them wanted to fight.

Tiki left the generals in charge of rebuilding the Macanna. She had other priorities. Before she could allow an attack on Donegal, she had to find Rieker, Dain, and Clara. Larkin had told her that Donegal kept his prisoners in only three places: the Palace of Mirrors, the White Tower, or the Plain of Starlight. The White Tower had been destroyed, so that left only two places: the palace or the UnSeelie stronghold on the Plain of Starlight.

Tiki left for the Plain of Starlight at night. She needed to travel light and fast—without Toran following to protect her. She would protect herself. On her back she carried a bow and an endless quiver of arrows. There were knives in her boots and attached to her belt. A light but deadly sabre hung from the side of her saddle.

Those weapons, along with her control of the four elements, would have to suffice.

The horse she took was black as ink and fast as the wind. The beast reminded her of the first time Dain had shown her Aeveen in the field near O'Donoghue's farm. The white horse had galloped toward them, and Tiki would have sworn her hooves never touched the ground.

Tiki was dressed in black as well, her hair braided down her back, no glamour to shield her features. She wanted anyone she met to recognize the Seelie queen and to know Donegal and those who helped him would suffer her wrath.

She'd never been so far into UnSeelie territory before—she knew only that the UnSeelie stronghold was located in the darkness on the far horizon. It seemed an easy-enough trip—around Wydryn Tor and through the Wychwood to the far side. It was when she arrived that her plan was still a bit murky, but she was determined she would not rest until her family had been found and was safely in her care again.

Night turned to day and then to night again. The horse never seemed to tire, and Tiki let the beast have its head. Memories pounded through her mind as the hooves pounded through the Wychwood. More than once, the wind dried tears from her face.

It was on the third day, when the sun should have risen above the horizon, but didn't, that Tiki knew she had reached the Plain of Starlight. She pulled the horse up and led it to a dark brook to drink. As the horse plunged his muzzle into the water, Tiki debated climbing down and getting a drink herself. Her body ached from the long ride, and her throat was parched.

Tiki eyed the surrounding forest. With a shrill *cawwww!* a black bird landed nearby on a stump of wood half submerged in the stream. The bird cocked his head, its one visible eye staring as if challenging her. As Tiki watched the bird's odd behavior, she noticed that the log the bird sat upon had an eyeball that was also staring at her.

Unsettled, Tiki tugged on the reins to pull her horse's head from the water. She nudged her heels into his sides, urging him back away from the water. As if in slow motion, other shapes became visible—a white bleached skull floated nearby, ears laid flat against a long head, flared nostrils just above the water line.

Tiki bit back a gasp of horror. A kelpie lurked just below the surface. If she had climbed down from her horse, would it have attacked?

She wheeled her horse around, anxious to be gone from the stream. The forest had changed as they rode—from healthy green trees to brown trees that had died where they stood. Barren branches reached out, reminding her of the Night Garden during winter, some blocking the trail.

Tiki ducked under several branches; then the trail forked. She pulled to a stop, unsure which direction to go. A breeze rattled through the dead wood and suddenly, dirty little men crouched among the branches, watching her.

"Who goes there?" one of them cried in a voice that sounded surprisingly like the *caw* of the black bird.

Tiki sat straighter in the saddle. "Tara MacLochlan. I seek the UnSeelie court. Can you tell me which way to go?"

The men muttered among themselves in birdlike chirps.

The same man spoke again. He leaned forward, his long toes wrapped around the branch to secure his place in the dead tree. "The court is in session at the Palace of Mirrors upon Wydryn Tor."

"I am seeking several of Donegal's prisoners." Tiki's tone brooked no argument. "Where will I find the Plain of Starlight?"

The men muttered among themselves again, their chirps sounding more alarmed this time.

"Has Donegal sent you?"

"Yes." Tiki toyed with the idea of shooting a bolt of lightning at the base of their leader's tree to encourage him to answer, but he spoke again.

"There." He pointed down the left fork of the road. "That path leads to the UnSeelie camp, but there's no one there. Donegal has sent everyone to attack the Plain of Sunlight."

Tiki's eyes narrowed into a glare of hatred. In her mind's eye, she could clearly see the devastation and death that Donegal had brought upon the Plain of Sunlight. "Why haven't you gone, then?"

The man flapped his arms like a bird, then hopped to another branch. "Can't fly, can't walk. The Winter King didn't want us."

"But you make wonderful sentries. Perhaps the Winter King has sold you short."

The men chirped among themselves in tones of surprise as Tiki nodded and kicked her horse into motion. Would recognize the UnSeelie stronghold when she saw it?

She need not have worried. Less than thirty minutes later, a familiar silhouette shadowed the path: bodies impaled on stakes. There was no way to avoid riding past the dead bodies. She averted her eyes as best she could as they drew closer to the first stake. Her horse shied away with a nervous whinny, and Tiki's focus shifted from avoiding looking at the dead bodies to controlling her mount. In the process, she inadvertently looked upon the face of the dead soldier, and a cry escaped her lips.

Bushy eyebrows, a beak-like nose, a jutting chin, and an odd hump on his back—it was the hobgoblin who'd watched when she and Rieker had gone in search of the cup. His long braid dangled in the air, as if he swung in play from a tree limb.

With a growl of rage, she swung her sabre free and sliced through the stake that held the dead hobgoblin suspended in midair. His body tumbled into the underbrush and disappeared as the vines on the ground wriggled with sudden life to wrap their arms around the corpse.

Tiki stared down the row of dead bodies that lined the path. Were these the hobgoblins who had resisted Donegal's attempt to make them fight for the UnSeelie court? Would she find Gestle, the hobgoblin who had helped her and Rieker save Dain from the White Tower, among the dead?

Her breath was ragged in her throat as she rode down the trail, slicing each stake in half as she passed, letting the bodies tumble to the ground. She couldn't possibly bury all these dead, but the forest seemed to be reclaiming its own.

Where before she had thought she would avoid looking at the dead, she now checked every face—afraid to find Gestle, while at the same time hopeful she would not.

The bodies didn't stop until she reached the stone archway that led into the headquarters of the UnSeelie court. She had not recognized Gestle's face among the dead.

Disturbingly similar to the opening into the Seelie court on the Plain of Sunlight, Tiki stared at the nondescript doorway that led into the UnSeelie stronghold. What would she find inside? More death? Or would she find the lives she so desperately sought?

"Don't leave me," Tiki whispered into the ear of her horse before she tied the reins to the saddle and set the horse free. "I might need you again."

The horse jerked its head as if in assent, then ambled over to a patch of trees that appeared half alive.

Tiki adjusted the strap of her quiver, the bow held tightly in one hand as she walked boldly in through the arched stone entry. Outside was shadowed with no moon or sun to light the way, but inside the doorway was pitch-black. Tiki stopped, waiting for her eyes to adjust, but it was so dark, she couldn't even make out which direction to walk.

"How does anyone bloody well see in here?" she muttered under her breath. She scooted one foot in front of the other, but it was hopeless. She groped along the wall until she found what she sought—a torch, waiting to be lit. With a flick of her wrist, fire spurted from the depths of the torch, the flames throwing a circle of light. "That's more like it."

She held the torch high—where was everyone? In the Seelie fort, there were guards at the entry and at many points along the way to the interior. Here, there appeared to be no one. Had Donegal taken everyone to the Palace of Mirrors for winter? Or perhaps all his troops were fighting the war.

The tunnel wound back and forth in a meandering path. Where the Seelie stronghold was surprisingly opulent, this was barely more than a tunnel carved within the earth. Vines sprouted from the walls, and the moist smell of dirt hung rich in the air. Tiki had just turned a corner when a huge shadow lunged at her with snapping teeth and sharp claws. She reacted by instinct—she reached across her body and grasped a dagger, flicking it back into the face of her attacker. There was a loud *pop* and the huge shape exploded into a much smaller figure that hit the ground and ran away.

"Spriggans," she muttered. Tiki yanked her bow up and aimed an arrow at another shadow farther down the path. The metal tip hit its mark, and the giant ogre popped and disappeared. One more came at her but Tiki made quick work of it with another arrow.

She turned the corner and stared. A vast room stretched before her. Devoid of life, the space was littered with debris: wine bottles, empty and strewn all about the floor as if dropped where they'd been finished; half-chewed bones and maggot-infested meat littered tabletops; chairs were tipped on their sides as if a party had ended in a horrific brawl.

But that wasn't what had riveted Tiki's attention. It was the paintings on the walls of the circular room. Amazingly lifelike, one was of Larkin, a red X painted over her face. Next to her were Dain and Rieker, both with a single black slash across their faces. A picture of Tiki covered the wall next to Rieker.

And next to her picture was an image of Clara, a red X covering her face.

Chapter Fifty-One

"Breathe—in and out," she commanded herself as she rode away from the stronghold of the Plain of Starlight. "He would not kill a little girl. She is more valuable alive than dead." She bit her bottom lip to stop the sobs that boiled in her chest. "Larkin told me so," she whispered, swiping tears from her cheek with the back of her hand. "Breathe—in and out. She is more valuable alive than dead." She urged her horse faster.

Aside from the pictures, Tiki had not found any evidence that Rieker, Dain, and Clara might be in that location. The only prison left was the Palace of Mirrors.

As winter had grown stronger, the Night Garden had become a frozen sculpture. Ice encased every thorn, bramble, and bloom. It was in the hour before midnight that Tiki went back to Wydryn Tor disguised as she had been when they'd visited the palace with Larkin glamoured as Fachtna. She looked like a small UnSeelie male with a large, hooked nose and white hair pulled behind her neck. Her eyes were black rather than vibrant green, and her shoulders bore a slight hunch, stretching the folds of her worn jacket.

Dark shapes of Donegal's soldiers patrolled the garden, something Tiki had never seen before. She had passed groups in the forest, as well. Luckily, she had been one where they had been many and therefore easy to hear from a distance, allowing her to circumvent their path without being seen.

She crouched low on the trail and made herself as small as possible, praying she could avoid detection. Raucous noise rolled from the Palace of Mirrors as Donegal's followers celebrated the Winter Solstice—the longest night of the year. Out in the Night Garden where Tiki crouched hidden, it was oddly silent, as if the world held its breath. She was counting the guards who surrounded the perimeter of the palace when a scratchy voice spoke close by her elbow.

"Alms for the poor?"

Tiki nearly screamed from fright. She whirled to stare into a bone-thin face. The hooked nose and fanged lower jaw were unmistakable.

"Ailléna! What are you doing out here? It's freezing."

The little redcap recoiled in surprise, her shaggy eyebrows pulling down over her nose in confusion. "Do I know yer?"

"Oh." Tiki put her hands to her face as she remembered her glamour. Did she dare tell the redcap who she was? Could Ailléna help her find Rieker and Dain? She made a split-second decision. "It's me—Tiki."

Ailléna tilted her head, her large hooked nose curling in doubt. "Who?"

"The Seelie queen," Tiki mouthed the words, but the frown on Ailléna's face got deeper.

"You are not my queen."

Tiki looked around in frustration. "Are you alone?"

The look on the redcap's face turned to uncertainty. "Yes."

Tiki whispered the words to remove her glamour just long enough for Ailléna to recognize her. "You helped us find *Corn na bhFuíoll*—the Cup of Plenty after it went missing." When the redcap's sizable mouth dropped open, Tiki quickly reapplied her disguise.

"Jumping Jack-in-Irons," the little goblin gasped, "what are yer doin' out here, Majesty? *Alone*? Donegal has his soldiers everywhere looking for you, the jester, anyone Seelie. You shouldn't be here, mum."

"I need your help."

"Certainly, Majesty." Ailléna bobbed her head up and down as she glanced over both shoulders with a look of apprehension. "Whatever yer need."

"First of all, you can't call me that anymore," Tiki whispered.

"Yes, mum—but what should I call yer?"

"Anything but that. How long have you been here on the Tor?"

"Since Donegal burnt the fields roun' the Plain of Sunlight." She shook her wizened head. "'T'weren't safe to stay without Larkin to protect me"—she hung her head—"bein' a redcap an' all." Her lower jaw trembled. "I still cannae believe she's gone …" Ailléna gave a great shuddering sigh.

"I know." Tiki closed her eyes and took a deep breath, but it did no good, for Larkin's face was always there, looking back at her with sardonic amusement. How the faerie would have laughed to know the sadness Tiki felt at her departure. "I will make Donegal pay," she promised.

"But why are you here, alone, Maj—er—uh, sir?" She crept up next to Tiki and stared at the palace through the frozen brambles. "You cannae be planning to attack the Winter King on yer own? That's madness."

"No, I'm looking for my friends—Rieker—you remember him?"

Ailléna nodded.

"And Dain—"

The redcap gave Tiki a hideous grin revealing all the fanged teeth that jutted over her upper jaw. "The 'andsome one."

"And there's a child—Clara. I don't think you've met her—"

"The mortal girl Donegal stole from yer?"

"Yes," Tiki said, "that's exactly who I'm looking for. Have you heard anything?"

The little goblin looked all around before she spoke, and when she did, Tiki could barely hear her. "The rumor is that while Donegal was fightin' with Larkin, somebody tried to cut the girl from her trap."

Tiki's heart caught. "What happened?"

"I's just 'eard the whispers outside the kitchens an' whatnot, but they say the ones who tried to cut 'er free are strung up in the Great Hall, and the little 'un is still hangin' in the golden net."

"She's alive?" Tiki's heart soared before it promptly plummeted. "Strung up?"

"The last I 'eard, she's alive, but I cannae be sure. The other prisoners' hands are tied by ropes so they cannae move."

Tiki took a shuddering breath. It was as she'd feared. That explained why no one had found her—they were all captives. It would be up to her to set them free.

"And what of Donegal?"

"I cannae say for sure, mum, but I've 'eard he's been in meetin's in the High Chamber since ... since ..." The goblin rubbed her clawed hands together. "The passin'."

"Since he murdered Larkin, you mean."

The little redcap averted her eyes. "Yes."

"I'm going to need your help, Ailléna."

"Anything, Majesty, but you know I can't go into the palace right now. They're not lettin' anyone in who isn't part of court."

"I know. That's all right. Here's what I want you to do ..."

Once she had given instructions to the goblin, Tiki cut through the frozen Night Garden toward the Palace of Mirrors. The garden was eerily quiet as she made her way close to the side of the building. As she passed one of the luminescent blooms encased in ice, she realized why it seemed so silent. The garden wasn't singing— the ice had muted their song.

Tiki drew in a deep breath of the cold air. Somewhere along the building, there was a door. She'd escaped out of the palace through it once with Dain. Now she needed to find it to sneak *into* the palace.

More than an hour had passed, and Tiki still hadn't located the door. The side of the building was immense, and the brambles seemed especially thick close to the palace. The thorns tore at her clothes like tiny fingers, and her teeth chattered with cold. Frustrated, she closed her eyes and tried to envision what she had seen when Dain had led her from the palace that night when they'd escaped from Donegal. It'd been dark, and the path had led through a maze of brambles for a short time before they'd reached the Tor's steep edge.

You have to jump.

Tiki's eyes flew open. She remembered. Dain had led her to the edge of the cliff where a secret path twisted down the side of the Tor. The door had not been far from the spot where Dain had told her to jump. If she started at the edge of the mountain, maybe she could work her way back to the door that led into the palace.

The moon peeked occasionally through the layers of soot-colored clouds that gathered above the palace and by the shadowy light, Tiki wound to the edge of the mountain, which cut away in a sheer drop. She inched forward to peer cautiously over the cliff. One wrong step and she would plummet to a sure death.

Below, she could make out the tops of the trees of the Wychwood Forest. Cut out of the side of the mountain was a rocky little trail.

This was it.

She searched the area where she stood. In the distance, the Palace of Mirrors loomed. From this perspective, it didn't take long to find the path that stretched back to the building. Tiki followed the trail, ducking under thorny branches thick enough to be tree limbs. She kept a constant lookout for guards or soldiers who might be patrolling the garden, but she was alone.

The trail wound back and forth, but it wasn't long until Tiki stood next to the palace. The building was elaborately decorated. Among the arches and columns were figures and gargoyles carved into the ancient stone. In some ways, the facade reminded Tiki of Westminster Abbey. But among the ornate design, there was nothing that looked like a door.

Tiki chewed her lip in frustration. Why couldn't she see it? She had to get inside—it had to be here. She imagined the grand hallway lined with doors. Dain had taken her through the last door—where was it?

Suddenly, the answer hit her—Larkin had spoken of those thirteen doorways, and especially the doorway that led up to Fial's spying post. *I'm surprised you were able to find that room. Fial had concealed those entrances with powerful magic. You should have been diverted to the Night Garden.*

The jester, so much more powerful than they had ever guessed, had protected all those doorways with some kind of concealing magic, both inside and out. She was sure of it.

She assessed the building again, but in a different way. This time she tried to see through a glamour. "I can do this," Tiki whispered to herself. "I am the true-born queen, I can see through glam—" She stopped as something peculiar caught her eye. She studied that section of the wall. Between each of the elaborately round columns were shadows—with straight lines. Shadows of straight lines that round columns wouldn't cast. She glanced down the side of the building and counted the strange sets of lines—thirteen. A thrill of excitement shot through her.

She'd found them.

Tiki hurried to the last section and studied what she believed to be a door. There was no obvious handle—no way to gain entry.

"Think like the jester. How would Fial disguise the handle?" The door was incorporated into the arches and peaks that made up the building. Tiki studied the intricate architecture. The answer was before her—but where?

Then she saw it—carved within a small, four-sided floret sat a man wearing a familiar three-point hat. In one hand, he held a staff with a Celtic cross at the top—just like the pin Rieker had found in the jester's spying room. In the other hand—two large keys.

Tiki reached for the keys. She wrapped her fingers around the cool stone and pulled. As silent as a whisper, the door opened.

She was in.

Chapter Fifty-Two

Tiki peered around the edge of the door to find a shadowed space behind one of the many huge columns that lined the hallway. She slipped inside and pulled the door closed. In the distance the raucous noise of the celebration in the Great Hall spilled down the hallway like water tumbling over a riverbed. She glanced around the column and into the hallway. A pair of UnSeelie lords, their heads bent together deep in conversation, strolled in her direction. Behind them a faun pranced alone, a petulant look on his face. Up ahead, two guards stood at the entrance of the Great Hall; another pair stood at the entrance at the opposite end of the hallway.

Tiki thought fast. She would need an excuse to enter the Great Hall to see if Rieker, Dain, and Clara were really being held as Ailléna had described. In a moment of inspiration, she whispered the words and changed her glamour. Taking a deep breath, she rounded the column and walked down the hallway as if she belonged here at the UnSeelie court. She ignored the guards and made to pass into the Great Hall, but they moved at the same time and dropped their speared staffs to block her way. The taller of the two spoke first.

"Name yourself."

Tiki arched a thick, woody eyebrow and stared him in the face. "Really? You don't recognize me?" Her blood was ice in her veins, and all the anger and hatred she felt toward Donegal fueled the emotion in her voice. "I suggest you learn before I'm forced to teach you."

"She's *Fachtna*," the other guard muttered. "Donegal's witch." He flipped his spear upright to allow passage.

"Precisely." Tiki nodded at him. She turned back to the first guard and pointed a knobby, branch-like finger that ended in a razor-sharp tip. "Perhaps I'll take your left eye to add to my collection and you may keep the scar—the better to remember me next time."

The guard jerked his staff away and stepped back.

Fachtna inclined her head ever so slightly but her expression didn't soften. "A wise decision." Tiki swept past them into the Great Hall. She hadn't taken two steps when her attention was drawn upward to the ceiling. There, to the right of the Dragon Throne, suspended high above the crowd like some ghastly chandelier, was the golden net. Inside the ropes, a small body hung, curled in a ball like a kitten.

Clara.

A wave of such immense relief went through Tiki, her knees weakened. She couldn't see the child's face, but the curve of her back, the blond curls that poked through the net, were unmistakable. Clara was alive.

Tiki dropped her eyes and forced herself to keep walking. How was she going to get Clara down without being seen? The room was crowded with all manner of cavorting UnSeelie fey. Guards were plentiful too, watching the goings-on with grim expressions.

Shaken, Tiki glanced at the Dragon Throne and stopped dead in her tracks. Behind the throne stood Dain and Rieker. Ailléna had been correct—they were "strung up"—both held captive by ropes that bound their wrists above their heads. Guards stood on each side of them. Tiki didn't give herself time to become scared. Larkin wasn't here to be brave for her anymore. She had to be brave for herself.

She sauntered toward the prisoners, quickly debating how she could get them free. Both Dain and Rieker had their heads down and hadn't seen her yet. A million questions swirled through her head. Did they know Larkin was dead? Would they recognize her in this glamour? What clue could she give them?

"And here we have the traitors." She spoke in the same arrogant tone Larkin had used when disguised as Fachtna. Actually, Tiki mentally corrected herself, Larkin had sounded arrogant all the time. Yet, somehow it pleased her that in this moment, she could pull off the same level of confidence that Larkin had exuded all the time. Perhaps she had learned more from the faerie than she realized.

At her words, both Dain and Rieker raised their heads. She saw a flash of recognition in Rieker's eyes before they went blank again. She leisurely circled him as though assessing his worth, then pivoted to walk in a figure eight around Dain.

"What fun and games does Donegal have planned for our little pets?"

The guards glanced at each other. "He hasn't said, mum, but I believe they're bait for the Seelie queen."

"*Her*," Tiki sneered. "She's not smart enough to confront the Winter King in his own court now that Larkin is dead. Your prisoners might starve to death before *she* ever shows up—and then what good are they to you?"

One of the guards coughed. Thickly built, with hair as black as a tar pit, he reminded Tiki of a bulldog. "You're right. She's probably hiding in London as she likes to do."

The other guard snickered. He was smaller than either Rieker or Dain, but well armed with multiple knives embedded in leather straps that crisscrossed his chest. The blades glittered in the torchlight.

"You're right, mum. We should probably feed 'em to the hounds like His Majesty did with the jester."

Tiki stopped and pointed a finger at him. "Now, that is a brilliant idea. Did you see it? Did the hounds like the taste of the Fool's flesh?"

The guards cast a wary glance at each other. "Didn't actually see it, but we all heard his cries when the hounds got him. Screamed like a little girl."

A chill crawled up Tiki's arms. Who had Donegal really fed to the hounds—and how callous and uncaring could these men be? But they were UnSeelie—they'd been taught to murder and kill their entire lives. Even if she could get rid of Donegal and create one realm, could the UnSeelies be taught to live a different way?

Tiki tossed her head at the prisoners. "Are they wounded?"

The black-haired guard jabbed the wooden end of his staff into Dain's ribs. "Not enough."

Dain's body jerked with the thrust, but he closed his eyes and clamped his lips shut.

"Donegal wants me to bring the prisoners to him," Tiki snapped. "A little interrogation, I believe." She held out her hand. "Give me their ropes."

"You can't mean to take them yourself," the smaller one cried. "They could attack you."

"She's Fachtna," the other one whispered. "They wouldn't dare."

"Thank you for your concern, but I don't think these two"—she sneered down her nose at Dain and Rieker—"are much of a threat. Besides, I'm not taking them far." She snapped her fingers and chains appeared around the ankles of both young men. "There—I'll fetter their feet if it makes you feel better." Tiki looked over at the guards. "The ropes, please?"

The guards looked warily at each other.

"Perhaps we should escort you," the shorter one said.

"No need." Tiki motioned at the ropes that held their arms. "Cut them loose."

The shorter one shifted his weight from one foot to the other. "But it'd be our heads if they escaped or did any harm to you, mum."

Tiki reached out and her arm extended until the knobby limbs of her fingers tightened around the guard's throat. "And it will be your head if you don't do as I ask."

The panicked look on the guard's face convinced the other to act. He hurried to the wall where the ropes where tied to a pulley and released the lever. As soon as the tension released, both Dain and Rieker grimaced as they slowly lowered their arms below their heads.

Fachtna stepped close and glared at both of them. "Test my patience and you will be dead faster than you can say 'Fate never crushed those who truth never deceived.'" She yanked the ropes out of the guard's hands and tugged Dain and Rieker behind her. "Follow me."

Every eye in the room was on Fachtna as she led the shuffling prisoners out of the Great Hall. Tiki fought the terrible sensation that the guards were going to call her bluff and attack from behind.

"Make way," she snapped, pretending she was Larkin and shooing people out of her way as they wove through the crowd. The guards at the entrance stood straight as she led the prisoners through the passageway into the corridor. She gave the ropes a light snap as she turned to the royal chambers. "Hurry up—the Winter King is waiting for us."

"Fachtna!"

Tiki jerked around in surprise. An unfamiliar guard dressed entirely in black hurried toward them, his long, straight black hair pulled behind his head. He wore a gold pin against his chest and gold buttons glistened from his vest. Fear coiled in her stomach. Tiki had never seen a guard dressed such as he, but the black and gold were too similar to the way Donegal dressed not to be of concern. Whoever he was, he was a man of power.

"Come with me." It was a command. "Donegal has left his chambers. He has requested your counsel in another location."

Tiki tried to hide how tense she was. "And who are you?"

The man stopped before her, briefly assessing Rieker and Dain, before he gave Tiki a stiff bow. "Perhaps you don't remember our previous introduction. I am Kieran."

Tiki blinked rapidly to hide her shock. "I do remember you now—as I recall, you were impertinent the last time we met."

His nostrils flared as though he found humor in her comment, but his lips didn't smile. "One of my many flaws. Come"—he turned and beckoned to her—"we must not keep the king waiting." As he straightened, Tiki got a closer look at the gold pin on his breast—a golden circle, with a man in a sitting position holding a staff topped with a Celtic cross in one hand and keys in the other.

Tiki pointed down the hallway at the thirteen doors. "Lead the way."

Chapter Fifty-Three

Kieran walked briskly as he led them down the hallway, stopping several doors past the entry that led up to the spying post. He pulled the door open, motioning with his hand, "After you—quickly, now."

The Night Garden lay frozen on the other side of the doorway. Tiki hurried through the opening but instead of walking into the garden, she stood in a circular room filled with more doors. As soon as Dain and Rieker were in the room, she removed the fetters on their ankles.

"Let me see your arms," Tiki said. "We need to get these off." The ropes were laced with iron and burned as she touched them. She couldn't imagine being bound for a long period.

Fial closed the door. "Quickly, if you please. Remove your glamour, Tara, so you will be able to see where you're walking."

"Fial?" Dain asked. "And Tiki?"

"Yes." Fial swept by them. "Better not to talk for now."

Rieker squeezed Tiki's hand as they followed the darkly garbed Fial around the circle to the right and opened the seventh door. "As quickly as you can go—hurry. We've not much time."

Tiki led the way down a flight of stone stairs, the tunnel becoming darker with each step, reminding Tiki of the UnSeelie home.

"Keep going," Fial said from behind. "We'll light a torch at the bottom."

The stones were rough and Tiki ran her hands along the walls to keep her balance. The stairway twisted down and around until she had the sense they were in the very bowels of the Tor. When they finally reached level ground, Tiki only walked far enough so the four of them could stand together, then she waited for Fial to take the lead.

He hurried in front and lit a torch that waited in a wall mount as if for that very purpose. Flames jumped and shimmied, lighting the darkness. He smiled at each of them one by one. "Good—very good. We are alive, we are together. Let us take care of these ropes." He handed Tiki the torch and ran his hands over the material still tied around Rieker's and Dain's wrists. The iron-laced ropes dropped free as if cut away.

"Thank you," Dain said as he rubbed his wrists. Rieker echoed his words.

"And now we shall take care of my brother."

"But we have to get Clara," Tiki protested. "She's—"

"I know where she is, my dear—believe me, I know where little Clara is. We cannot get to her. There is only one way to free the child—we must take on Donegal in his own den."

Rieker spoke for the first time. "What's your plan?"

Fial nodded at Tiki. "Tara has been gathering our generals. They wait at the Plain of Sunlight for her order to attack. I have been marshaling any UnSeelies who might defect to our side. The hobgoblins are with us as well as many of the homeless faeries. We'll see who else might join us."

"And what are we going to do?" Dain asked.

Fial looked at Tiki. "You have the Four Treasures?"

She nodded. "They are mine to command."

"Good. We will get word to our soldiers to gather just beyond the Night Garden. The four of us will be inside the palace—they will be outside. Dawn arrives at five thirty-five. We will strike exactly one hour before."

"Where?"

"In the Great Hall, of course. We'll cut Clara down first, then as she is carried to safety"—Fial's face hardened—"we will show that murderer the same mercy he showed Larkin."

"But he hasn't been in the Great Hall," Tiki said. "They say he is in the High Chamber—"

"I promise you—he will come out. We will give him a reason to come out."

Tiki transported to the Plain of Sunlight and relayed the plan to the Macanna generals.

"You must be prepared. The UnSeelie troops are everywhere. Dig in if you must—whatever you need to do to survive."

"We are ready," they assured her.

She went by Larkin's chambers for one last look. As she stepped into the drawing room that was a perfect reflection of Grosvenor Square, Tiki's heart caught in her chest. Would she ever see this room again, in either world? Memories danced before her eyes of the times she'd spent with her family here, of the hopes and dreams she'd held for their future. Tears welled in her eyes.

The Faerie Queen's Mirror was on a nearby table where she'd left it and on impulse, she went to the mirror and lifted it. But instead of her face, she saw Larkin's beautiful features speaking to her: "I want you to be the queen you were born to be."

Infinite sadness filled Tiki. "I will be, Breanna," she whispered. "I am the Faerie Queen." Tiki blinked and it was her own teary reflection staring back at her. Shaking, she took one last look around the room.

"Majesty—" Toran had a pleading look on his face. "Let me come with you. It's my job." He hesitated. "And you might *need* me."

Tiki remembered the torment she had caused Callan, her first bodyguard, by denying him the satisfaction of fulfilling a responsibility he was honored to hold. He had died for her, and she would never forget his sacrifice, but part of her understood that he would have died in a different way if he hadn't given his life for hers.

"Meet me at the Palace of Mirrors one hour before dawn, and you may guard my back from that moment forward, as long as I'm in the Otherworld."

Tiki returned to the tunnel where Fial, Dain, and Rieker waited.

"They are ready," she whispered.

"As are we." They sat in a circle, safe for the moment within the depths of the rock mountain. "It is fitting that we will end the Winter King's reign on December 21—the night of the Winter Solstice." Fial's lips twisted in a grim smile. "On the night when he should be at his most powerful, he will cease to exist." He nodded in satisfaction. "Here's my plan."

Tiki and the others listened carefully. When Fial finished, Tiki nodded. "I agree. And here is my plan."

They had little more than an hour to wait for the designated time to strike. Though Tiki was afraid to have Clara out of her sight for that time, Fial reassured her.

"She has more value to him alive than dead," the older faerie said. "Nothing will happen to her."

"I was thinking about Larkin—" Tiki started, but Fial held up his hand.

"We cannot speak of her yet. When we have won this battle, there will be time for all the talking we need to do. For now, let's save our strength."

Rieker and Dain exchanged glances but neither spoke. Tiki sat between them, holding tight to their hands. She bowed her head and thought of all that had occurred since she'd stolen the ring. Everything that had happened had pointed her to this moment. She would not fail her family or the Seelie court. She would not fail Larkin.

Chapter Fifty-Four

It was an hour from dawn when they retraced their steps up the stone stairway to the room off the grand hallway. They had agreed not to wear glamours but to attack Donegal in their true forms—as representatives of the Seelie court and themselves—for all to see and follow if they chose.

Fial had not changed his appearance after they'd made the decision, and his likeness to his brother was apparent, now that Tiki knew the truth. She remained silent, though, leaving it to the jester to choose when, where, and with whom he would share his secrets.

They all wore black, giving themselves the advantage of being harder to see in the shadows that enveloped the palace during the winter months. Tiki's hair was pulled behind her head and braided down her back, emphasizing the curve of her cheekbones.

"It's good to see your emerald eyes again," Rieker said, running his thumb across her cheek.

Tiki put her hand over his and leaned in to his caress. "It won't be long now and we'll be done with this forever. And then we will make a home with our family and live in peace."

Rieker nodded but his eyes were shadowed. "I look forward to that day, my queen."

He refused to leave Tiki's side, so it had been agreed that Dain would take Clara to safety.

The celebration of Winter Solstice was winding down, though stragglers still danced and drank in the Great Hall. The musicians had dwindled and now only a fiddle, a reedy flute, and a panpipe played on. The notes combined in an eerie, mournful sound that grated on Tiki's already frazzled nerves.

"How will you get Clara down?" she asked, rubbing her hands together to fight off the chill that pervaded the hall.

Fial spoke with calm assurance. "I will create a bird with a scissor-like beak that will cut through the rope holding the net. We will have to be prepared to catch her when she falls. Donegal's guards will attack immediately, so we must have our soldiers ready."

Tiki nodded. "Then we should start in the Night Garden."

Fial led the way through a hidden door, and they found themselves in the garden on the side of the building.

"What is it you need to do, Tiki?" Dain asked, peering at her curiously.

"It is time to call the Four Treasures."

She raised her hands above her head. "I speak to you, Air, as the breath and wind of all things living, to heed my command: breathe a warm wind through the Wychwood and all along the mountaintop before me until the ice has melted and the sun shines bright upon the Tor."

A warm gust of wind eddied around Tiki, lifting her braid from her back, before blowing over the side garden, melting the ice as it went. The wind swirled around the Tor, ice turning to water in its wake, and the black clouds that had hovered for so long were pushed toward the horizon of the Plain of Starlight.

Dain watched wide-eyed as sun broke through the departing clouds. Immediately the melody of the Night Garden could be heard as the blossoms were released from their icy shells.

"Witness the Four Treasures—our Faerie Queen can command the elements." Though Fial's face looked weary, he smiled in satisfaction and nodded. "I knew you could do it, sweet Tara—as you were meant to do."

Tiki pulled the Faerie Flag from inside her bodice where she'd placed it as a last bit of insurance when she'd returned from the Plain of Sunlight. She slowly unfurled the fragile material and held it above her head where the wind made the silk sing.

"I speak to you, Earth, as the element that provides strength and life to all manner of plants and animals that live on and within you: I command that you bring to me an army."

The wind grew in strength, tossing the bushes back and forth. The trees that lined the Tor bent against the onslaught, and the gust blew a thousand leaves from their branches until the sky was filled with foliage. As each one touched the ground, a soldier stood in its place—armed and ready to fight. In as long as it took the leaves to blow to the ground, there stood one thousand soldiers. They spoke as one: "We are yours to command."

Tiki raised her voice so all could hear. "I am the queen here. I want anyone who tries to stop me or my people to be removed."

Her heart was ice in her chest as she led the way around to the front of the palace. She would not waver. She would not flinch. Clara was coming home with her—no matter what.

At the sight of Tiki, the Macanna generals emerged from the trees where they had been waiting for her signal, armed and ready to fight. Tiki allowed herself a grim smile of satisfaction at their shocked expressions when they spied the vast army that followed her. The ground shook as they approached the front of the palace, and the UnSeelie guards who stood in position along the entrance stared in horror at the approaching throng. One guard darted into the palace and disappeared while cries for reinforcement echoed across the Tor.

Like a flight of birds, UnSeelie soldiers boiled from the depths of the Wychwood, their weapons glinting in the half light.

A contingent of Macanna flanked Tiki as she marched up the palace steps. The UnSeelie guards barely moved to bar her way before they were struck down by the Seelie army.

Beset by an unshakable sense of urgency, Tiki ran through the columns into the Great Hall, only to skid to a stop. The room was filled with UnSeelie soldiers, armed as heavily as the Seelie guard. Donegal sat on the golden Dragon Throne, a taunting smile on his face. And most horrifying, positioned directly beneath the golden net that was holding Clara was a roaring fire.

"*Tiki!*"

Tiki's eyes were riveted upwards at Clara's shrill cry. The fear in her voice made the hair on Tiki's arms stand up.

"*Tiki—save me!*"

Donegal's evil laughter filled the room. "Now what will you do, little queen?"

"*Teek—I've called and called Larkin and she hasn't come! Help me!*"

Tiki lifted her arms. "I speak to you, Water, as the element that sustains and purifies—cleanse this room of fire." She flung her hands at the fire that crackled beneath Clara, and a torrent of water flowed from her fingertips until it looked like a river filled the room, squelching the flames. The fire and all of the flames of the torches evaporated into a hissing gust of smoke.

Out of the billowing cloud, a large black bird with a silver beak flapped giant wings, arching slowly up to perch on the top of the golden net.

"What is that?" Donegal cried before he searched the crowd. "FIAL!" he roared. "WHERE ARE YOU? COME FACE ME LIKE A MAN!"

The soldiers on both sides stood frozen, watching the moment play out, unsure whether to attack.

The great bird turned and cocked its head so its silver eye could look at the Winter King. When it moved, its beak sliced through the rope that held the golden net suspended, and Clara plummeted toward the floor. Its perch gone, the bird flapped its great wings and dove straight for Donegal.

A cry went up from the crowd.

Tiki, Rieker, and Dain darted forward at the same time, their arms outstretched to catch the falling child.

Donegal jumped from the throne with a shriek and ran from the attacking bird.

"STOP THAT THING!" he roared as he shoved soldiers out of his way. "KILL IT!"

It was the battle cry for which the soldiers on both sides had been waiting, and the world exploded in a flurry of battle-axes, swords, whips, chains, and knives.

In the space of a heartbeat, Dain cut through several strands of the net, creating a hole big enough for Tiki to reach in and pull Clara free. She hugged the little girl close to her heart and breathed in her scent. "You're safe now," she whispered in Clara's ear. "I promise I'll keep you safe now."

A group of Macanna formed a tight circle around Tiki, battling any UnSeelie who dared to approach as she hugged and reassured Clara.

"Hold tight," Tiki whispered in Clara's ear. She looked at Rieker and Dain. "Change of plan," she said calmly. "I can't have her anywhere near this world right now. I'll be right back." Before they could reply, Tiki closed her eyes and transported to the farm in Richmond.

They arrived inside the kitchen, behind where Mrs. Bosworth stood at the sink peeling potatoes.

"Mrs. B.!" Clara cried.

The older woman jumped at the noise and let out a scream as she whirled around. Her jaw sagged when she saw Tiki standing there with Clara and dropped both her potato and peeler onto the floor with a clatter.

"Who might you be?" she shrieked. "And what are you doin' with my little darlin'?" The expression on her face went from shocked to determined. She marched toward Tiki, not recognizing her true self—without the glamour she'd grown up wearing in London. "Give her to me this instant. We've been worried sick—"

Tiki kissed Clara on the forehead. "Go to Mrs. B. I'll be back soon."

Clara clung to Tiki. "You always say that. Teek— please stay."

"I can't right now. But I *promise*—I'll be back with all of you soon. Now, be a good girl and go."

"Who are you?" Mrs. Bosworth demanded, pulling Clara from Tiki's arms. "Why have you got Clara?"

"I am a friend," Tiki said. "Take good care of her—don't let any of them out of your sight until Tiki and William return. And tell Shamus to keep the iron close." Tiki blew a kiss at Clara and disappeared.

Chapter Fifty-Five

"Clara." It was a whisper.

The little girl turned from where she sat playing with Doggie in front of the fire. It had been almost four hours since Tiki had dropped her off. She and the others had finished supper and were now gathered in the drawing room. Toots and Fiona were playing checkers on a table in the corner. Mrs. Bosworth sat nearby, intent on her stitching, while both Shamus and Mr. Bosworth snored from their chairs.

A familiar face stood in the hallway, a finger held to her lips indicating silence. She beckoned with her hand.

Clara hopped up and hurried in that direction, her stocking feet silent on the wood floors.

"Hush, not a word, now," the visitor whispered. She slid her long, slender fingers into Clara's little hand and led her down the hallway away from the others.

"What are *you* doing here?" Clara whispered, unafraid. The woman knelt and opened her arms. Clara didn't hesitate before throwing her arms around the visitor's neck and hugging her tightly. "I've missed you, Larkin." She leaned back and ran her little hand along the woman's cheek. "I was afraid you were hurt."

"No, I'm fine, my dear, just as you are. But Larkin has gone—you may call me Breanna from now on. I'm going to stay here with you and make sure everything is all right until Tiki and William can come home and take care of you." Breanna gently pressed her lips to Clara's forehead. "Never be afraid again. You'll be safe with me, my little darling."

Chapter Fifty-Six

When she returned to the Palace of Mirrors, Tiki arrived standing on the Dragon Throne. The room was chaos—men and women fighting and yelling, weapons clashing, shrieks filling the air. Smoke hung thick above the melee, making it difficult to see. An UnSeelie soldier stabbed one of the Seelie fighters with his bayonet straight through the heart in front of Tiki. Instead of falling to the floor in a puddle of blood, the wounded man disappeared. In his place, a leaf with a hole through its center drifted lazily to the floor.

"Teek!" Rieker darted through the crowd, his sword drawn to fend off attacks. Dain followed close behind, protecting his back. "Teek—get out of here!"

"Where's Donegal?"

Rieker pointed to the far end of the Great Hall where the Winter King was being buzzed by three large black birds. Donegal threw a fireball at them, but the flames were met with a splash of water and turned to black smoke before they came close to the birds.

"SHOOT THEM!" the Winter King screamed, turning for the door.

Tiki jumped down. "We need to help Fial get him outside." She swerved through the masses to one of the arches that led from the room. Once through the passageway, she sprinted down the grand hallway,

Rieker and Dain close on her heels. She rounded the corner just in time to see Donegal run out through the huge double entry doors.

Tiki, Rieker, and Dain raced out behind Donegal. The Winter King reached the stairs that led down to the Night Garden and came to an abrupt halt to survey the scene before him. Fial sat on a magnificent black horse whose eyes were the color of fire. The beast snorted and smoke curled from his nostrils; he pawed the ground as if anxious to run.

Seelie guards stretched as far as the eye could see, cutting off any entry or escape from the palace. Behind the first wave of soldiers, another layer stood with their backs to the inner circle to guard against an attack from their flanks. Above the Tor, the sun shone in golden brilliance.

Fial flicked his wrist and a thin, lead-laced braid of leather wrapped itself around Donegal's neck.

"Checkmate, dear brother," Fial said coldly.

Behind Donegal, the giant doors to the palace slammed shut. More Seelie soldiers moved to stand in front of the barred doors.

"Once again, you're fighting for the wrong side, Fial," Donegal spat. "You'll never learn, will you, *Fool*?"

"Your words mean nothing to me." Fial shrugged. "Your life means nothing to me." He blew into his cupped hands and seven sleek black birds flew free, their daggerlike beaks flashing silver in the sunlight. Fial's eyes narrowed. "But rest assured, I'll show you the same mercy you gave Larkin and so many others."

Donegal's head shifted to follow the flight of the birds now circling above the group. "Your magic doesn't scare me," he snarled. "Those birds will dissolve in a puff of smoke at the slightest touch." He tried to pull the whip away from his neck but the leather wouldn't give. In frustration, he wrapped his hands around the whip and stomped down the stairs toward Fial, shooting a ball of fire at his brother. "Get out of my way."

Fial deflected the fireball with a flick of his wrist, then yanked on the whip, forcing Donegal to his knees before him.

Tiki called out. "Elder Dryad, heed my call. Today I fulfill my promise to you. Find me now, my friend."

The UnSeelie King grabbed the noose around his neck, trying to slide his fingers beneath the leather to loosen its grip. He stared at Tiki. "*You*," he growled. "I should have known."

The wind grew stronger, gusting the leaves from the ground and swirling them in little whirlwinds. As if on command, the first bird dove—straight for the Winter King. Donegal swung, trying to defend himself against the attack, but the bird's daggerlike beak sank into his shoulder before it dissolved in a puff of smoke. Green blood burst from the wound and ran down the UnSeelie king's arm.

Fial snapped the whip free from his brother's neck as the other six birds wheeled around to position themselves to dive. A blast of wind shrieked through the trees, eerily similar to a woman's laughter. Donegal clutched his shoulder and threw another fireball at the jester, but Fial easily deflected the attack. The second bird dove, followed by the third, then the fourth.

The UnSeelie king turned and ran. He looked over his shoulder at the plummeting birds, unaware of the tree that suddenly stood in his path with a face visible in its deep brown bark. Its branches were outstretched like the arms of a lover. As he stepped near, the branches snaked around his body and yanked him to the tree.

His scream was one of pure terror. He struggled against the limbs that bound him, kicking and struggling, but in slow motion, the branches retracted back into the tree's trunk, pulling the Winter King along. As he disappeared into the woody bark, a woman with shimmering hair the color of molten steel stepped away from the tree.

She glanced down and felt her arms and legs before she threw her head back and screamed with laughter. "I am freeeeeeeeeeeeeeeeeeeeeeee!" The woman whipped around to face Tiki and bowed her head. "Our bargain has been met, Seelie Queen. Consider me a friend for life."

Tiki nodded at her. "A friend for life."

The witch laughed—a glorious, gleeful howl. "I will be back for you, sisters," she called out, then snapped her fingers over her head and was gone.

A cry of terror erupted from the tree where Donegal had disappeared. Tiki stared back at the black eyes that stared from the trunk, making no effort to hide her loathing. She raised her hands.

"I speak to you, Fire, as the element that can both create and destroy, to heed my command: light the bonfire that waits yonder and burn anything that touches the flame until there is only ash left for Air to scatter."

A great mound of sticks that Ailléna had gathered at Tiki's request stood stacked in a pyramid nearby. As Tiki spoke, the wood burst into flame. The fire leapt toward the sky, dancing and flickering like a hungry beast.

Fial stepped down from his horse, pulled a quiver free from the saddle, and slid it over his shoulder. From the leather holder on his back, he pulled a thin ax. His face was set with grim determination as he approached the dryad.

"No!" Donegal shouted from within the tree. "What do you think you're doing? Let me out of here! I COMMAND YOU TO LET ME OUT OF HERE!"

Fial threw the ax. It turned in perfect circles and sliced a limb clean from the tree.

A hideous howl of pain erupted, filling the sky. Fial pulled another ax free and threw again at the tree. "This is for my wife"—he threw a third—"and my children. This is for everyone you have murdered and threatened and tortured all these centuries." As he reached for another ax, other axes flew through the air to join with his to slice the branches from the tree.

The ring of the axes as they bit into the wood mixed with the tree's screaming. When there were no branches low enough to entrap someone and pull them into the trunk, Fial drew the final ax. He stepped close and with a mighty swing, he buried the ax in the trunk. Other soldiers joined him—each taking turns burying their axes deep in the bark of the screaming tree.

"Stop this! *STOP, I TELL YOU. WHERE ARE MY GUARDS? HELP ME! I AM THE KING!*"

As the crescent-shaped cut within the bark grew, a loud creak echoed as the tree began to sway. Men pushed on one side of the trunk, while others continued to chop at the bark. The tree tipped further and further to one side.

"*I COMMAND YOU TO STOP!*"

With a final woody *crack* that reverberated across the Tor, the tree toppled to the ground and was silent.

"Chop it into firewood and take it to the fire," Tiki called. The ring of axes continued for another few minutes, then one by one, the pieces of wood that had once been a tree were carried over to the bonfire and thrown into the flames. As each chunk of wood landed in the fire, a spray of sparks and flames shot into the sky, as if in celebration.

Tiki, Dain, and Rieker picked up the last piece together. She motioned to Fial. "Come with us." They walked to the bonfire, heat rolling off the greedy flames like waves. "Ready?" Tiki asked, looking from one to the other.

"Never more," Rieker said.

"Absolutely," Dain said eagerly.

Fial nodded wearily. "Let it end."

They swung the segment of tree back and then together threw it into the fire. They watched as the orange flames licked the bark before it consumed the wood.

Tiki slid her hand into Rieker's and reached over and took Dain's. Fial slid his arm around Dain's shoulders, and together they watched as the fire burned until there was nothing left but ashes.

Tiki spoke softly, but her words were heard by all. "We are free."

Behind them, the Macanna, the hobgoblins, the soldiers, and the homeless faeries erupted in cheers.

Chapter Fifty-Seven

It was two days later that they gathered in the Palace of Mirrors.

"Hear me, one and all." Tiki sat on the Dragon Throne in the Great Hall. She was dressed in a glittering gown of gold—in homage to Larkin—a golden circlet woven in her black hair. Rieker and Dain stood on one side of the throne, Fial on the other. Toran stood next to Fial and the Macanna proudly surrounded her. The dead had been removed, and the hall was overflowing with all species of fey, stretching out the doors and filling the Night Garden that was now lush and verdant.

"I am Tara Kathleen Dunbar MacLochlan, Queen of Faerie."

A cheer echoed through the hall, rattling the windows.

"I claim this throne in winter and summer, spring and fall. I claim it for both Seelie and UnSeelie—for everyone and anyone who lives here in the Otherworld."

Another cry went up—louder this time.

"From this day forward, we will be united as one court—one world. We will work together so that all may live in peace and harmony."

"TARR-UH, TARR-UH—" The chant started and swelled in volume.

Tiki held up her hand, waiting patiently until the crowd quieted.

"There is more—the most important part. I will forever be your queen, but I have made a decision. I will lend my guidance, my strength, and my love, but I will not rule over you. It's time for Faerie to rule itself.

"We will form committees and groups—a government—that will be the voice of our people. You will select representatives to guide our world to a better future. And to preside over these committees is the person I trust most in this world to seek and find the peace we all want. A man who is both Seelie and UnSeelie, who has the most knowledge of Faerie, the most wisdom to envision and guide our future. A man of honor and unbelievable strength—Fial Lasair Cathall Winterbourne."

Chapter Fifty-Eight

"When did you decide to turn control of the Otherworld over to Fial?"

Rieker, Tiki, and Dain sat in Rieker's study in Grosvenor Square. It was Christmas Eve and they had just finished decorating a tree with the children and the Bosworth's. Outside, snow fell in sparkling white, fluffy flakes, turning the landscape into a breathtaking winter sculpture.

"For the longest time, I suspected there was more to the Faerie Queen's Mirror than just to read the smoke in the Cup of Plenty, but it wasn't until Donegal was dead that I realized it was never him on the mirror's frame—it was Fial." Tiki held up the mirror that sat on a small table next to her, pointing to the face carved into the bottom of the frame. "It's so obvious now—there's even a jester's mask carved into his crown."

"I noticed that when Leo gave me the mirror," Dain cried, "but I wasn't smart enough to put it together."

"That's when it all made sense," Tiki said. "Fial knew all the secrets of both courts. Finn and Eridanus had entrusted him with knowledge about the location of the Four Treasures. He was there to guide me when I needed help. He gave up everything for a future he believed in—there was no one more perfect to rule

Faerie." Her lips twitched in a mischievous smile. "And just to be sure—I put the mirror in front of his face."

"And what did that prove?" Rieker asked.

"I saw his reflection. The only faces I've ever seen the mirror reflect are mine and Fial's."

"Ah," Dain said. "The Faerie Queen or the Faerie King?"

Tiki nodded. "As you know, Fial is distantly descended from Eridanus. My guess is that's why those two likenesses are carved into the frame—Finn and Eridanus meant for one or the other of us to rule. As Finn's daughter, I am a true-born queen, the only one who could make the Stone of Tara cry out. From what Fial and Larkin have told me, I was meant to rule, but I know in my heart that Fial is more suited to joining these courts together than I."

The patter of stocking feet against the wood floors could be heard through the open door.

"Tiki, Tiki, Tiki!" Clara ran giggling into the study, Toots on her heels. "Come quick!"

"What is it?" she asked, leaning forward to catch the little girl's hands as she slid to a stop in front of her.

"Leo is here! He says he must speak to you and Wills *immediately*."

Tiki glanced at Rieker. This was unexpected. Had something gone wrong already?

Tiki and Rieker excused themselves, leaving the children with Dain, and hurried out to the foyer. Leo stood in an overcoat dusted with snow.

"Leo," Rieker said, extending his hand. "What a pleasant surprise! How did you know we were back?"

Leo swept his hand aside and uncharacteristically embraced Rieker in a tight hug. He leaned back and clapped him on the shoulders. "Have you forgotten? My mother has an advisor with good connections." He set Rieker aside and held his arms out to Tiki. "And the beautiful Tara. I'm so happy to see you both safely home again."

Tiki embraced Leo, happiness and relief filling her. Leo was exactly right—she was home.

"Come into the study. My brother is visiting." Rieker led Leo to the study where Toots and Clara skipped out to meet them. "What are you about tonight? It's Christmas Eve."

"So it is, so it is," Leo said with a happy smile, "but when I learned you'd returned, I just had to pop in for a minute and say hello." He looked from Rieker to Tiki. "You do remember, we've got a wedding to plan."

At Leo's request, the wedding was to be held in St. George's Chapel at Windsor Castle.

"I've given it a lot of thought, you see. We have occupied this castle for over eight hundred years. St. George's Chapel is where we marry and bury our family. It seems the right place for my dearest friends to be married." He grinned at them. "One day I will be buried here myself, and it pleases me to know that I will rest in a place that has shared such joy with those I love."

Rather than wait for summer, the wedding was planned for shortly after New Year's. The day dawned bright and clear, a soft breeze blowing the few clouds toward the horizon. Snow still covered the ground, making the world look magical—as though it were covered in sparkling frosting.

"Tiki"—Fiona was weaving Tiki's hair in fine braids and pinning them up in an elaborate hairdo—"I'm so nervous. My first wedding and my first ball. I can't believe it! And the bloody Queen is going to be there!"

Tiki laughed. "I promised you'd attend a ball one day, Fiona. And you'll look as beautiful and royal as any of the blue bloods. Hurry up with my hair so I can do yours."

Clara skipped around the room with Doggie. "And somebody has to do mine too!"

"And then …" Tiki paused, a grin twitching at the corners of her mouth, "we have a guest who needs her hair done."

Fiona frowned. "Who's that?"

"Her name is Bridgit. I saw her working in the kitchens at the Palace of Mirrors and knew I recognized her. It wasn't until after Donegal was dead and we actually met the servants that I knew who she was. Mr. Potts is going to have a big surprise at the wedding."

The sun was high in the sky as Tiki stood in the entrance of the chapel with Fial, waiting for the time when she was to walk down the aisle. An orchestra played, and Clara blew Tiki a kiss as she turned to skip down the aisle, throwing rose petals.

"See you at the other end," Toots said, once again straightening the Ring of *Ériu* and another solid gold band tied onto the white satin pillow he held. His green eyes were wide and nervous as he looked down the long stretch between the pews.

"William, Dain, and Shamus are at the other end waiting for you," Tiki said, giving him a pat on the shoulder. "They'll probably want to talk about horses when you get there."

Toots's face lit up. "D'ya think?" He turned with a new sense of confidence and walked boldly down the row.

"Are you ready, my dear?" Fial smiled gently as he offered his arm to Tiki. He looked elegant in a black tuxedo, a white rose tucked in his lapel. His black hair was combed back from his face and tied behind his neck, as regal as any king.

Tiki slid her hand up under his elbow and hugged his arm close. "I am. My only regret is that Larkin's not here with us."

A smile turned the corners of Fial's mouth. "Actually, my dear, you're right. Larkin has died, but Breanna has come and would love to walk you down the aisle with me."

"Hello, Tara." The voice was the same, but different somehow. There was a sweetness to it, a lightness and joy—that had been lacking when Larkin spoke.

Tiki whirled in disbelief.

The woman who stood before her was breathtakingly beautiful—soft blond waves of hair framed an exquisite face with guileless blue-green eyes. Her lips curved in a gentle smile. "Allow me to introduce myself." She held out a slender hand. "I am Fial's wife, Breanna. I was your mother's best friend."

Tiki stared at the woman before her—so familiar, yet someone she didn't know at all. For the first time, she saw uncertainty in those eyes. Tiki let out a cry of pure joy and hugged her tight. She whispered in her ear, "We have a lot to talk about, Breanna."

Breanna laughed, the sound like wind chimes. "Yes, we do. And we have all the time we need to do it."

Fial kissed Tiki on the cheek and patted her hand. "I am so proud to have you as my daughter. I couldn't hope for a better match for my son, William."

Breanna moved to the other side and kissed Tiki's other cheek. "And I feel the same. We are very thankful for the strength and love you have shown our family. Your mother and father would be very proud of you."

Tiki smiled. "And I couldn't ask for a better family," she said. "We'll have many happy years together."

The music changed, announcing Tiki's entrance, and the congregation rose to their feet.

Tiki took a deep breath and began the walk down the aisle. Though the church was full, she had to bite her lip not to laugh at the attendees who couldn't be seen—faeries filled the aisles, hung from the columns, and even stood on the altar behind the minister. Toran, Gestle, and Ailléna stood near the front, close to Rieker and Dain. The little goblin waved wildly and jumped up and down in excitement when she saw Tiki. Gestle leaned over and spoke in Ailléna's ear, and she pulled her arms in, looking chagrined. But it didn't last long. She waved again until Gestle reached over and held her hand, causing her to smile happily at him.

Johnny stood behind Fiona, invisible for now, though Fi knew he was there. The plan was for him to escort Fiona to the ball in person. From there, no one knew, but Tiki was confident they could manage to live happily between the worlds. Dain had already promised to teach the young boy how to navigate on his own.

Clara stood between Fiona and Toots, holding their hands, looking like a young, sweet version of Larkin, with tiny blue forget-me-nots woven into her blond curls.

Mr. Potts sat clutching tightly to the hand of his daughter, Bridgit, his eyes wet with tears of joy as he smiled at Tiki.

Leo, Arthur, Mamie, and Queen Victoria sat in the front row, but Tiki looked past the guests up to William, where he stood with Dain. They were both dressed in black tuxedos—one brother with dark hair and the other blond—but the same height, the same build, with features similar enough that they were a blurry reflection of each other, and of Breanna and Fial.

A warmth spread through Tiki's chest—a love that filled her completely for the family that surrounded her. She would never regret her decision not to rule the kingdom of Faerie. This world was where she belonged. Her mother and father had wished for the world of mortals and faeries to live in peace, and she would gladly be the one to meld the worlds.

She would always have a place in her heart for the Otherworld and all who lived there—but her life and family were here, and that's where she would stay.

Fial kissed her again when they reached the altar. "Once for me," he said. Breanna kissed her too. "And once for me. We both give you our love." They released her hands and William stepped forward and slid his long fingers around hers.

"Are you ready?" he asked.

Tiki smiled at him. "Absolutely."

The pastor spoke eloquently of patience and commitment, of family and duty and mostly of love.

"Do you, William, take Tara to be your wife for all time?"

"I do."

"Do you, Tara, take William to be your husband for all time?"

"I do."

"With these rings that you place upon your fingers, may they symbolize your commitment to each other through the circle of life—through good times and bad—to remain true and loving to each other."

William slid the Ring of *Ériu* onto Tiki's finger, the red stone glowing softly in the light of the chapel. Then Tiki slid a burnished gold band onto William's finger.

The pastor smiled with a pleased expression.

"I now pronounce you husband and wife. You may kiss your bride."

William leaned close. "I love you, my Faerie Queen."

"I love you too, my faerie king."

They kissed amid shouts and cheers. Applause filled the room and in the distance, Tiki could hear the chant of "Tarr-uh and William! Tarr-uh and William!"

Chapter Fifty-Nine

'

"A honeymoon with the whole family?" Wills laughed. "I've never heard of such a thing."

"Please!" Clara cried, jumping up and down. It was the day after the wedding, and the ball had lasted until dawn. No one had actually gone to bed yet, though Fial and Breanna had departed shortly after midnight saying they had their own honeymoon to go on. "Leo said we could *all* go."

"Yes, well, Leo talks a lot now, doesn't he?" Wills winked at Leo who sat slumped in a nearby chair looking exhausted.

"But it will be so much fun!" Clara danced around the room. "We can dance some more."

Wills raised his eyebrows at Tiki. "And where has Leo plotted to take us?"

Clara twirled her way back to William's chair. "He says he has a little castle in Scotland called Balmoral where we can stay."

"Really?" Dain sat up in his chair, looking interested. "I would love to visit Scotland again."

"Please?" Toots asked hopefully. "He said there are horses and dogs there too. Loads of them."

Even Fiona looked hopeful. "And it's a real castle. Can you imagine?" She looked shyly at Johnny who sat by her side. "We could pretend to be royalty."

Seated in a chair by the fire, Shamus laughed out loud and smiled at Juliette, who was snuggled in the chair with him. "Not me."

Tiki smiled. "No offense, Leo, but I don't think I'd choose to be royalty even if I could."

Wills reached over and threaded his fingers through Tiki's. "I agree."

Leo waved his hand. "None taken. Not sure I'd choose it if I had a choice either."

Tiki laughed. "But I would choose to be with the family I love more than anything. So, I think it's a brilliant idea for all of you to come on honeymoon with us. We shall leave tomorrow."

Rieker snorted. "You all can leave for Balmoral tomorrow." He threaded his fingers through Tiki's. "And we'll meet up with you in a few days. But Tiki and I are going to begin our honeymoon *alone!*"

Later that morning, after the others had gone to bed, Wills and Tiki walked hand in hand past the great round bailey at the center of the castle and out onto the parapet. Vast fields stretched before them in pastoral serenity.

"Now that Fial is caring for Faerie, the homeless fey are being fed, and Seelie and UnSeelie are working together to rebuild what Donegal destroyed," Tiki said. "I asked Lark—I mean, Breanna, if she was going to assist him, and she told me she had no desire to rule Faerie. After all these years of making everyone believe that was her greatest desire, it turns out she just wants to spend time with her family. They are both so excited to make up for all those lost years with you and Dain and Clara."

"I know we have so much to learn about my mother and father," Wills said, "but for once, I feel like we have time. And speaking of time"—Wills glanced down at Tiki—"when we return, I'd like to get back to work on the Thomas James Ragged School. Have you noticed how many hungry children there are on the streets of London? Someone needs to help them."

Tiki leaned her head against his shoulder. "I agree. One of the things Larkin asked me when she was trying to help me find my way was if I would choose a child or a kingdom." Tiki gazed out over the English fields and imagined she could see them stretching all the way into the Otherworld. "What I've learned is that I don't have to choose. I can have both."

The End

Author's Note

Thank you for reading *The Faerie Queen*. I hope you've enjoyed Tiki's story. You might find it interesting to know that the Faerie Flag of Dunvegan Castle is a real artifact and considered the Clan MacLeod's most prized possession. The legend of the flag does say the flag was a gift to an ancient MacLeod relative from a faerie. The flag is presently on display at Dunvegan Castle in Scotland. You can read more about it on the Dunvegan Castle website: http://www.dunvegancastle.com/content/default.asp?page=s2_5

St. George's Chapel at Windsor Castle is where much of English royalty has been married and buried. The longest occupied castle in Europe (for over one thousand years now), Windsor Castle is the current Queen of England's residence and both Prince Leopold and Prince Arthur are interred in St. George's Chapel.

Also, the White Drawing Room in Buckingham Palace does have a concealed door. There are ebony-veneered cabinets with gilt-bronze mounts positioned behind tall mirrors at each end of the room. In the northwestern corner, the cabinet and mirror move as one to reveal the secret door, which is used as a private passageway for the royal family when they want to move discreetly between rooms.

There is a Faerie Bridge on the Isle of Skye—supposedly the spot where the faerie wife who gifted the Faerie Flag to the MacLeod's bid goodbye to her mortal husband.

Thank you for reading Tiki's story of the faerie ring. If you enjoyed this story, you might consider posting a positive review online for others to see and learn of the series! This is, in part, what allows authors to be able to continue to publish stories! Thank you!

Always believe!

Kiki Hamilton

Made in the USA
Coppell, TX
03 January 2023